Vanessa Gordon lives in Surrey and spent many years working in Classical music as a concert manager, musicians' agent and live music supplier. She has travelled all over Greece and has visited as often as possible over the last fifteen years.

The Martin Day mystery series is set on Naxos, the largest island in the Cyclades. It is an island of contrasts. The modern port of Chora is crowned by a Venetian kastro which is surrounded by an interesting old town. On Naxos you can find uninhabited hills, the highest mountain in the Cyclades, attractive fishing villages, popular beaches and archaeological sites. There are historic towers and welcoming tavernas, collectable art and ceramics. Naxos has produced some of the finest marble in Greece since ancient times.

Now Martin Day has moved in.

BY THE SAME AUTHOR

The Meaning of Friday

The Search for Artemis

Black Acorns

The Disappearance of Ophelia Blue

The Disappearance
of Ophelia Blue

A Naxos mystery *with Martin Day*

Vanessa Gordon

Published by Pomeg Books 2022 www.pomeg.co.uk

Copyright © Vanessa Gordon 2022

Cover photograph and map © Alan Gordon

Cover image: The Portara on the islet of Palatia, Naxos

ISBN: 978-1-8384533-6-7

Pomeg Books is an imprint of
Dolman Scott Ltd
www.dolmanscott.co.uk

'Understand and judge not'

Georges Simenon

I am very grateful to everyone who has helped in the creation of this book. Some have contributed enormously with their editorial comments and proofreading: Kay Elliott, Alan Gordon, Alastair Gordon, Alastair and Helen Ward, and Christine Wilding. Each brought their own expertise to the editorial task and it was great fun working with them. Thank you to Koula Crawley-Moore and Efthymios Stamos for their help with modern Greek, and my new friends on Naxos and Paros for their friendship and enthusiasm, especially Jean Polyzoides. Sue and Martin Garnett, Claire Gates, Martin Holding, Rhona Luthi, and Cristine Mackie have all supported me tremendously this year, and I really appreciate it.

Special thanks to Robert Pitt, in whose company I learned to love Greece and develop my enthusiasm for its history and archaeology, and who enabled me to hold a real Cycladic figurine (very carefully) in my hands.

As always, this book is for Alan and Alastair.

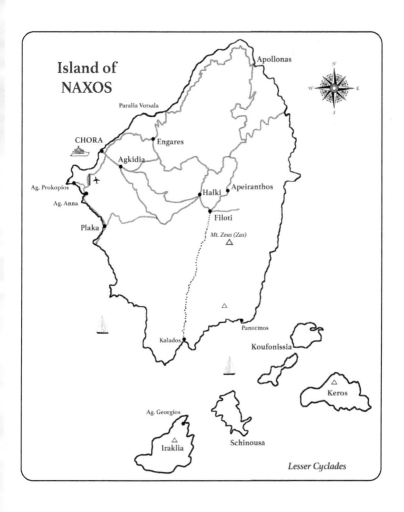

Island of
NAXOS

Apollonas

Paralia Votsala

CHORA

Engares

Agkidia

Ag. Prokopios

Halki
Apeiranthos

Ag. Anna

Filoti

Plaka

Mt. Zeus (Zas)
△

△

Panormos

Kalados

Koufonissia

△
Keros

Ag. Georgios

Schinousa

Iraklia
△

Lesser Cyclades

A NOTE ABOUT GREEK WORDS

NAMES for men in Greek often change their ending when the man is spoken to directly or a familiar form is used, such as Vasilios - Vasili, Aristos - Aristo, Alexandros - Alexandre.

PLACES
Chora and *Halki* begin with the same sound as in the Scottish 'loch'
Agios Ioannis, *Agios Georgios* are St John, St George
Spedos is pronounced spEE-doss
Bourtzi comes from the Ottoman-Turkish and means tower

GREETINGS & EXPRESSIONS
Kyrie and *Kyria* are forms of address like Monsieur and Madame
Kyrios is the word for Mr when not addressing him directly
Mou means 'of mine' and is often used after a name as a term of affection, as in
Agapi mou - my dear, my love
File mou - my friend
Kalimera - hello, good morning (*Kalimera sas* - formal or plural)
Kalispera - good evening (*Kalispera sas* - formal or plural)
Yia sou - hello (*Yia sas* - formal or plural)
Ti kaneis - how are you? (*Ti kanete* - formal or plural)
Pos paei - how are things? (poss-PIE)
Para poli kala - very well indeed
Efharisto poli - thank you very much
Hairo poli - pleased to meet you
Kalos irthatay - welcome
Kali orexi - bon appétit
Stin yia sas/mas - good health, cheers
Oriste - a common way to answer the phone.
Synharitiria - congratulations

Kali epitichia - I wish you success
Signomi - excuse me, sorry
Panagia mou - an explanation of shock, Holy Mary!
O Martin eimai - I'm Martin
Lipon - now, well, let's see
Telia - perfect
Perimenetay - Wait!

GENERAL

estiatorio - restaurant
psarotaverna - fish taverna
kafenion - traditional cafe
mikri agora - mini market
plateia - town square
spilia - cave
tholos tomb - underground bee-hive-shaped tomb
maquis - scrub vegetation
levanda - lavender
yiasemi - jasmine
asterias - starfish
komboloi - popular string of beads
tavli - Greek game played on a backgammon board
volta - evening walk
kastanozantha mallia - auburn hair
briki - metal pot used to make Greek coffee on the stove
Meltemi - prevailing wind in the Cyclades
Demotiki - modern Greek language as it is spoken today
Katharevousa - more formal modern Greek language
bousoules - spiral or circular marks carved into rock
paravoli - parabola

FOOD & DRINK
kafes - coffee (*Elliniko kafes* - Greek coffee*)*
sketo - unsugared, plain
kitron - a large citrus fruit famous on Naxos; a liqueur
mastika - a tree resin; liqueur made from the resin of the mastic
trees of Chios island
tsipouro - distilled spirit (ts-EE-puro), not to be confused with
tsipoura - sea bream (tsi-PUR-a)
gavros - mackerel
pestrofa - trout
dendrolivano - rosemary
trahanas - a dried stuffing made with wheat and yogurt
miso kilo - half kilo: wine is measured by weight in Greece
myzithropita - a dessert like a cheesecake, made with mizithra
cheese. Pita means pie
koulouraki(a) - Greek biscuit(s) (from *kouloura*, a coil)
orzo - small pasta
horiatiki (salad) - the traditional Greek salad
politiki (salad) - salad with a tangy, vinegary dressing
dakos - rusk used in a salad
melitzanosalata - aubergine dip
fava - yellow split-pea dip
feta, arseniko, kefalotyri, graviera, kopanisti, mizithra - Greek cheeses
feta ravasaki - feta cheese in pastry parcels with sesame and honey
ouzomezethes - small bites to eat (with ouzo)
mezethes - small savoury plates of food (sing. *meze*)
orektika - appetisers similar to *mezethes*
sto fourno - (cooked) in the oven
yemista - stuffed; vegetables stuffed with rice and baked

1

The island of Naxos in the Cyclades was enjoying one of the best Augusts in recent years. Tourism was at an all-time high. The white sails of windsurfers moved languidly in the bay, and a ferry of the Blue Star line bringing visitors to the port left a creamy wake in Homer's 'wine-dark' sea. The Aegean shimmered like black fabric against the cloudless sky.

Ophelia stood among the holiday-makers who had gathered on the islet of Palatia. The breeze threw her hair into her face whenever she lowered her hand, like in a painting she had once seen of Helen of Troy. Helen's was a sad story which had long resonated with Ophelia. Homer's heroine had to make a difficult choice between love and duty, and in choosing love she caused countless deaths and condemned herself to a lifetime of guilt.

She turned from the sea and wandered over to the Portara of Naxos. A huge marble doorframe topped with a massive lintel, the Portara was the most famous piece of antiquity on the island. It faced directly out to sea and was visible from every direction, because the Temple of Apollo for which it was the portal was intended to show that

Naxos was a place of importance. The temple, however, was never completed; nothing remained of it now but the foundation blocks that suggested the glory it might have been. The noble Portara stood alone, surrounded on three sides by the sea, an impressive and dignified symbol of disappointed ambition.

She walked back along the modern causeway towards the tavernas and cafés of the town. A bouzouki player was busking on the pavement, singing some old song of love that she recognised. She threw some coins into his music case.

"*Efharisto poli*, Kyria!" called the musician, and his eyes followed her as she walked away. Turning back to look at him, she fixed his image in her mind and added it to her memories of Naxos. This was the most beautiful island in the Cyclades: its tall hills and wild valleys had changed little since the Bronze Age, and its coastline was as unspoilt as when the first ships traded here. Its history was rich and its antiquities beyond compare. She had spent her life studying them.

She carried on more cheerfully towards her hotel. It was then that she recognised a fair-haired man sitting at a pavement table in a bar called Diogenes. He was laughing with the waiter, facing away from her, engrossed in conversation. It was certainly him, older now but still somehow the same. Before he could see her she ducked into the nearest shop, a gloomy place selling tourist items from beach towels to replicas of the Portara, and pretended to browse.

"*Yia sas*!" called an old lady who appeared from behind a rail of swimwear. She looked Ophelia up and down critically. "Can I help you?"

"*Kalimera sas*," replied Ophelia. "No, thank you. I'm just looking."

There was nothing in the shop she wanted, that was certain. The real question was whether there might be something she wanted from the fair-haired man.

2

"This is it, Martin, no more secrecy."

Day, one hand on the steering wheel, ran his hand through his hair.

"I'm not sure I'm quite ready, to be honest. It's been fun, nobody knowing, like having a secret affair."

"It really has, but we can hardly avoid telling our closest friends, can we?"

Day urged the Fiat up a steep right-hand bend and parked next to the old Mercedes that belonged to his friend Aristos. There were no other cars around, suggesting they were the first to arrive. The village of Agkidia, its white villas scattered among fields and gardens across the plain, was spread out below them, and in the distance the port town of Chora with the Kastro on its summit sat solidly on the horizon. By contrast, their friends' house had an air of seclusion. The front door was rarely used and the way in was a tall flight of stairs that led straight to the garden.

Helen and Day exchanged a smile. Over the winter in London they had made sure that Day's desire to change the nature of their relationship was the right thing for them both. They had kept to themselves, living like new lovers. Most of their friends were in Greece, and they had said nothing to the few in London.

As they took the stairs at the side of the house, it seemed unlikely that this privacy would survive the afternoon.

The Curator of the Naxos Archaeological Museum, Aristos Iraklidis, looked up from pouring a small amount of wine into his wife's glass. He finished the operation with a little twist of the bottle, a technique perfected by many years of practice, just as they reached the terrace.

"Aristo, Rania, *ti kanete?*" called Day from the top step.

"*Para poli kala, file mou*! Welcome back to Naxos! You've brought the summer back to us."

"Congratulations on your anniversary!" said Helen, kissing Rania on both cheeks. "Forty years of marriage - that's a real cause for celebration."

Rania opened their gift and held the glass vase to the light to admire its colour. They had bought it in Bath just before their return to Naxos. It had a flattened rim which suggested the shape of an ancient Greek pot, and its rich blue hue seemed to swirl around the bowl like the sea.

"Thank you, it's beautiful. You're very kind. Come in, come in."

Aristos Iraklidis, revered on the island and often known simply as The Curator, had been in charge of the Archaeological Museum for many years. Day had met him professionally when he first moved to Athens, but had come to regard him as a close friend. He was into his sixties now but he looked younger. His shirt was the azure blue of the Greek flag, which flattered his deeply tanned complexion, slightly wayward white hair and generous grey moustache. His dark eyes were still those of a much younger man.

Day had brought Helen to visit Aristos and Rania for the first time last summer. The terrace still looked the same, sheltered from the sun by its vine-draped pergola, its wonderful old olive tree in one corner, the ornate garden with scarlet bougainvillea and Aristos's olive trees and vineyard beyond.

Aristos took Helen to inspect the new vines he had planted, and Rania put her hand on Day's arm.

"You're rather pale, Martin, you need some good Greek sunshine. Still, you look happy. I'm very pleased to see it. Last time I saw you was in October, wasn't it? You were quite upset by that business at the tower."

She was right, he had been stressed before Christmas, but something told him she was asking about his current blatant happiness. When he hesitated, uncharacteristically for a man who always had something to say for himself, Rania gestured towards Helen in the garden.

"I feel as if we've known Helen for ever," she said, "yet it was only last summer that you brought her to meet us. The cold English winter hasn't done her any harm, in fact she looks extremely content." She paused expectantly, and Day waited to see whether she would ask him outright.

"Is she staying for the whole summer?"

Day smiled, thinking that the moment had come to give her the whole story, but at that very moment they heard people coming up the steps to the terrace. It was the only other guests invited to the anniversary celebration, Nick and Despina Kiloziglou and their 11-year old son, Nestoras.

"Hey Martin, how you doing, mate?" called Nick, his Aussie accent a legacy of his childhood in Sydney. He shook Day's hand and clapped him on the back. "Good to have you back."

"It's great to see you both," said Day. "My god, Deppi, you look radiant. That's what they say, isn't it? You really do! When's the baby due?"

"Early July. You must come out to Plaka and see the new house before there's a new baby to deal with. I see Helen over there. Let me just put this food in the kitchen for Aunt Rania, and we'll catch up with you both."

Day watched them go into the house and heard voices from the kitchen, Rania and Deppi discussing the food. Nestoras took his chance to follow one of the cats into the garden.

An old lady with a stick came out of a ground floor bedroom door, lowered herself into a chair and propped the stick within reach against the wall. She closed her eyes with a smile to enjoy the warmth of the sun that fell gently through the pergola. Day recognised the most senior member of the Iraklidis family and walked over to her. Aristos's mother rarely appeared when there were visitors, preferring the quiet of her own room. Day had only met her once before, on Rania's birthday last year, and he remembered that she spoke no English.

"Kyria Anastasia, *kalispera sas*," he said, bending down and shaking her hand. "*O Martin eimai.*"

The old lady smiled at him as if she needed no reminding. She was Day's ideal of an elderly Greek lady, majestic in her traditional black dress, her face a beautiful arrangement of wrinkles earned during a long and sun-drenched life. She must be, he guessed, in her late eighties. He talked to her in his highly idiosyncratic mixture of Ancient Greek, *katharevousa* and *demotiki*; it was a benign blend of classical literature, the formal modern Greek language, and the everyday spoken one. This hotchpotch, delivered with embellishments and courtesies, clearly delighted the old lady. She responded in the simplest and clearest Greek that Day had heard in a long time; he would never tire of hearing the language spoken like this. He lodged on the low wall near her chair and they talked for a few minutes before Aristos called everyone to the dining table. Day helped Anastasia from her chair, and soon everyone except Nestoras, who was still somewhere in the garden, was seated in the cushioned white armchairs round the long wooden table.

Aristos emerged from the kitchen with two bottles of cold white wine. A cluster of glasses already stood on the marble table made by his friend, the artist Konstantinos Saris. A perfect meander pattern decorated its deep white rim, and its well-proportioned pedestal seemed both massive and delicate. Day laid his hand on Helen's on the arm of her chair, no longer interested in secrecy.

"Rania and I are delighted to have you with us today," announced Aristos, who alone remained standing. "Thank you for being here to share our anniversary. Please raise your glasses. To family, friendship and a long and happy life!"

"*Stin yia mas!*"

"*Synharitiria!*"

Amid toasts and congratulations, the meal began with the *mezethes*. There were little chickpea balls, a *melitzanosalata*, tender pieces of octopus in a lemon coating, homemade *dolmades*, grilled vegetables and fresh cubes of local cheese.

From the other side of Helen, Nick leaned round to Day, his enthusiasm obvious.

"Hey, I've just heard your good news, Martin. Congratulations! What a turn-out for you."

Even the old lady stared at Day. He hoped he wasn't blushing. The time had come to tell them all about Helen and himself. It seemed to be becoming more and more difficult, though he could not have explained why.

"I've just told Nick about the *reward*, Martin," said Helen quickly, before he could speak.

"Oh, yes, that. It was a complete surprise."

"What was?" asked Aristos from the end of the table, looking to Helen for the story. Everyone was waiting.

"Martin had a letter from a lawyer in America last month. It was about the stolen antiquities that he tracked down last year. The lawyer said that the owner of the collection had died, leaving instructions that Martin should receive the reward that he offered for the recovery of his treasures."

Day said that the police had done all the hard work.

"Come on, Martin," laughed Helen, "it was all down to you, even if you did take too many risks." She smiled at the others, shaking her head. "Despite this sudden boost to his income he's still taken on two major pieces of work for the summer."

Aristos nodded. "Martin would be lost without his work."

"What do you have lined up, then, Martin?" Nick asked. "Is it enough to keep you out of trouble?"

"The reward is going straight into my currently empty pension pot," said Day, "Work needs to continue as normal. I've got the contract to finish the project that Edward Childe set up before he died, which is a TV series on Greek marble sculpture. I can see it taking several years and quite a bit of travelling round Greece."

"Sounds interesting," said Nick. "And what's the other job?"

"My agent in London wasn't convinced we'd get the Childe contract, so he arranged for me to write and present another TV series: each episode will be filmed at a different excavation site in Greece, one which is still active. We'll be disrupting the excavation teams and I'm supposed to smooth the way."

"Both jobs will take you away from Naxos quite a lot," noted Rania.

"Oh, there's plenty I can do here, I'm in no rush to go anywhere. This island is my delight as well as my home. And Helen will keep me from working too hard, won't you Helen?"

Everyone laughed. Day's friends were not afraid that he might suffer from overwork. Why else, after all, had he moved to a quiet Cycladic island? Day loved his work but he had his priorities, and professional ambition was not something that interfered with them.

The table was cleared and Rania went inside to fetch the main course, roasted Greek lamb with potatoes. Fragrant with herbs and garlic, the aroma of the meat was rich with lemon juice and white wine, and the potatoes had been cooked in the tray with the joint. They had absorbed the meat juice and were full of its flavour, but their tops remained crisp. Nestoras was the only person at the table who noticed Day, who loved potatoes in any form, quietly helping himself to one or two more.

"So, tell us about London, Helen," said Aristos, sitting back for a small rest from the serious business of enjoying his wife's cooking. Day glanced at Helen, who seemed to hesitate in the same way as he had himself.

"We had a good time," said Helen. "The highlight was Alex and Kate's wedding in November. You met Alex last year when he came to see us. The actual ceremony was private, but Martin and I went to the champagne reception in the British Museum, where Alex works, then to a place in Chelsea Square for dinner, about a dozen people in a private room. It was really very special."

"Then Helen spent most of December and January at her publisher's beck and call," continued Day. "Book signings, radio interviews, that kind of thing. If she isn't careful she'll be quite famous soon. I just did my usual kind of work. And we had a very good Christmas …"

It had been a Christmas he would never forget, because it had been the real beginning of their new relationship. He took another sip of his wine and was about to make their announcement when he realised that the conversation had taken another direction.

The lamb course was followed by a dessert. Deppi had made a *myzithropita,* a delicate Greek cheesecake from a traditional recipe from the nearby island of Syros where she grew up. It was a rich combination of the soft local cheese, honey, cinnamon and grated orange peel. Nestoras had a large portion and a second helping. Day was quite sorry to have no fondness for desserts.

They lingered well into the afternoon. Sunset would not be till eight o'clock, but people began to take their leave around six. Kyria

Anastasia was the first to excuse herself, and shortly afterwards it was the Kiloziglous. Once Nestoras had been found in the garden, the family left amid promises to meet up soon.

Helen and Day stayed for another hour. Over a final glass of wine with Aristos and Rania they talked about Naxos, London and life in general, but the subject of their relationship did not arise. On the drive back to Filoti they had to laugh and admit their total failure to introduce the subject.

"You were so funny, Martin. At the beginning you cleverly avoided Rania's hints and questions, then later, when I could see you were dying to tell everybody, you didn't manage it."

"Nor did you! There just never seemed to be the perfect moment…"

"I don't think you need worry, darling. I suspect we don't have a secret relationship any more."

3

Day woke to find that he had slept longer than Helen and she had already got up. He slid his hand across to the side of the bed that for so many years he had shared with no-one, and found it cold. He imagined her making coffee, or already drinking it on the balcony, or on the sofa in the main room. He indulged in a few moments of quiet contentment. He had always been happy with his own company, but when his relationship with Helen had changed from friendship to love, and she had quite suddenly become essential to his happiness, his life had become immeasurably better.

He reached out for his phone to see the time, despite knowing that this was irrelevant to his island existence. There was a new message from Maurice, his London agent, but it would keep for later. He got out of bed and opened the bedroom door.

"Morning!" called Helen. "Coffee nearly ready, but have your shower first if you like."

He said he'd take a quick shower and found a clean shirt on his way to the bathroom. The warm water was insufficient to drench him, the water system being quite old, but it certainly completed the task of waking him up. He was not a morning person, although since living with Helen in Hampstead over the winter he had begun to improve. He quickly dried himself and was soon dressed and ready for the day.

Helen was sitting at the balcony table with a large cafetière of coffee, her hands round a cup. The morning was still cool, but the sun had just emerged over the hills to the east, banishing some of the shadows and creating new ones that stretched long and thin across the ground. In a few weeks the balcony would be warm at this hour, but for now she needed a jumper round her shoulders. Day put his hand beneath it and briefly stroked her neck.

"You're up early, for you," she murmured. "It's only half past seven."

"I missed you. Have you been up long?"

"A while. I was woken by the braying of a donkey somewhere, and I knew at once I was back in Greece. I've been watching the sun come up."

"We've only been here a week and it already feels longer, almost like we never left. The island has enfolded us again. Do you feel that?"

She smiled. "Absolutely. Although I notice you haven't touched any work yet, Professor Day!"

Day winced. He could never quite lose the 'Professor', which he had certainly never earned in any university, having acquired it when working on a documentary for a history channel. They had given him the title without consulting him. At some level, of course, he quite liked it. Cristopoulos had used it sometimes, but Day had never known whether he was being serious or not.

"You're right. I shall start work this afternoon. I've just noticed a new message from Maurice on my phone - surely he can't expect any results yet? Anyway I thought this morning we could go and see Vasilios and Maroula over at Paralia Votsala, if you like? We could get some food at the supermarket on the way before it gets busy."

Day clearly had little appetite for starting work.

The supermarket was on the outskirts of Chora, just off the road from Filoti. There were already quite a few cars on the gravelled parking area, and fresh produce was still being unloaded from vans and stacked by the front door. A local hotelier was intercepting what he needed before it could even be laid out. Day and Helen had a system for food shopping. Helen would pick up the meat, salad and what Day called 'cooking stuff', while he shopped for snacks and drinks. First he put a six-pack of mineral water into his trolley, not because there was anything wrong with the local water but because it was easier to chill it in the fridge. As Helen went to the meat counter and began to ask for what she wanted, Day walked directly to examine the wine, where he quickly became absorbed.

"Right," he said when they met up again, "I have water, drinks, nibbles, lemons and that kind of thing. What else do you want me to get?"

"Coffee? Bread? I suppose it's no use giving you the job of fruit or vegetables, is it? I'll do that, and I'll meet you at the till. Oh, you get the olive oil too."

Day nodded; he loved a really good olive oil, mopped up with fresh bread or drizzled over rocket. He studied the shelves carefully, finally choosing a small tin of Cretan Extra Virgin which he hoped would be full of flavour and that tempting green colour that he associated with certain good oils. A packet of coffee and two bags of the delicious local flatbreads completed his task.

He looked with interest at the contents of Helen's trolley as they waited at the till. There were packs of meat, hand-wrapped and labelled, and similar parcels from the cheese counter. He approved of the bunch of fresh rocket and the bag of dark red tomatoes, but he could never really understand why she bought so much fruit.

From the supermarket they drove north along the coast in the direction of Engares. As usual they had the road almost entirely to themselves. For most of the time the coast was out of sight, but after Engares they took a small road towards the sea that was signposted to Paralia Votsala, or Pebble Beach. A new sign had appeared that read 'Elias House Accommodation', replacing the older one to 'Nikos Elias Museum'.

"Vasilios has been busy," noted Day approvingly.

The Elias House, formerly the home of the historian Nikos Elias, now belonged to Day. He had converted it into visitor accommodation which, whenever possible, he rented out to scholars, writers or artists in keeping with its past. Day's friend Vasilios, whose taverna lay at the other end of the bay, had accepted the job of looking after the property. It was an arrangement that worked well for them both.

The road down to the sea at Paralia Votsala ended abruptly in a T-junction, nothing ahead but a narrow strip of stony sand that fringed the water of the bay. Day paused here to glance left towards the Elias House. White and sprawling, it was tucked between the cliff and the sea, and even at this distance it brought back powerful memories. Helen let him gaze without interruption until he put the Fiat in gear again and turned towards the pretty taverna in the other direction. Aptly named Taverna Ta Votsala, it was the only other building on the bay. Despite its isolation it was never short of customers, and even now they could see a few cars parked outside and people sitting at the tables that stretched along the shingle under the tamarisk trees.

"My good friends!" called Vasilios, a smiling old man in a white shirt, coming towards them. He wrapped them each in a familial embrace. "It is so good to see you! Come in, take a seat, I will bring your coffee. You like the same as usual?"

He gestured them to a table flanked by blue-painted wooden chairs and turned away towards the bar. From inside the house a woman appeared, drying her hands on her apron, his wife Maroula.

"Martin, Helen, *ti kanete*? We're so happy that you're back with us again. Vasilio has been doing some repairs on the Elias House, and I have aired it ready for your first guests. I believe they arrive next week? They will find the house in the very best condition…"

"I'm sure they will, Maroula, thank you!" said Helen. "Can you join us for a coffee?"

"Thank you, Eleni mou. I'll come over in a few moments."

She bustled back to the bar and Day looked at Helen. "Eleni? I think you've just become an honorary Greek. Or maybe you've been adopted. They both look well, don't they? In fact, it feels like only yesterday that we were here. Except there's a bit of storm damage over there on the side of their kitchen. Perhaps I should offer a bit of extra cash to Vasilios when the moment is right…"

He said no more because Vasilios appeared with the tray of coffee. He set it down on the table and stood smiling until invited to sit down with them. Maroula arrived with cups of Greek coffee for herself and her husband, and four pieces of homemade cake. During the exchange of news that followed, Helen nibbled her cake. Day was just giving her the little biscuit that had arrived with his frappé when Maroula took him by surprise.

"So, Eleni mou, you and Martin are now engaged?"

Helen laughed and nearly spilt her coffee. Vasilios glowered at his wife and began to apologise.

"Don't worry, Vasili, we don't mind being asked. The answer, Maroula, is that we're not engaged, but we are … together."

Briefly she wondered whether Vasilios and Maroula might disapprove of their informal arrangement, but her fears proved groundless. There was no outpouring of congratulations, but something better: gratified smiles suggesting that this was not a surprise, and nods of vindication and approval.

"*Synharitiria!* Congratulations! May you stay together on Naxos for ever!" said Vasilios. His wife patted his shoulder in agreement, and more coffee was offered.

An insistent noise from Day's pocket dragged him away from the idyllic prospect of life on Naxos. He took out his mobile and saw that it was a call from a UK mobile number. The ringing stopped before he could answer, and he put the phone on the table.

"Sorry," he said, "it was a call from England, I expect it's about work."

Vasilios and Maroula strolled back to the bar so that he could return the call, and Helen went to visit the bathroom. Day looked at the number on his phone again, but it was not one that he knew. He pressed the call button and listened to the ring tone. When it stopped there was a woman's voice at the other end.

"Hello, is that Martin?" she said. Day tried to understand how he recognised her voice. "Is this the right number for Martin Day?"

"This is Martin Day. Who's that?"

"Ophelia. Ophelia Blue."

"My god, Ophelia? How wonderful to hear from you. How are you? How did you find me?"

The woman at the other end laughed and said she was well. "We have a mutual friend, Alex Harding-Jones. We met in London and your name was mentioned. I told him our connection and asked for your number."

"Brilliant. I can't quite believe it even now. Are you still in London?"

"No, at home in Cambridge. I met Alex when I was at UCL for a conference. And you, Martin, you're settled in Greece, I understand?"

"Yes, I moved to Athens some years ago and now I have a house on Naxos. I kept the small apartment in Athens, but frankly I love island life, especially in the summer. You know Alex got married last November?"

"Yes, he told me. You were there, he said, with your partner."

"That's right. Helen. So, what's your news?"

"News? Well, life goes on in Cambridge much the same as when you were here. We can't possibly catch up over the phone, you know, it must be eighteen years since we last met. That's in a way why I'm calling you. I'm coming to Naxos. In fact I'll be there early next week. It's the university vacation and I'm taking a break. It would be good to meet you, if possible? I have something of a professional puzzle I'd like your help with."

"It would be really great to see you, Ophelia. What kind of professional puzzle?"

"Much easier to tell you in person. Would you mind? I'm certain you'll find it intriguing, and if what Alex told me is even halfway true, then you're rather good at solving puzzles."

Day grinned but decided not to comment, wondering what Alex had said about him.

"As you like. It really is so good to hear from you again. You must come and stay with Helen and me in our house in Filoti, one of the villages in the mountains. Helen will be very pleased to meet you."

"That's kind of you, I appreciate the thought, but I've booked myself into Yiasemi Villas near Agios Prokopios. I've stayed there before, they're very friendly. Perhaps you can suggest a quiet bar in Chora where we could meet one evening?"

Day named his favourite bar, Diogenes, told her how to find it, and fixed the date and time. Ophelia said nothing more on the subject of her visit. She told him that she was still teaching in the same Cambridge department and saw his name occasionally on a book cover or a history programme, but he had the feeling that she wanted to close the call and save the real exchange of news for when they met. Far too quickly for Day's liking, she hung up.

His surprise at her call had changed into excitement by the time Helen returned to the table. He was still working out their relative ages. He had known Ophelia during the last two years of his four year degree at Cambridge, when he would have been twenty to twenty-two. She had been older, a recently-qualified research assistant of twenty-seven, when their relationship had begun. Now he was forty, and Ophelia therefore forty-seven.

"Everything all right?" asked Helen, sitting down and slipping off her shoes, laying her bare feet on top of them to keep them off the stones.

"Absolutely. Slightly in shock."

"Why? Who was the call from?"

"A woman called Ophelia, Dr Ophelia Blue, from my old Cambridge college. She met Alex recently and got my number from him. She said she's coming to Naxos and asked if we could meet up. Alex has clearly told her I'm some kind of detective and Ophelia has a professional puzzle that she wants to ask me about. I don't know anything more, she wants to tell me when she gets here."

"How odd. Still, you sound pleased about it. How do you know her?"

"Ah. Well, I have to confess …"

"What?"

"I mentioned her before, that night when we went to the restaurant in the old town, just before we left for London. Do you remember I mentioned falling for a young lecturer at my college, but as she was a member of staff we couldn't see each other openly? That was Ophelia."

"Oh. And you say it didn't come to anything?"

"Nothing very serious. We were on and off for a couple of years. She'd just had a very good relationship with a brilliant fellow classicist which had ended… and I was around, that's all."

"So you did have a relationship with her?"

"Yes. It had to be very discreet. Things were quite strict then. Just before I graduated we decided to end it anyway. That's when I went to London to teach Ancient Greek to school children and thankfully met you - which was clearly the best thing I could have done. I heard Ophelia started to see somebody else soon afterwards, somebody much less naive than I was. I haven't heard from her since."

Helen smiled, rather to Day's surprise. He was relieved, not only that she had accepted his explanation, but also that Ophelia had declined his impetuous invitation to stay with them. There was very little in his personal history that could possibly upset Helen, but his relationship with Ophelia had the greatest potential to do so.

"I've arranged a place and time for you and I to meet her..."

"Both of us?

"Yes, of course. We'll meet her and find out what her conundrum is, and if it's interesting you and I can work on it together. Ophelia's subject is the history of the Aegean, so there's every chance I'll know something about whatever it is, or she wouldn't have called me. I wonder what can be so important that she needed to come here in person? Maybe she just wanted a little holiday. I hope you like her, Helen. You will come along and help me, won't you?"

"I expect so. Do I need to keep an eye on you, Martin? You do seem very excited."

He shook his head ruefully and leaned towards her, kissing her lightly on the lips.

"Absolutely no need to worry, darling," he said.

4

The police station on Naxos occupied a building in one of the older squares in Chora town. If it had not been for the blue-painted grilles across the ground floor windows, and the signage announcing it to be the *Astynomiko Tmima Naxou,* 'Naxos Police Station' written underneath in English, it could have been mistaken for a small business. The motorbike rental company next door seemed to be busier, but this was misleading. Inside the police station a revolution was taking place. A new inspector had taken over, and he was effecting changes.

Martin Day swung his car into a vacant parking space surprisingly close to the police station. Shortly before leaving for London he had parked in the same place to say goodbye to the retiring Chief of Police, Tasos Cristopoulos. Although Inspector Cristopoulos had initially disliked Day's involvement in police matters, they had come to regard each other with respect, even friendship.

Day had assured Cristopoulos that he would welcome his replacement to the island. With a little homework online Day had learned that this was Kyriakos Tsountas, and that he had come from Volos, south of Thessaloniki. There was a hint of an incident in Volos, of which no details were given, that may have led to Tsountas's transfer to the vacant position on Naxos. This added to Day's appetite to meet him. Day knew that Volos was a port town and one of the most populous cities in Greece. He wondered whether the peaceful island of Naxos might seem something of a backwater to Inspector Tsountas.

One of the first changes he noticed at the police station was that an officer now stood on duty outside the entrance. Last year, with Cristopoulos in charge, Day had been able to walk into the station unchallenged, but that had all changed. The young officer hesitated. He knew very well who Day was, but had new orders. While nodding his recognition, he asked the reason for Day's visit.

"I just want a quick word with Inspector Tsountas," said Day.

The young policeman stiffened but gestured Day inside, indicating that he should take a seat against the wall. The desk officer completely ignored his arrival. Day glanced at the door of what used to be Cristopoulos's office, a room he had visited on many occasions, his opinion often welcomed and valued. He waited, looking round.

The station had been freshened up with new paint, and there was no sign of anything superfluous such as coffee cups or newspapers. Day concluded that the new broom was sweeping clean. The interior of the station had always been quite impressive, especially the senior staff offices and the IT equipment, but now an aura of professionalism was conveyed in everything from the polished door handles to the formality of the desk officer. No portly figure emerged to greet Day from the office of the Chief of Police, and the wall clock ticked on.

"Kyrie Day," said the desk officer at last, replacing the telephone into which he had been murmuring. "I'm sorry you've been kept waiting. Please follow me."

Day was shown into what had once been Cristopoulos's office. Where Inspector Cristopoulos had once sat dwarfed by the two computer screens between which he had peered, his short stature belying his influence and effectiveness, a younger man now stood, presumably Inspector Kyriakos Tsountas. The computer screens had been relegated to a table against the wall. Tsountas had reorganised his office so that his desk was a bare playing field on which he conducted every event. He was not in uniform and was dressed almost entirely in black. He was wearing an unreadable expression, a far cry from Cristopoulos's frank, ironic glance. His dark hair, beard and moustache were perfectly trimmed, and his eyes regarded Day without curiosity.

"Good morning, Kyrie Day. I am Kyriakos Tsountas. How can I help you?"

As he had not been invited to sit, Day stood facing the new inspector. Summoning his most professional manner, he explained his desire, as a former friend of Cristopoulos, to welcome Tsountas to the island. He began to wish he had not come: this man seemed to want no welcome from anyone. There was a knock on the door and the young officer from the front desk handed Tsountas a cardboard folder. Glancing at it with slight contempt before throwing it on his desk, Tsountas gave a sigh and invited Day to sit down.

"Forgive my formality, Kyrie Day, it was good of you to come. I believe you worked with my predecessor on several occasions. I'm … I'm very pleased to meet you."

"I played a small part, enough to appreciate the professionalism and effectiveness of the Hellenic Police."

A flick of one brow indicated that Tsountas had heard. Day had a sense that he was about to be interrogated.

"You're an archaeologist, I believe?"

"That's correct, I'm freelance. I write, do research, and present a few programmes for film and TV."

"And you live here on the island." It was a statement. Tsountas had done his homework too, perhaps while Day waited outside his office door. "You have a house in Filoti and an apartment in Athens."

Day nodded. He summoned a professional smile and tried to regain the upper hand.

"You've come from Volos, I understand, Inspector Tsountas? Congratulations on your appointment."

"Thank you. Volos is a very different place to Naxos, as I expect you know. It's an important industrial centre and a highway between Europe and Asia. Here in the Cyclades life is about as different as it's possible to imagine."

"Naxos is neither a hub nor a highway, of course, but nowhere is immune to the unexpected, and Naxos has seen its share of excitement."

Tsountas replied with a small upward movement of his chin. Day had still to see a smile cross the handsome face or illuminate the eyes that regarded him from beneath heavy lids. A pair of frown lines separated the black brows and crowned the straight Greek nose. Day began to think that he might be looking at an insecure or angry man, though arrogance was what he mostly sensed as he listened to Kyriakos Tsountas. He decided it was time to leave.

"I won't take up any more of your time, Inspector, but if you and your wife would like to join my partner Helen and me for a meal, it would be our pleasure. If you don't yet know many people on Naxos, ..."

"I'm not married, Kyrie Day," interrupted Tsountas, "and though I appreciate your invitation, I fear I am too busy…"

"Of course. Well, goodbye, Inspector Tsountas."

Day jumped crossly to his feet, unaccustomed to being treated with so little courtesy in Greece, the land of hospitality to strangers. Tsountas stopped him with a small gesture.

"I do appreciate your welcome. My predecessor told me about your significant role in the resolution of a recent case of murder and antiquities theft. As a highly respected member of the community I'm sure our paths will cross in the coming months, one way or another, as I begin to know the island. I look forward to meeting your partner - Helen, did you say?"

"Yes, Helen. She's a writer."

Tsountas nodded and they stood awkwardly eyeing each other.

"I've been wondering whether you are by any chance related to Christos Tsountas, the great Greek archaeologist?"

Tsountas looked at Day with a strange smile, shook his head and leaned back against his desk.

"No, we are not related, but it is strange that you should ask. That gentleman has cast something of a shadow over my life. You might find the story amusing, as an archaeologist yourself. My father was insistent, you see, that I should train in your subject and attempt to follow in the footsteps of our more famous namesake. I, however, had no talent or inclination for it, nor did I relish such an opportunity to fall short. This was a source of great annoyance to my father, who was profoundly disappointed in me. As a direct result, I joined the police force."

Tsountas gave a small smile, his first of the morning, but it was with obvious irony.

"I am a most ambitious police officer, Kyrie Day, perhaps too ambitious. I have something to prove, but it is not that I am the next excavator of Greece."

"You have no interest in ancient history, I quite understand. There's no reason why you should, of course. Except that in your country it's impossible to ignore."

"Indeed. However, I shall leave it to you and your colleagues to unearth antiquities, and I will continue to concern myself with whatever crime should occur on this island, perhaps some petty theft or domestic dispute. I look forward to continuing our conversation another time. Once again, thank you for your visit."

Day left the Police Station and stepped out onto the road, intending to return to his car. Instead he walked past it towards the shore. He needed a coffee, and remembered a place overlooking the sea where he had been several times before. He had much to think about, even though he remained in ignorance of whatever scandal may have brought Tsountas to Naxos.

At the café he took a table facing the bay, sat on a traditional chair, and lodged his feet on the lower spindle of another. It was a Greek custom of which he approved, a position in which one could gently rock while watching people pass by or just staring out to sea. He ordered a frappé and stirred it thoughtfully. Tsountas had certainly won no awards for charm, yet what else could be expected of a senior policeman in his position? What could Tsountas have done to deserve such a posting, such a sideways move in his career, one which clearly dismayed him? It would be interesting to hear how the new inspector coped, but Day felt no urge to speak to him again.

He finished his drink and sat watching the few boats that moved in the bay. It was still too early for the arrival of summer visitors in any quantity. A chill sat teasingly behind the warmth of the April sunshine. Beyond the harbour wall the sea shone with breeze-driven brightness that conveyed a hint of the cold water beneath. He breathed deeply to enjoy the sea's freshness to the very depths of his lungs, and relegated Inspector Tsountas to the back of his mind. For a while he thought only of Ophelia. Extracting some coins from his trouser pocket, he threw several onto the table to pay for his drink and the customary tip. As he walked away the waiter gave him a friendly wave, continuing his conversation with the local man who sat on the chair nearest the bar. The tourist season had indeed not yet begun.

He put on his sunglasses as he returned to the car. In London he had probably never taken them out of their case. On the drive eastwards across the island towards Filoti, however, they earned their place. Day found himself smiling, and even humming something unidentifiable under his breath.

Helen was sitting at the large table in the main room, computer open in front of her, wearing her dark-rimmed anti-glare glasses. Day found this oddly irresistible and went to stand behind her, his hands on her shoulders.

"You look very studious, Miss Aitchison. Not to mention sexy!"

She laughed and pulled off the glasses with one hand while closing the laptop with the other. "How did it go with the new inspector?"

"I managed to keep my composure," he said. "I'll tell you all about it."

They went out onto the balcony. The hills on the other side of the valley were as green as Day had ever seen them. Later in the summer they would become parched by the heat, bleached and yellowed and almost golden in the evening light, grey and bare at the peaks. A small collection of blue-painted bee hives on a high slope to the left caught the midday sun.

"So, everything's changed in the police station now that Cristopoulos has gone. I don't just mean new paintwork, I mean the bearing of the men, the whole atmosphere of the place. I so wanted Cristopoulos to pop his head out of his office and call me in like he used to, as if he'd known for hours that I was on my way. His dapper little jacket and his way of peering out from between his computer screens, all gone. The new man wears black, and it isn't accidental. He's black all over - hair, beard, moustache, eyes. Character. He fixed me with one of the most steely stares I've ever encountered."

"My goodness. I gather you didn't like him."

"Not much, but it's fair to say he wasn't in the least interested whether I liked him or not."

"So what did he say?"

"At first he just wanted to get rid of me, didn't even invite me to sit down. I thought I'd be on my way pretty much at once. Then something happened, someone gave him a folder, and that seemed to change him. I think he felt appalled at the banality of it all, something like that, and it was marginally less boring to be talking to me. He already knew quite a bit about me. Just as I was about to leave I asked him whether he was any relation of Christos Tsountas. I was just making polite conversation."

"Sorry, who is this Christos Tsountas?"

"Christos Tsountas was an important Greek archaeologist," said Day, enjoying the chance to share some of his knowledge. "He worked at the end of the nineteenth century, died in the 1930s. He's the one who discovered and identified the Bronze Age palace of Tiryns. He invented the term 'Cycladic civilisation' that we all use now. He's one of the greats."

Helen smiled at his enthusiasm. "So are they related then?"

Day shook his head.

"Tsountas smiled for the first and only time when I asked him. The name has been something of a problem for our inspector throughout his life. Apparently there was a family expectation that he would become an archaeologist, and his father was deeply disappointed in him because he refused to do so."

"That's dreadful, and cruel!"

"Indeed. Our Tsountas rebelled and joined the police instead."

5

Day woke slowly and luxuriously from his siesta, Helen beside him still asleep. He listened to her gentle breathing and the equally peaceful sound of the doves on the roof somewhere above the room, their drowsy, flirtatious murmuring drifting in through the open bedroom window.

His wakefulness conveyed itself to Helen who managed to smile, the first stage of waking. He rolled over towards her, moved her hair from her neck with one finger and kissed her there lightly.

"More please ..." she said without opening her eyes.

Day was about to obey when, with the unfailing timing of inanimate objects, the ring tone sounded loudly from his mobile. He considered ignoring it but picked it up from the bedside table to silence it more quickly. He saw the name on the screen just as the ringing ended: Ophelia.

"Who was it?" asked Helen.

With some embarrassment, Day told her. A notification arrived that Ophelia had left him a voice message which, after some hesitation, he brought up. He put it on speaker so Helen could hear.

"Hi, it's Ophelia. I'm in my hotel on Naxos. I know we were going to meet tomorrow evening in the town, but I thought - would you and Helen consider coming here this evening instead? I'm in my little apartment in Yiasemi Villas, which is on the road between Chora and Agios Prokopios, and we could have drinks and something to eat on my balcony. It has a really good view and it would be lovely to have some company. If you can come, I'll get some food from the hotel for us. I hope you can. Any time after six. Let me know?"

Day looked at the time, already nearly five o'clock.

"What do you think, darling?" he said. "Whatever you want to do."

"Why not? I'm curious to meet this Ophelia anyway. Say that we'll come, and I'll steal the first shower."

Day chuckled as they locked the house and got into the car to drive to Yiasemi Villas hotel. He had dressed in a rather good shirt, an indulgence in the January sales from some gentlemen's outfitters in Hampstead, which begged to have the cuffs nonchalantly turned up. He had accordingly done so. Helen, however, had completely outdone him. Though her skin was still pale from the winter months in England, her silk shirt somehow turned this to advantage. It was the colour of the sky at dawn, a luxurious material that shimmered with shades of pink, blue and pale grey. They looked like they were going to a wedding, he thought, smiling as he opened the car door for her.

It was, after all, quite an occasion, and the importance of it was not lost on Day. They were about to meet someone who had been significant at an early and turbulent stage of his life, and Helen clearly guessed what this meant to him. In the pit of his stomach he was excited, even apprehensive. His mouth was quite dry. He needed a gin and tonic. Ophelia would remember that, at least.

They took the road through Halki then down past Sangri to avoid driving through the town. After the airport and the disused campsite they came to the wetlands nature reserve, shimmering on both sides of the road. This shallow, reedy lake, a refuge for migrating birds, was already drying out with the approach of the warmer weather. The bus from Plaka passed them, empty today but ready for its summer duties carrying tourists to and from the beaches. The road wound round, past the windsurfing bay, until they turned inland again. A tall hill stood between the road and the sea all the rest of the way to Yiasemi Villas.

A gravel drive led into the hotel, which was a collection of small villas scattered among trees around a central swimming pool. They parked by the reception and went inside to ask for Ophelia. Well-made wooden tables of an earlier era and comfortable upholstered chairs set the tone of the hotel. They were directed to Ophelia's villa, *Levanda*, which involved a walk through a Mediterranean garden already full of flowers. Day took Helen's hand.

"It might be that one over there," he said. "Yes, the name is on the wall. Look, all the villas seem to be named after local plants."

Levanda, or lavender, was a small, white, two-storey villa perched at the top of the hotel garden, facing over the reception towards the road. As they approached it Ophelia appeared on the balcony and waved to them. Day stopped in surprise and returned the wave. Helen released his hand and placed hers in the small of his back with a little laugh.

"Honestly, Martin," she whispered, "it'll be fine!"

She was right. From the moment Ophelia opened the door and invited them into the villa, they were all quite comfortable together. A flight of steps led into the living area and kitchen, from which a glass door opened onto the balcony. They could see a table already prepared with glasses and small plates, and on the kitchen counter were two trays covered in foil, a bowl of fruit and a bottle of red wine.

"Helen, I'm so pleased to meet you," began Ophelia when they were inside, lightly embracing her. "And Martin, who would have thought we would meet again here on Naxos?"

Day hugged her slightly awkwardly, a greeting that Ophelia emerged from with a relaxed movement and gestured them towards the balcony.

"Look, isn't this such a beautiful place?" she said. "Can I make you a gin and tonic to start with? Helen?"

Helen had begun to enjoy herself. Ophelia went inside to make the drinks and she leaned against the wooden railing to enjoy the view. Directly in front and quite close was the rocky hill that they had driven past, its slopes grassy at the bottom rising to bare rock at the top. It blocked the view of the sea here, but was full of interest and colour in the slanting light. Somewhere on the hill a goat was bleating unseen among the dusky boulders and purple shadows. The name of this hill, she was told, was Stelida.

To the right of Stelida hill was the windsurfing bay of Agios Georgios and the wider sea beyond. She looked along the coastline, past rocky outcrops, to where the white houses of Chora rose from the ferry port and spread over the low hill of the Kastro. She could easily pick out the sheer brown walls of the castle itself, and the striking Portara arch on the strip of land that jutted out below the town.

She went to the end of the wide balcony to look at the inland view. She heard it before she saw it: a tiny white plane that appeared from the right, gained height and headed out over the Aegean. The evening departure from Naxos airport. It made her very glad not to be leaving.

"Ophelia's right, this is a wonderful view," she said, returning to sit down next to Day. "I love that hill opposite and the strange trees among all the villas."

"They're a kind of cedar, Naxos is quite famous for them. There's a small forest of them on the other side of Plaka."

"I'd like to see that. Perhaps we could visit Deppi and Nick at the same time."

"The cedar forest is quite a bit further south of their house, near Alyko beach. I seem to remember there's a place down there actually called Cedar Beach."

"There's so much of Naxos I've never seen, Martin!"

"We have all the time in the world," he said. "Some of it is wonderfully remote, barely accessible by road, but we'll explore. We're so lucky to live here."

Ophelia returned carrying three tall glasses pleasingly covered in condensation. She took the chair opposite Helen with her back to Chora and the mountains, and raised her glass.

"*Yia mas!*" she said. "Thank you so much for coming."

As Helen made small talk, Day studied his former tutor. She was rather different now from how he remembered her, but he supposed that was hardly surprising. The woman who had been twenty-nine when he last saw her was now an established historian of nearly fifty with a considerable scholarly reputation. There were creases on her forehead that he did not remember, but she was still very attractive. Her hair was as remarkable as it had been then, long and wavy and a light coppery red. He wondered if the right word was 'Titian'.

He snapped out of his private thoughts when he heard Ophelia and Helen talking about the hill of Stelida. As the sun started to sink in the sky, the hill had appeared to get closer.

"I feel we could almost touch it from here," Helen remarked. "It's a trick of the light."

"I know that hill quite well," said Ophelia, turning to explain to Helen. "When the French excavated Stelida in 1981, they realised that the entire mound was a prehistoric quarry. It's the oldest site to be excavated in the Cyclades by a long way. We'd assumed till then that early humans couldn't cross large areas of water, but discovering that the ancient quarry on Stelida was used as a tool-making centre by the Neanderthals challenged all our prior assumptions. The only explanation was that archaic humans crossed the Aegean."

"I remember reading about that excavation," Day recalled. "Not my period, of course. Did you say you knew the hill well?"

"Yes, my husband and I knew someone who had worked on the original excavation, and he showed us round Stelida one day. It was fascinating. The entire hill is made of a rock called chert, Helen, which the Neanderthals used for making tools. There was no sign that anybody ever actually lived on the site, it was simply their quarry and workshop. Pieces of emery were also found: that's the hard rock used for honing softer rocks into shape. It meant that the emery must have been extracted from the ground and then carried here from the centre of the island, where the emery is found. That in itself was a massive achievement for the time."

Helen looked again at the side of Stelida hill and tried to imagine the place peopled by Neanderthals. It was impossible.

"There seemed to be a lot of building work on the far side of the hill," she said. "I saw it from the road. Isn't that a problem, given the historic importance of the area?"

"Modern construction has to be carefully done," Ophelia agreed. "Stelida has protected status. But as always in Greece, there have to be compromises. Now, shall we have some food?"

They brought out the trays that the hotel had prepared for them, which turned out to be a generous buffet of cheeses, meats, olives, bread and fruit. Day picked up the bottle of wine with interest. It was a dry red from the Moraitis winery on nearby Paros. He offered to open it for Ophelia, and she handed him the corkscrew with a small smile.

The sun was about to set, almost sitting on the line of the surface of the sea. The temperature had begun to drop, an April freshness rolling in from the Aegean, but as the russet of the last rays of light lavished the dark surface of the water with a fleeting richness, and the white walls of modern Chora turned pink with the setting sun, nobody on the balcony noticed the chill. Day poured wine for them all and they sipped quietly, knowing the sunset would be over all too soon. It was easy to feel, together on the balcony at Yiasemi Villas in the silence of the garden, that the nightly ceremony was being performed exclusively for them. They watched the orange globe lose its shape as it slid below the horizon, and its terracotta rays change almost at once into grey. When the show was over, Day raised his glass.

"To old friends," he said, "and the reliable setting of the Aegean sun which we are so fortunate to enjoy together."

"Old friends and new," agreed Ophelia with a smile to Helen. "Now, help yourselves to food. And tell me how you came to be living here on Naxos."

The answer suddenly seemed long, far too long for Day. He shot an appealing glance towards Helen, who summarised the story.

"So last year Martin bought the house here on Naxos and I came for a holiday. In the end I stayed all summer. He couldn't get rid of me."

"And I didn't want to," Day added with a grin. "I think Helen and I might be here for ever. Where else would you want to live, once you've lived in the Cyclades?"

"I completely agree," smiled Ophelia, and though she looked about to say more, she lifted her glass of wine instead and took a thoughtful sip.

"You mentioned your husband, Ophelia," said Day. "Would I know him?"

It was entirely possible, in the small world of Greek archaeology, that Ophelia's husband would be someone Day had heard of, perhaps had even met. He was surprised that news of her marriage had never reached him, but he did make himself exceptionally elusive to academia.

"I'm sure you'll have heard of him. His name was Tim Mitchell. No? Tim was a Yorkshireman. His family had never had anyone go to university before. They didn't know what to make of it when poor Tim got a scholarship to a good school and went on to do a degree in Classics. He took a doctorate in the Greek Bronze Age, and his first job was a lectureship at Nottingham. That's where we met."

She poured a little more wine into her glass before offering the bottle to Helen, who took it from her and helped herself. Day showed no sign of recognising the description of Ophelia's husband, as indeed he did not. Ophelia continued talking in the darkening evening.

"Tim was somehow larger than life. He was funny and outspoken, and a fanatical supporter of students from under-privileged backgrounds who wanted to study the Classics. You may have seen some of his contributions to the Journal of Hellenic Studies, Martin?"

Day nodded politely, awaiting the arrival of any useful memories. He decided he was getting out of touch.

"Sorry, but you're talking about Tim in the past tense," said Helen quietly.

"Yes. We were married for twenty years, but we've parted ways. Poor Tim became ill, he had problems with stress that affected him deeply. He decided he needed to make a fresh start in the US, took a job in New York. We didn't divorce, but it was a permanent separation."

Day reflected that New York sounded an unlikely place to look for a stress-free life, but said nothing.

"I'm sorry to hear that," said Helen. "Especially after twenty years together."

"Yes, but they were good years. We never had children, but we adopted the most wonderful boy. Our son Raj was ten when he came to us, now he's a confident young man of twenty-six working in London. I'm very proud of him."

"How long have you been on your own?"

"Four years. But I'm not on my own. I have Raj in London and plenty of company in Cambridge, particularly my friend Mary Merriman. But enough about me. What have you been doing with yourself, Martin?

39

Alex told me about the book you've been working on together, the Greek vases project for the BM. You seem to have made yourself a nice life outside academia."

"It didn't appeal to me, Ophelia, academia and all that. I didn't want to be constricted by courses and exams and research grants. But it's hardly a dull life here in Greece…"

"So I heard from Alex! You've become something of a detective, he said."

"Not really. Things just happened that I had to resolve. Friends of mine were affected, I couldn't stand by and do nothing."

Ophelia nodded, smiling.

"Alex told me that you found a tholos tomb and some stolen antiquities?"

"Well, the possible location of a tholos tomb, yet to be confirmed by excavation. But yes, I did find some stolen artefacts. They were part of the private collection of a retired American who was targeted by some very professional thieves. Sadly, he died before he knew that his precious items had been recovered."

Ophelia looked thoughtful.

"Funnily enough, I've had two break-ins at my house in Cambridge," she said, "and I once thought I was being followed, though I probably imagined it. Luckily, nothing was stolen in the break-ins, they just made a mess. You hear about that kind of thing, but you never expect it to happen to you. No burglar would want my things, anyway, I have nothing worth stealing. My prize possessions are strange rare books, just oddments in my field that take my fancy. It gives me hours of pleasure hunting on the websites of antique book sellers, usually in

Greece or Turkey or Germany. I never guessed it could be such fun until I started!"

This led Day to mention that he had bought a first edition of *The Antiquities of Athens* by Stuart and Revett when he was teaching in London. "It was so much more than I could afford! But worth every penny, and it eventually helped me understand what I needed to do."

"What was that?"

"Go to Greece."

They finished the food and the bottle of wine, and Ophelia offered coffee. It was getting quite cold and almost time for them to leave, but Day accepted. He never drank coffee at night, and Helen wondered about his answer until she realised that Ophelia had still said nothing about her reason for coming to Naxos. Day took his chance when the coffee was served.

"So, what's this 'professional puzzle' you mentioned? I'm not sure how I can help, living out here and being outside academic circles. I guess it's something to do with Hellenic studies?"

"Oh, you know what?" said Ophelia. "It's such a saga, I think it would be better kept for tomorrow, at the bar. I'll bring some papers and explain it then. It would be a shame to spoil such a peaceful evening. It's been so good to catch up with you, Martin, and to meet you, Helen. And it's getting a bit chilly now, isn't it? Will tomorrow still be OK?"

And so they agreed to wait until they met in Diogenes bar in Chora the following evening.

"Wonderful," said Ophelia. "I've done the right thing in coming to see you, I know you're exactly the person to help me, Martin. It's a good puzzle. Definitely something to get your teeth into."

6

Day and Helen strolled to their favourite café in Filoti the next morning in the hope that over coffee they would gain the motivation to settle down to work. Helen had started writing a new novel in London, but had done nothing on it for several weeks now. Coming back to Naxos had been a welcome distraction for them both, but it was time to establish a routine. For Day, having accepted a lot of work that would see him through a pleasant summer on the island, it was more a case of not knowing where to start. His first task, he decided, was to make a plan.

Café Ta Xromata on the main road through the village was aptly named. Xromata in Greek meant colours, and the couple who owned the café had decorated accordingly. Woodwork and seat cushions were resplendent in lime green, yellow, orange and lilac. Somehow it worked, probably because every other surface was white. The tables at the front of the café spilled out under a white canopy and provided a good place to watch passers-by. Inside, where the coffee bar and snack cabinet were located, the far wall overlooking the valley was made almost entirely of glass and was perfect for colder or windy days.

Today they chose an outdoor table at the edge of the village road and sank into the cushions of many colours. The owner came out to take their order, and soon brought their coffee and complimentary slices of cake. As usual, Day nudged the plate closer to Helen.

"So, today we're both going to get down to some work, aren't we?" said Helen, sipping her cappuccino and looking over the rim of the cup dubiously. "Any idea what you're going to do? I don't envy you those enormous projects."

"Yes, that's the problem. I think I should prioritise the work for Maurice, though. The first thing will be to decide which excavations might possibly work for the programme, before contacting the people in charge to see how they'd feel about the intrusion. It could take a long time, so I should get on with it."

"Has Maurice given you a deadline?"

"No, thank goodness, but excavations take place in the summer so we'll have to do the filming in August. It needs to be set up by then. How about you, do you think you'll be able to settle down to writing?"

"I think so. Listening to Ophelia last night, especially when she told us about her husband, I could feel myself starting to take an interest in life outside our bubble again. You haven't been good for me, Martin, I've been quite distracted."

He grinned without sign of regret.

"What did you think of Ophelia?" Helen asked. "Was she as you remembered her?"

"Well, obviously a lot of water has passed under the bridge and we're both nearly twenty years older. I remembered her as more carefree, but it sounds as if life's been hard on her recently. If anything, seeing her again has pushed that era further back into the past for me."

"No thrill at all?" she teased.

"I'd be lying if I said it wasn't exciting to see her again. She was a big part of my early life. It would be sad not to have those good memories, wouldn't it?"

"Very sad. How old were you?"

"I was about twenty when it started and it lasted a couple of years. The last two years of my time at Cambridge."

"Was she your first serious girlfriend then?"

"More or less."

"More or less 'first', or more or less 'serious'?"

Day looked at her, surprised, and reconsidered the quip that had sprung to mind.

"As you know, I wasn't a happy teenager and university was my escape. Let's just say that Ophelia was a large part of the escape."

Helen smiled. "Did you know about her marriage?"

"No. I heard that she'd met someone almost as soon as I left Cambridge, but that's all. It was a sad story she told, wasn't it?"

"The way the marriage ended, certainly. They were together a long time, though, and the adopted son seems to have been a success. The way she spoke about her husband made me think she really loved him. Probably still does."

"I agree, I had the same impression. Tim Mitchell. Actually, I hadn't heard of him, though I could hardly say so."

"There's no reason you should have, is there?"

"Only that everyone tends to know everyone else in the field, if only by reputation."

Helen put her empty coffee cup on the table and watched a group of three young mothers with pushchairs heading towards the *mikri agora*, the little supermarket at the other end of the street. In the *kafenion*, the older men sitting with their *komboloi* beads turned their heads to watch them pass.

"Martin, do you think Ophelia's real reason for coming to Naxos may have been to get back together with you? I mean, she didn't describe the puzzle, and we still don't know what it is. All she said of any importance was that she's on her own now. Don't you think it's possible?"

Without giving Helen's quite reasonable suggestion a great deal of thought, Day shook his head. The excitement he had felt when he had first heard from Ophelia, and again when they were about to meet her at Yiasemi Villas, had been all about the past. The idea that this would be of present or future relevance to him was so inconceivable as to be quite startling.

"Absolutely not, no, I really don't think so."

They left money for their coffee on the table and waved to the proprietor as they left. Day was quiet as they walked home: Helen had a good instinct when it came to people's motivations, and the thought that she might be right now was unsettling. He would do as he often did, immerse himself in work and think about it later. If he didn't do that, he would waste the rest of the day in speculation that would lead nowhere and solve nothing.

Helen got down to work without mentioning Ophelia again. She was still absorbed when Day pushed back his chair, closed his laptop with a sigh and uncharacteristically offered to make a cup of tea. There was just time to drink it together on the balcony before getting ready to go out. For once they sat in silence. The mule that they often saw under a tree in the valley was in its usual place, tethered in the scant shade and enjoying the sweet spring grasses.

Showering helped to wash away the tiredness of the hours spent at their screens. By the time they were heading to the port and Day's favourite bar, he was excited again, this time on account of the so-called professional puzzle about which he would soon be hearing. He didn't doubt the existence of such a challenge and he hoped the real reason that Ophelia had come to see him was because it was something only he could solve.

The staff at Diogenes were not as busy that night as they would like to be, and certainly not as busy as they would be in just a few weeks, once the tourist season on Naxos really got under way. Day and Helen took their favourite table, a table for four from which it would be easy to see Ophelia as she arrived. Alexandros, the only full-time waiter who was not a member of the owner's family, came over to them at once.

"*Kalispera*, Alexandre! *Ti kaneis?*" said Day, shaking hands. Alexandros was a familiar sight and a welcome one, arriving to work at Diogenes every summer from his home in eastern Europe. With a glance to Helen, Day ordered two gin and tonics. When they arrived, Alexandros left a large bowl of salted nuts in front of them and dropped the till receipt with a practiced hand into a small glass on the table.

Day checked his phone for the time. "Still ten minutes or so before Ophelia is due. I haven't forgotten your question this morning, darling. I really don't think that's why Ophelia has come here. Even if it were, I wouldn't be remotely interested. I give you my word."

"I know, Martin." She smiled and picked up her glass, slightly raising it to him before taking a sip.

"I'm actually intrigued to hear about this puzzle of hers," he went on. "I hope it's a juicy academic argument, some scholarly scandal or other. Even if I don't know where to start, it sounds quite fun."

"As if you need anything more to do at the moment! I know you, though, you would find it irresistible, like the puzzle that Nikos Elias left you, with his mysterious clues to the hidden burial site. Oh well, not long now and we'll know what the new mystery is to be. It must be important for Ophelia to come all the way to Naxos herself."

"Yes, I suspect she's brought some books or papers with her, otherwise it would have been easier to send everything electronically." His voice dropped to a melodramatic whisper. "Unless it's too scandalous to send!"

They talked of other things, waiting for Ophelia to arrive. On the pavement, people had started to enjoy the evening walk known as the *volta*, the chance to go out with your partner or your family, meet and chat with neighbours, and generally be sociable at a particularly pleasant hour of the day. It was an opportunity to wear your best clothes, to flirt, to be seen. For the people-watchers at the cafés, it was an entertainment in itself.

Day began to look out for anybody with distinctive red hair. Alexandros came over to ask if they wanted more drinks, and they told him they were expecting a friend. Half an hour passed after the agreed time.

"Have you looked at your phone to see if she's sent a message?"

Day picked up his phone and checked. "Nothing."

"Perhaps you'd better call her in case she's sitting in another bar."

He brought up Ophelia's mobile number and called it. When there was no answer it occurred to him that she might not want to take an international call, so he sent her a text. When there was no still response and no sign of her, Day suggested that Helen should stay at Diogenes in case she arrived, while he walked along Protopapadaki, the wide pavement where Diogenes was located, to look for her.

First he walked in the direction of the Portara, because the bus from Yiasemi Villas terminated near there. When he reached the terminal he found only a single bus parked and locked with nobody inside, and there was no sign of Ophelia. He cursed his stupidity. If she had walked from the bus terminal along Protopapadaki, she would have walked right past Diogenes and they would have seen her. He retraced his steps, shook his head to Helen as he passed, and continued along the busy pavement. All the length of the popular road he checked the cafés for Ophelia. He was sure he had not missed her. He wondered whether he should move inwards to the lanes behind Protopapadaki and look for her there, but decided against it. There could be no mistake. They had talked of Diogenes being on this popular street, close to the civic platform with three brass flagpoles, a distinctive landmark. She had seemed to know where he meant. Why had she not found it?

Returning to Helen he had to report defeat.

"Another drink here, or shall we go home?" he asked her, his voice flat.

"It's been an hour, it doesn't look as if she's coming now. Let's go home."

Day sent a text to Ophelia's number to let her know, and to ask when they could meet the following day.

By the next morning there was still no word from Ophelia. Day had left texts and voice messages, none of which had raised a response.

"There might be something wrong with her phone," he said. "I think I'll go to the hotel."

"I'll see you later, then."

"You don't want to come?"

"I'll stay and get on with this," she said, nodding towards her laptop which was already open on the table. "It might be better if you talk to her alone. Give her my best."

Day took a last mouthful of his coffee, picked up his mobile and car keys, and left the house. On the road, as he waited to pull out from his parking space while the bus from Apeiranthos passed by, the morning sun cheered him. The prospect of a long talk with Ophelia about Bronze Age Greece was a pleasant one. The mystery of her non-appearance the previous evening would soon be resolved, he thought.

He headed south, taking the small roads again. The road twisted between fields and finally brought him to the wetlands reserve and Stelida. The gravel drive of Yiasemi Villas crunched pleasingly beneath his tyres.

There was nobody in reception this time, so Day decided to go straight to the villa. He took the steps two at a time, crossed the Mediterranean garden where a busy gardener was making the most of the cool morning, and knocked on the door of *Levanda*. There was no sound from inside. He walked in the direction of the pool and the bar, thinking that Ophelia might be having breakfast. A man was cleaning the enormous pool with a device resembling a vacuum cleaner on a long hose, and they exchanged a nod of civility. Day reached the entrance to the bar, from where he could see the guests who were having breakfast at small tables along a sheltered veranda. There was no sign of Ophelia.

He experienced his first stab of anxiety. It was surely unlikely that she was still asleep. He retraced his steps to reception, aware of the stare of the pool man. The door stood open.

"Good morning," said the young woman who owned the hotel, recognising him from his previous visit and courteously using English. "How can I help you?"

"I'm a friend of one of your guests, Ophelia Blue. I visited her two days ago."

"I remember. *Kalimera sas.* Is Miss Blue meeting you here at reception?"

"No. Actually, we were meant to meet in Chora last night but she didn't arrive. My partner and I are a little concerned, especially as we haven't been able to contact her. There's no reply from her villa, and she doesn't seem to be having breakfast…"

"I'll call the staff at the bar. If they've seen her this morning, I'll be able to tell you."

She spoke into her desk phone and waited for the answer. Replacing the receiver, she shook her head apologetically.

"Miss Blue hasn't been to breakfast this morning," she said. "If you like, we can take the keys and make sure she's all right?"

"Thank you."

With a set of keys in her hand, the hotel owner led the way back across the garden to *Levanda*. She stood back to let Day knock again, and when there was no reply he nodded to her to use the key. Calling a warning, he went inside. The kitchen was immaculate, not so much as a glass remained unwashed, and the curtains were drawn over the glass door to the balcony, which he checked. He went downstairs where he found the bedroom and bathroom equally tidy. The sheet on the bed was crumpled but neatly pulled over the mattress. He opened the wardrobe, then the drawers, and even looked at the hook behind the door. Ophelia's things were gone.

"It's so odd," said Helen, "What did the owner of the hotel say?"

"She's as puzzled as we are. Ophelia has paid in advance for her whole visit, but was meant to stay another three days. Nobody seems to have seen her or spoken to her since breakfast yesterday. Ophelia didn't want her room cleaned, so there's no way to know when she was last there. The owner said it's not unusual for guests to make a new plan and leave early, but they always let the hotel know."

7

Day lay next to Helen, staring up. The house in Filoti still retained many of the features of a village house and the old wooden beams of the original ceiling were still there, painted white. He had never really noticed them before but now he was familiar with their every knot and crack. He had been awake since first light.

He reached for his mobile, careful not to move the sheet that covered them both. As he had come to expect, there was no reply from Ophelia. After failing to find her at Yiasemi Villas he had tried to call her mobile many times and sent a series of messages, but her phone appeared to be dead. Now he made a decision, one which he had been mulling over in the night. He would have to take his concerns to Inspector Kyriakos Tsountas.

He left without stopping for a coffee, joining the morning traffic on the road to Chora as people made their way to work. Not being an early riser, Day was astonished at the number of vehicles on the country road from the villages. Sun-bleached old cars, vans of all kinds, and heavily-laden motorcycles shared the winding road. The ubiquitous small hatchbacks that had become popular in recent years, both as private and hire cars, were everywhere. As Day owned one himself, he fitted in like a local. The thought gave him a fleeting smile.

This was the first time that he had come to Naxos Police Station to report a problem. He hesitated to say 'report a missing person', because it sounded too dramatic, yet otherwise why had he come?

He was admitted to the building and approached the young desk officer, who was intent on his computer screen. There was nobody else in the room, and the chairs lined up along the wall were empty. Behind the desk, the half-glazed door to the office that had once belonged to Inspector Cristopoulos was firmly closed. Day waited to be acknowledged.

Just as the young officer raised his face from the screen, the street door slammed and Kyriakos Tsountas entered the station. The young officer's posture stiffened to attention.

"Kyrie Day, *kalispera sas,*" said Tsountas, unzipping his black jacket. "I didn't expect to see you again so soon."

He raised an interrogative eyebrow to his officer, but when no explanation was offered he gestured Day ahead of him into his office.

Day had just time to reflect that Tsountas was still completely dressed in black, even to the short padded jacket he wore over his shirt. The inspector shrugged this off and hung it with little care on the hook behind the door.

"I'm here to report someone missing," said Day at once, having decided on a direct approach since parking the car and entering the station. "It's a friend who came to Naxos from the UK to visit me. She hasn't been seen for the last two days and didn't keep an appointment with me the night before last. She's not answering her phone either."

Tsountas looked at him directly for the first time and sat down behind his desk, indicating that Day should take the chair facing him. Day gathered his thoughts in order to make the most compelling case.

"Her name is Ophelia Blue, she's a university lecturer from Cambridge. We used to know each other quite well but I hadn't heard from her for twenty years. Her call last week was a complete surprise. She said she was coming here to speak to me about something important. My partner Helen and I met her at her hotel, and we arranged to meet again the night before last at Diogenes bar, where Ophelia said she would tell me why she had come to see me. She never arrived. I went to her hotel yesterday and everything has gone, all her clothes, all her belongings, everything."

The inspector's expression was professionally blank, his eyes slightly narrowed.

"Miss Blue is a lecturer in archaeology?" He made it sound almost sinister.

"Greek history," said Day.

"At which hotel was she staying?"

"Yiasemi Villas, Agios Prokopios."

"Was there any sign of a struggle in the room? Anything to make you think that your friend had been forced to leave?"

"No, in fact it was very tidy, even though Ophelia had turned down room service."

"I see."

"I spent yesterday calling her mobile, sending texts, checking with the hotel - there's still no sign of her. If she came all this way to ask me something specific, why would she not do so? I want to report her as a missing person."

Tsountas shrugged in a way which angered Day.

"Given what you've told me, Kyrie Day, I'm afraid we cannot do that at the moment. Your friend is an adult with the right to come and go as she pleases, and that's what she appears to have done. I suggest you try her home in the UK, I expect she will be there."

"I beg your pardon?" said Day, losing patience. "Could you at least check the ferries and the airport, find some proof that she left the island? Could you check the hospitals? Her mobile phone records? I tell you, this is not like Ophelia, and it's been two days already. I was expecting rather more help."

Tsountas raised his hand slightly to caution against Day's raised voice, and perhaps also to concede a point.

"Very well, we will make some checks."

He picked up his desk phone, spoke into it curtly and replaced the receiver.

"Give a statement to the desk officer and leave us your contact details. Miss Blue's too."

Day curbed his anger. It cost him no small effort. He left the police station without destroying his new acquaintance with the inspector from Volos, but with no great hope of his support. He walked towards the *plateia* regretting the retirement of Inspector Tasos Cristopoulos.

He ordered a double espresso in Café Seferis, the best café in the square and one that the police themselves often used. He picked up a copy of *Kathimerini*, one of the major Greek newspapers, just to distract himself. His coffee was brought to his table with a glass of water, a small biscuit wrapped in plastic, a bowl of sugar cubes and the till receipt. The only one of these he needed was the water. As he drank deeply, drops of condensation fell on the newspaper, blotting the face of a politician recently elected to the New Democracy Party. Day read the article mechanically, gradually becoming calmer.

There was nothing to be gained from antagonising Tsountas, he knew that. Thankfully the interview had just about remained civil, and at least the police would make some enquiries. For Ophelia's sake Day must put aside his mounting antipathy for the inspector. He remembered to breathe, and with that his thoughts cleared. He had lost interest in the newspaper. What did he actually *know*?

He knew quite a lot about Ophelia herself. She was a highly regarded lecturer in his old department, and a member of his old college, Jesus. For a couple of years she had been his girlfriend. He stopped to analyse that thought. How did the word 'girlfriend' creep up on him? It was an inaccurate description of their passionate but dysfunctional relationship. He sighed and decided to keep going. What else did he know? She had quite recently been abandoned when her husband, suffering some sort of mental problem, had left her. She had a close friend called Mary and an adopted son called Raj, both of whom she seemed to value highly. He knew nothing about her current work, which was something he should find out about because it might give him an idea of why she had come to see him. He had once read that to find out how a man died, you must find out how he lived. He hoped to God that Ophelia was not dead, but to find her he thought he would have to find out more about her current life.

As he continued to think, he began to recall more details. Ophelia had said that she collected rare books, that her house had been broken into, that she thought she had been followed. Followed where? In Cambridge? London? Naxos? He had not thought to share any of this with Tsountas.

"*Signomi*," said the man at the next table. "Are you finished with that newspaper?"

Day nodded and handed over the paper. The man took it without a word. Day sat back to recover his train of thought.

He did not believe that Ophelia had come to Naxos to rekindle their relationship. He really thought she had come specifically and deliberately to speak to him, but he could think of no reason whatsoever for her to seek his help on any academic matter. Day was as far from academia now as he had ever been in his life, and she knew that. He wrote books for non-specialised readers and his films were accessible and enjoyable to a wide range of people. Popular archaeology, he supposed. His strengths were investigation and research, but those were abilities that Ophelia herself possessed in abundance and many other people besides. So why had she thought he could help her? Alex Harding-Jones, good friend that he was, had elaborated amusingly on Day's recent exploits on Naxos, his involvement with the police in resolving a few cases of mystery and murder, and Ophelia had referred to it more than once. Could that be it? It hardly qualified him for a 'professional puzzle', whatever that was.

He checked the time. If the police found any trace of Ophelia, especially if she was in the hospital, he wanted to be in Chora rather than at home half an hour's drive away. He decided to take a walk, to clear his head and pass some time while staying close to the station. He put a few coins on the table for his coffee and left the café, heading towards the coast. He sauntered down Galanadou street and turned left onto Aristidi Protopapadaki, looking aimlessly into shop windows, and within ten minutes he was standing on the shore looking out across the water. There was a chill in the air, as if Chora had not fully woken up from winter, an impression confirmed by the abrupt disappearance of the sun. Since he had left Tsountas the blue sky had been overtaken by cloud and was now two tones of grey. The sea shone like pewter except where a streak of silver showed where the sun was hiding somewhere above. Rain was promised, or at least some change in the weather.

He paused for a while looking at the untidy surface of the sand leading down to the damp flat margin where the tideless sea had washed away the footsteps of early walkers. The distant port was no more than a dark coruscation between sea and sky, its features unidentifiable in the dullness. As the weather worsened he was filled with frustration: he needed to be active, not wait around for the police. He turned and took a shortcut back to the police station past the newly white-washed walls of a beach bar, between shiny two-star hotels awaiting the summer rush, seeing almost nobody on the pavements.

As he approached the police station, already reaching for his car keys, an officer who had been taking a cigarette break collided with Inspector Tsountas who was emerging from the main door. There was a moment of embarrassment, the officer took a backward step, and Tsountas glared at him. Still glaring, Tsountas noticed Day. With an effort he changed his expression to a professional one.

"Kyrie Day! I can give you some information. There's no sign of your friend at the hospital nor at any clinic on the island, so we can be confident that she has not been involved in an accident. There's no record of her in any accommodation on the island, nor has she hired a vehicle. Her name doesn't appear on the passenger lists at Naxos airport, nor on any ticket outlets for the ferries. Despite being negative results, I hope they put your mind at rest."

"I'm not sure they do, Inspector Tsountas. If Ophelia hasn't moved to another hotel or left the island, where is she? Did you have any luck with her phone?"

"The phone is switched off, and hasn't been used in twenty-four hours. The last call was to you, at the time when she invited you to Yiasemi Villas."

"Then her disappearance is bizarre. What's the next step?"

"For the moment we have done all we can do."

"What about the British Embassy? Don't you let the embassy know when a foreign national is missing?"

"Kyrie Day, I'm sorry, but as I explained earlier, we cannot officially regard Miss Blue as a missing person. I understand your concern, truly, but she is an adult who has every right to move around as she pleases. There is no indication that she has come to harm. Let us hope that she returns soon, and you find your concerns were unwarranted."

Day clamped his jaws together and nodded, staring at the ground so that Tsountas would not see his expression.

"Let's hope so indeed," he muttered.

8

"Kyriakos Tsountas," said Helen, savouring every syllable with a smile. "What a good name. Very dignified."

"Are you trying to annoy me or is it accidental?" snapped Day, collapsing into a chair. "Sorry, I don't mean that, but the man has just told me that Ophelia isn't officially a missing person. He says she's probably just gone off somewhere - like she's trying to avoid me."

"Hey, calm down. Is he going to help?"

"He's made some basic enquiries," said Day grudgingly. "She's not had an accident, nor booked herself on a ferry or a plane. Her phone hasn't been used since she called me that night. She doesn't seem to be staying anywhere else on the island, and she hasn't hired a car. He says there's no evidence that she's come to harm, so there's nothing more he can do."

"I see." She regarded him for a moment. "I have a feeling you're about to take the matter into your own hands."

"I would, if I only knew where to start. I need to think. First I need to eat. Have you had lunch?"

Day rarely recognised when he needed food, but the coffee in Café Seferis was disagreeing with him. He got up and went to the kitchen where he put some pieces of ham and cheese on a large plate, and some rocket in a bowl with a liberal glistening of Cretan olive oil and a few pinches of oregano. Next, two flatbreads went into the oven and while they crisped up he brought out a jar of capers, two small plates, cutlery and the salt grinder.

"What's happened to the weather?" he muttered. "It looks like a storm coming in. We'd better sit inside."

He went back to the kitchen for the bread and the pepper grinder, applied oil to the flatbread, added a few capers to his own plate, and was finally happy with his creation. They ate and chatted while outside the wind began to rattle the cane canopy over the balcony.

"A package was delivered for you this morning," said Helen. "I forgot to tell you."

"Really? I'm not expecting anything, I suppose it must be from Maurice. Any sender's address?"

"I don't think so. It's in the front room, on the table behind the door."

Day went to get the parcel and returned with a puzzled expression on his face.

"This is a Naxos postmark…"

Helen turned back to him from the kitchen counter where she had just placed their empty plates. Day was opening the parcel none too carefully. It was securely wrapped and resisted his impatient hands.

Inside, tucked in a plastic bag to keep the contents dry, was a small hardback book with a cheap, dark-blue cover, and an envelope on which his name was hand-written. Day picked up the envelope first.

"This looks like Ophelia's handwriting," he said. He extracted a single piece of paper from the envelope, read it silently and passed it to her.

**Malcolm Street
Cambridge**

Dear Martin,

I'm afraid by now you will be very puzzled and perhaps anxious, but I urge you not to worry on my account. I want you to have this book and the letter inside it, in the hope that you, with all your intelligence and curiosity, will make out the truth. Do this for me, please Martin, for old time's sake.

Confident as I am of your success, all that is left for me to ask you is, if you can, not to think badly of me. I hope you will come to understand, at some level, my heart and mind.

Ophelia

Helen read the letter with a frown and gave it back to Day. He put it on the table, pulled out a chair and sat down to examine the book. He scanned the front cover and opened it, noting that it was completely written in Greek. Inside lay a lightweight envelope of the kind used some years ago in Greece, unsealed and unstamped. It was addressed to 'The Director, British School of Archaeology, Souidias 52, Athens'.

With Helen looking over his shoulder, Day unfolded the letter that he found inside. It was handwritten in English in a flowery script that was hard to read and conflated the English and Greek alphabets.

"Never posted," remarked Day. He held the letter so they could read it together.

Kalados, Naxos
25 November 2001

To The Director, British School at Athens

Dear Sir,

I am taking the liberty of writing to you on the subject of my research. You know of my publication 'Το Κάλλος, ένας Κυκλαδικός χώρος', and will recall our personal conversations on the subject. The British School, and in particular the Library staff, gave me a very warm welcome over many years, and you yourself greeted my efforts with sympathy and encouragement. I thank you very sincerely for that kindness.

I realise that my early efforts offered little sign that I would be successful in my search; however, I have since been blessed with a discovery. I want to share my happiness

with you, that the Kállos of Naxian folklore not only exists but is in relatively good condition. I have seen this with my own eyes.

I hope you will forgive me, but I have taken the decision to allow the whereabouts of the Kállos to remain unknown for the time being. The danger of looting is as severe today as it was in the past, and moreover I have reason to believe there is an imminent threat to the find. If word of its location were to escape now I fear it would fall into the wrong hands. It is my responsibility to protect what I have spent half my life trying to find, leaving it to others to complete my work.

It only remains for me to thank you, for without the forbearance and help of the British School the outcome would have been different. Like seafaring Odysseus (the nickname I know I was given at the School), I roamed for many years in search of beauty and fulfilment, only to find it at last at home.

I trust you will remember me kindly, as I certainly remember my friends at the School.

Yours truly,
Christos 'Odysseus' Nikolaidis

Day laid the letter on the table and picked up the book again.

"And this must be the book he was talking about. The title means 'The Beauty, a Cycladic place', or 'place' could mean 'site'. Published in

1999, two years before the date of the letter. That tells us he must have found the actual location between 1999 and 2001, don't you think?"

"I'm completely at sea, Martin."

Day took another look at the small book. It appeared to have been printed privately, rather than produced by a publishing company. The printing was attributed to a firm in Athens of which Day had never heard. A quick check online told him the company no longer existed, and he turned back to the book. It was in italicised print, *katharevousa* Greek, and a small font, on flimsy paper. Though extremely hard to read, a glance at the preface told him that it was an account of Christos Nikolaidis's search for something known as The Kállos of Naxos.

"Why do you think Ophelia sent you this, Martin?"

"I can only guess that this is the 'professional puzzle' she wanted to hand over to me. You're not the only one completely at sea, of course. Me too. I mean, look at this."

He picked up the packaging in which the book had arrived, the brown padded envelope and the plastic inner wrapper.

"This plastic bag is from a British supermarket chain, and Ophelia's letter is addressed from her house in Cambridge. I think the whole thing was parcelled up before she left home. If so, it means she brought it with her to Greece and posted it on Naxos. It also tells us that she never had any intention of showing it to us at Diogenes. She planned all this before she even got on the plane at Heathrow. I just don't understand."

"This unposted letter written by Christos Nikolaidis," said Helen. "It's addressed to the Director of the British School, but Nikolaidis doesn't address it to him personally. Doesn't that seem strange when he says they knew each other quite well?"

"Yes, it seems very odd, but maybe they had a formal relationship. The Director's role is a very senior one. The last few lines don't ring quite true to me, though."

"It looks like Nikolaidis intended to send the letter, otherwise he wouldn't have addressed the envelope, so why would he just leave it inside a copy of his book?"

"Perhaps he just forgot about it."

"Surely not. He must have thought of little else. Perhaps he changed his mind about sending the letter because he had decided to make his discovery public. And yet that can't be right, because he didn't do that. Oh it's impossible! How can we ever know?"

"Ophelia probably found herself thinking the same thing!" Day grumbled, re-reading the letter. "This is addressed from Kalados, in the south of Naxos. Presumably he lived there."

"That only tells us he was there when he wrote the letter."

"We can't be certain about anything much, can we?" sighed Day. "He's got a good point about looters, though. There's a lucrative market in illegally-exported Cycladic artefacts, as much today as in the past. I can understand his concern. But why not tell the British School or the Greek Archaeological Service where to find it? They are exactly the people who could have ensured its safety."

"Mr Christos Nikolaidis sounds a bit eccentric, Martin, don't you think? Hence the nickname they gave him at the School. Perhaps he wasn't quite right in the head."

Day laughed. "They were probably teasing him behind his back because he was coming and going for years like the ghost of the place. Our profession attracts that type, I've seen a lot of them.

Anyway, everyone haunts the BSA library from time to time, myself included."

Day replaced the faded envelope and its curious contents inside the front flap of the book and sat back with a sigh.

"I can only think of one reason why Ophelia left me this puzzle. I live here, on Naxos. I'm ideally placed to follow the trail left by Nikolaidis."

"You mean, she wants you to find the lost artefact? But why wouldn't she talk about it with you? And why does she ask you not to think badly of her? Funny, both she and Nikolaidis ask to be remembered kindly."

"Nikolaidis has just told a top archaeologist that he's found something important and is not going to give it to him."

"Good point. What about Ophelia, though?"

"No idea, frankly. Perhaps Tsountas was right and she did leave deliberately. It fits what we know now."

"Who knows, Martin. This could still be an elaborate way to bring you back into her life!"

"It really doesn't feel like it," grinned Day, "but if I can solve the puzzle she might come back and then we can ask her. There's one thing to take comfort from, though. I don't have the feeling any more that she's come to harm."

Heavy spring rain began to fall outside. Day poured a glass of water and headed to their bedroom with his computer. He lay on the bed with his laptop next to him unopened. Helen put her head into the room to say that she was going to work on her novel for the rest of the afternoon, and smiled when she saw him lying on the bed looking at nothing with a serious look on his face.

"What are you doing?"

"I'm ordering my thoughts," he replied. "To do that, I need to lie here quietly. Then, a little research into our new friend Christos Nikolaidis, I think. I'll tell you what I come up with over dinner at O Thanasis. Good idea?"

"Very good idea. We'll get very wet walking to the taverna, but the food will be worth it. Good hunting, then! Wake up in a good mood, please. You're going to solve this, I know you will."

After a while, Day typed 'Christos Nikolaidis' into the search engine. An hour later he was still reading, but becoming increasingly drowsy and rather tempted to succumb to sleep. His mind full of the life of another man as obsessed with Greek antiquity as himself, he put aside the computer and set about his siesta. Instead of sleeping, however, he found himself thinking about Ophelia, her curious package, and her even more curious disappearance.

9

The air in Filoti that evening was fresh and cool, the brief but determined downpour having left the central hills of Naxos well watered and ready for a new burst of spring flowers. The dust on the road had been washed away and the pavement gleamed, reflecting in its glassy surface the dying light of the sky. Day and Helen walked towards the centre of the village past the hardware shop that sold everything from coffee pots to goat bells, and the greengrocer where only a few crushed leaves remained of the pavement display.

Day was deep in thought. Helen assumed he was thinking about Ophelia and her challenge, but she would have been surprised to learn that he was thinking of the many occasions when he and Helen had walked to Thanasis's taverna before the change in their relationship, and how grateful he was that she was beside him now.

He was thus particularly vulnerable to a wave of sentimentality when they entered the taverna. The old framed photographs on the walls, the typical Greek chairs with their woven seats, the old wooden bar gleaming from years of polishing, and the blue and white cloths on the tables filled him with pleasure and immense relief. A portly

Greek looked up from laying a crisp white paper cover over a table and expertly fixing it in place with a piece of elastic.

"Ah, *kalos irthatay!*" he called. "Koula *mou*, here is Martin!"

It was Day and Helen's first visit to their favourite local taverna since being away for the winter. Thanasis shook Day's hand and gave Helen the traditional double kiss. His wife Koula joined them from where she ruled the roost over one of the best kitchens on the island. Hovering behind her stood their son Vangelis, who usually served in the restaurant.

"It is very, very good to see you," said Thanasis. Koula, who spoke very little English, clapped her hands together. Day summoned some Greek in response, and they were gestured to their favourite table by the wall next to the window. Thanasis arrived with menus and Vangelis brought water, glasses, and a basket of bread and cutlery.

"We've made a few changes to our menu," said Thanasis proudly. "I suggest you look at what we have added … Look, there's this, and this, and this!"

Day followed his pointing finger, and indeed there were items that were new to him and sounded good. He felt better immediately and the wave of emotion settled.

"Can I bring you some wine, perhaps?" asked Thanasis.

"Yes, please, a *miso kilo* of your red, I've been looking forward to it," said Day. The local wine from the barrel that was served in a metal jug was gentle and full of flavour; fresh 'and' – extremely drinkable, and it had the additional advantage of never giving him a hangover.

"So, Madame, are you hungry?" asked Day when they were alone again.

"Yes, particularly for one of Koula's special creations. Do you feel like fish or meat tonight?"

"Meat, I think. Let's take a closer look at this new menu of theirs."

As they began to read, Thanasis came over with a tray of small dishes which he transferred reverently to the table.

"Please, I would like you to try these *ouzomezethes*," he said. "They are new, different from last year. This is *gavros marinatos*, marinated smoked mackerel, which comes from the island of Limnos. We have recently made a connection there. And this is *pestrofa* - I don't know what that is in English. Vangeli!"

The father summoned the son to supply the translation, but Vangelis shook his head and got out his phone. After a quick search he announced that *pestrofa* was trout.

"Yes, trout," confirmed Thanasis, expelling the short English word from his mouth as if he found it distasteful. "Small thin pieces, served with homemade *fava*. My wife's cousin has moved with her husband to Epirus, and this is how we now get the fish. We only have a small amount."

"Wonderful," said Helen. The delicate pieces of preserved fish looked delicious. Thanasis returned to the bar and Day sat back happily. Within a couple of minutes Vangelis had brought a jug of wine to the table. The light red wine looked appetising in the pale gold of the metal jug, and the bubbles were still bursting at the surface from being filled from the barrel. He put Helen's glass nearer to his own and poured for them both before proposing a toast.

"Here's to us, *agapi mou*!" he smiled.

"And to our return to Filoti."

They helped themselves from the three small dishes and tried each in turn. The mackerel was good, pricking the tastebuds at the sides of their mouths, its oiliness a good excuse for another sip of wine. The trout, however, was in another class. Sprinkled with a squeeze of lemon, it thrilled the tongue with its combination of gentle fishiness and the excitement of the unidentifiable dressing in which it was served.

"I could eat this for my main meal," said Helen happily, scooping up some of the *fava* dip with her bread.

"But think what you'd miss! Let's see what's new on the menu. And you have to let me have chips, it's been four months since I last had Koula's chips!"

"When have I ever prevented you from eating chips, Martin?"

Day's one weakness, if it could be said to be his only one, was for Greek chips. He enjoyed them when he was happy, when he was sad, when he was stressed and when he was relaxed. In short, at any time.

"Have you seen this, Helen?" he said, "*Gourounopoulo sto fourno 'skordati'.* Traditional roast shoulder of pork cooked in the oven with lots of garlic. I think I can smell it from here!"

"Something certainly smells good. Here comes Thanasis."

Day asked the taverna owner about his roast pork.

"Yes, it is the pork shoulder, which has the best flavour of all pork, in my opinion, rubbed with salt and pepper, lemon, orange juice, and *dendrolivano* ... Vangeli!"

"It's OK, Thanasi, I know that one, we call it rosemary."

73

"Ah, good. After that, you make little cuts like this …" He demonstrated the action of stabbing the flat of his hand with an imaginary knife. "And you put in pieces of garlic. You know? We use quite a lot of garlic, so you can taste it. Then it cooks in the oven for nearly four hours, the last of the time on a high temperature so it's very crisp and golden. I recommend the roasted potatoes, nothing more. You will not need more food tonight. The *gourounopoulo* is very satisfying."

He smiled broadly and nodded, but Day was hesitating. The Greek's smile became a look of concern.

"Martin? There is a problem?"

Day came to a decision and looked across to Helen. "No, Thanasi, that sounds excellent. Thank you."

Thanasis deftly cleared the empty dishes from the table and went to convey the order to the kitchen.

"No chips? Are you all right?"

"The roast potatoes here are excellent," he smiled. "Anyway, I make a point of accepting the advice of the cook."

"Unlike that of the police," she murmured so that nobody else could hear. "What did you find out this afternoon?"

Day poured a little more wine into her small glass, gathering his thoughts.

"I read quite a lot about our friend Christos on the internet. He was born and grew up here on Naxos. If he were alive he would be about eighty now. He went to the University of Thessaloniki where he took a degree in Greek History and Art. After that he returned to Naxos and got a job as a teacher at the public high school, where he stayed for the rest of his working life. All that time he was an amateur archaeologist, exclusively interested in the Cyclades. He didn't marry or have any children, but he seems to have been well-liked. On his fiftieth birthday he did an Open Water Swim which made it into the newspapers. Apparently he was a very strong swimmer and a keen competitor, and worked with the local kids to encourage them in the sport."

He was interrupted by the arrival of their main course. His account was shelved for the duration of the meal by mutual consent; it would be a crime not to give this food their full attention. To describe the dish as meat and potatoes would have been insulting; it was a delight to all the senses, including the eyes. The edges of the thickly-sliced pork had been deeply scored into small rectangles which were darkly roasted and crunchy, and soft slivers of garlic were visible between them. The golden roast potatoes were decorated with sprigs of rosemary. The aroma that rose from the dish was tantalising. Vangelis, the bearer of this treat, grinned as he gave them each a warm plate and wished them '*Kali orexi*'.

Only when they had done justice to the feast and Day was toying with the idea of one last roast potato did Helen ask him to continue with what he had found out.

"It's clear that Christos's book was quite controversial. He was claiming that there was a site in the Cyclades where something of 'international historical importance' was buried. Those aren't my words, they appear on every website I looked at. But he hadn't found the precise location, his book was just an account of his theories. Nobody in the profession would risk taking him seriously on so little evidence, but there were a few amateur enthusiasts who thought this was going to be the next Knossos and made a real fuss for a while. There were also many detractors and the argument became heated. Only the British School at Athens made any attempt to support him, giving him an honorary research membership which meant unlimited time in the library.

"Only a few copies of the book were printed, and it was done at Christos's expense. His idea was to get somebody interested in making a financial commitment to helping him. There are no copies available online at the moment. Christos was never believed, and no funding came his way."

"So, for years he tried to find the Kállos alone?"

"Yes."

"Did you say he's dead now?"

"He died seventeen years ago, although his body was never found. It was assumed he'd swum far out in the open sea, which was something he loved to do, and was drowned. There was a nice piece in the local paper about him when he was eventually considered to have perished. Funny how people speak of you far more generously after you've gone. I feel very sorry for poor Christos."

"You have a fair amount in common, apart from the swimming."

"I can't imagine what you mean, Helen! When have you ever seen me swim?"

"Exactly. You're not very good on a ferry, never mind in the water!"

"You have a point. Shall we order a little more wine?"

She considered. "No, I think we should head home soon."

The look she gave him made Day immediately wave to Vangelis for the bill.

10

Day was in the kitchen, looking rather too tall for the space he was trying to work in. Aristos and Rania were coming for dinner, and Day had decided that he would do the cooking. He had announced his intention to make 'something Middle Eastern'.

His idea was to prepare food that was impressive and different, since attempting to cook Greek cuisine for Rania would be foolish. Guessing that the Curator would have conservative tastes in food, which was a pity since Day had a repertoire of Indian dishes, he remembered a recipe that he had once enjoyed at a friend's house. He had brought back from London a particular spice which he had not yet managed to find on Naxos, sumac. A visit to the supermarket in Chora that morning had then provided him with chicken, green peppers, onions, chilli flakes, garlic, thyme and lemon. Day had bought these in quantity, on the basis that if he had a culinary disaster there would be enough spare ingredients to make something else.

Helen had retired with her book to the balcony and Day had begun his preparations. He decided that marinating should be the first step, so mixed some olive oil, lemon juice, chopped garlic, thyme and sumac - guessing at the amounts - and applied this to the chicken. Having done so he put on the kettle and made Helen a cup of tea. He felt rather pleased with his progress as he took the cup out to her.

"Are you sure I can't help?" she asked.

"No, no, it's all in hand."

Back in the kitchen he surveyed the mound of remaining ingredients and began to chop. Unsure of quantities, he erred on the generous side. As he peeled the onions and cut them into chunks, he reflected that it looked rather a lot. He washed the green peppers, removed the insides and chopped these too before throwing them, with the onion, into the largest baking pan he could find in the oven drawer. This reminded him to put the oven on to warm up.

He had a sudden qualm that the dish would not be flavoursome enough. Pulling out a clean bowl he spooned in some chilli flakes, salt, pepper and more sumac, and mixed them all together. With his hands he extracted the chicken from the marinade a fillet at a time, and rubbed some spice mixture into each sticky piece with his hands, putting the finished chunks of meat on top of his vegetables. To Day it looked extremely impressive, and he had a little private smile. Now he was left with some dry spices and some marinade. I'll mix them and add them to the pan, he thought, and did so. He poured over a generous quantity of red wine and some hot water from the kettle, and put the pan in the oven.

Aristos and Rania arrived bearing a gift of homemade *koulourakia*, traditional Greek biscuits flavoured with orange and vanilla. Day asked what he could get everyone to drink, and proposed a nice white wine he had chilling in the fridge.

"Rather than open one of yours, Martin," said Aristos, producing a gift of his own from a bag. "why don't we try this? I'd like to hear what you think of it. Panayiotis, who owns the wine shop in the *plateia*, is deciding whether to stock it, so I bought a few bottles from him last week. It's from Nemea, your favourite and mine, but from a new winery that hasn't supplied Naxos till now."

Day was only too happy to take part in such a trial. One of the many things he shared with Aristos was an enjoyment of wine, and in particular discovering new wineries. Aristos removed the cork and poured a little into the four glasses on the table, and Day held his glass up to the sun to admire the colour. He found himself looking instead at Helen, who sat in that direction with Rania. The Curator's voice cut into his thoughts.

"I think I should tell you, Martin, as one of your oldest friends on Naxos, that we've noticed something of a change in you since you got back from England. I hope you don't mind that I mention it?"

Though he had spoken quietly, Helen and Rania broke off their conversation. Helen smiled with a long look at Day.

"I'm sorry," she said, "we should have told you at once. We took the winter in London to decide if it was the right thing to do, and it turned out that it is."

A huge smile covered the Curator's face.

"Oh Martin!" Rania chided, pretending to be annoyed. "I gave you several chances to tell me at our anniversary meal. This is excellent, excellent news. You must tell Nick and Deppi too, they've been wondering like we have."

"I will. Sorry. Good news, though, isn't it? I'm a lucky man."

"Any chance of a Naxos wedding?" asked Rania.

"Good God!" said Day without thinking. As the others laughed, he took a decent swallow of his wine.

"Delicious!" he announced.

He checked on his Middle Eastern Chicken; it looked far from cooked. He turned the oven up and returned to the balcony with a bowl of salty nibbles.

"Aristo, I've asked many times to pick your brains and you've never hesitated to give me the benefit of your knowledge. I'd like to again, if I may? The dinner is going to be a little while - have another glass of wine and let me tell you about something strange that's happened recently."

"Of course. What's the problem?"

"A couple of weeks ago I had a phone call from a friend in Cambridge, someone I haven't seen or heard from since I graduated."

"An old flame," added Helen, before realising that she needed to rephrase for their Greek friends. "A former girlfriend of Martin's."

"Her name is Ophelia Blue and she was my tutor. The less said about our relationship the better, but it ended when I left university. Then not long ago she called to say she was coming to Naxos to see me."

Rania threw an involuntary look at Helen. Day hastened to reassure her.

"This wasn't some kind of romantic thing. She said she had something that might interest me, she called it a professional puzzle. I thought it must be an academic problem in our field, though it did seem strange that she couldn't have found someone closer than Naxos to help her with it."

"She came in person?" said Rania.

"Yes, she arrived quite soon after the call," said Day, and told them the whole story as succinctly as he could.

"Are you happy about all this, Helen?" asked Rania when he finished.

Helen nodded. "Actually, I rather liked Ophelia, but we need to know what's happened to her."

The Curator was a patient man, but he had no interest in the romantic turn of the conversation and urged Day to continue.

"The first thing I want to ask you, Aristo, is this: have you heard of a man called Christos Nikolaidis?"

"Nikolaidis? The one who wrote that contentious book? Yes, I knew him a very long time ago, in fact it must be twenty years or more. He spent many hours in the museum for a few months. He was interested in any discoveries made on Naxos, in particular the exact location they were found, he would make a note of them all. He was also interested in whatever I could tell him about Naxos history, though he was quite knowledgeable himself. A good soul, I'm sure, but a bit of a loner and, in my opinion, misguided. Why do you want to know about him?"

"I'll tell you in just a moment. One more question first. Tell me what you remember about his book."

"He was looking for something to do with a local legend, I think. As far as I know, he was never taken seriously by anyone in the profession. There was a bit of excitement for a while about buried treasure, and I did read the book, but it was all nonsense."

"Nobody was willing to look into it?"

"Sadly for him, no. I felt rather sorry for the man. He was clearly giving his life to this search."

"Do you know if he had any family? Friends?"

"He was born here, I believe, then went away to get some qualifications before coming back to live on the island. It's a common enough pattern. I don't think he married or had children, although I seem to remember he lived down near Kalados. He was a school teacher. Then I read that he'd died. Do you remember that, Rania? Didn't he belong to a group who called themselves open water swimmers, or something like that, and he was thought to have drowned?"

"Oh yes!" said Rania. "They looked for the poor man but they couldn't find him. There was a memorial at the cathedral. On the islands it's a very terrible thing to lose someone to the sea."

"You say you read the book, Aristo?"

"Yes, but I'm afraid I haven't kept it and I can't really remember it now. What's your interest in this man, Martin?"

"Ophelia sent me a copy of his book."

"You mean, she gave you one?"

"No. She sent it in a parcel which arrived just after she disappeared."

"So you conclude that she thinks you can find what Nikolaidis was looking for," stated the Curator.

"Perhaps, but what makes no sense is her disappearance. The police have checked the hospital, the ferries, the airport, there's no sign of her. She's vanished, when it would have been so simple to talk to me about this. The parcel was particularly odd because it was wrapped in Cambridge before Ophelia came to Naxos, which means she never intended to give it to me in person. I feel she was just checking me out before leaving me to it."

"Are you sure," said Rania, "that Ophelia's motive wasn't personal? Perhaps she left because she found you were with Helen."

Day caught a look from Helen. He took his time to reply.

"I suppose it's possible, but I really think I would have known, and I didn't. I only sensed a kind of nostalgic goodwill when she spoke to me. I don't have the greatest emotional intelligence, but I think I'd have picked up something like that. What do you make of it, Aristo?"

"Well, there's nothing you can do about Ophelia's disappearance, I think. You have to focus on what she left in your hands, especially because she went to a great deal of trouble to get it to you. Do you know how she came to own a copy of the book? It's as rare as a trustworthy Turk."

Everyone winced and Aristos held up his hand apologetically. Day forged on.

"She collects rare books to do with the period of history she's interested in. Normally that would mean old books, and this book wasn't old, but it's certainly rare and she loves the Cycladic era. I assume she discovered a copy for sale and bought it."

"It sounds like she acquired the book and just acted on impulse. She wanted your help to complete Nikolaidis's search. She may have felt embarrassed about asking you in person. If she's on the staff at Cambridge, of course, she doesn't have much time to complete the search herself. In fact, you'll probably find she's back at the university for the start of the next term."

"I certainly hope so," Day said, remembering that Tsountas had said the same thing, "but I think she would have called me. I've asked the police to tell me if they find any trace of her, but there's been no word yet. Well, it's good to have your thoughts and what you remember of Christos. Look, I don't know why she couldn't just talk to me about it, but I'll accept her challenge. Maybe if I can solve the puzzle it will lead to Ophelia."

With that he grinned with a confidence he did not feel and excused himself to check on the dinner. He heard the conversation continue outside on the balcony.

The Middle Eastern Chicken was looking good, so he loosened the roast potatoes that had stuck to the pan and put it back into the oven while he made the salad. That done, he carried the plates and cutlery to the balcony and set them out on the table. He saw Helen looking at him over Rania's shoulder and winked at her. She returned the wink.

The last thing to do was open the bottle of wine he had chosen to go with his meal. That done, he carried first the tray of chicken, then the salad, and finally the wine and a bottle of water to the balcony table.

There was enough to feed everyone for several days.

When at last Day and Helen were alone again, night had fallen. Such birds as there were had long since carried out the nightly routine of flocking and chattering as the sun set until finally falling quiet in their night-time roost. It was a ceremony of nightfall that Bronze Age man must have heard, trading and settling on the coasts and islands of the Cyclades. Day sat with Helen on the balcony, listening to the deep, warm, quiet Naxian night, musing on the reassuring certainties of nature. Here at least those certainties did not yet seem fragile.

In the darkness mitigated only slightly by the single weak bulb on the house wall behind them, Helen sipped from her glass. Day looked at her.

"Are you sure you're okay about Ophelia?"

"Oh yes, I'm sure," she said, withdrawing her hand from his and pushing her hair back from her cheek. Day found this less than reassuring.

"So how are we going to begin?" she continued. "With the book, I mean. It seems to be the only place to start if we want to find her."

"We need to know that book inside out. I'll translate every word of it carefully, starting first thing tomorrow morning."

"Okay, I'll read it as you translate it."

"You will?"

"Of course. This is one mystery you're not going to tackle on your own."

"I think we should also try to find out more about Ophelia, especially her work, which might explain her interest in Christos and throw more light on the whole thing, including this Kállos legend. Do you agree?"

85

"I do. You know something, Martin? Ophelia might be the only person in the world who knew that Christos *actually found* the Kállos. She read the letter, didn't she? I think we have to assume that. Knowing the Kállos exists might be quite a burden of responsibility for her, as a historian. She might feel it her duty to finish what Christos started."

"You're right. As always, you've seen something important. I always said we'd make a great team! So, we have a plan of action, a starting point. Let's hope we also have a great deal of luck."

He stood up and switched off the balcony light. Taking her hand again he drew her into the house.

"Come on," he said, "time for bed."

11

"Good grief, Martin, you're up early!"

Helen emerged from the bedroom and found Day in the main room already at work on his computer. She stood behind him, resting her hand on his shoulder, and peered at his screen.

"You've started work on the translation already? Well done! How's it going?"

"Not too bad. The Greek isn't difficult, but the print is terrible and his tone is a bit strange. Slightly clipped and mysterious, over-careful perhaps. I'm just reading about what set him on the track of the Kállos in the first place. There were stories that had been handed down from person to person, each version slightly different from the last, as tends to happen. The stories told of something hidden, something impressive. I'll just have to translate word for word and we can analyse it afterwards."

"That sounds like the right thing. I'll make some coffee."

Day translated a piece of particularly colloquial Greek that Christos had transcribed verbatim from an old man in Engares, and was quite pleased when he had finally made sense of it.

"Any idea how long it will take to translate it all?" asked Helen from the kitchen.

"At this rate, a very long time, but it may speed up. The language is one thing, and quite difficult when he quotes exactly what old folk said, but this tone of his is infuriating. I hope he writes more clearly in the later chapters. This is an intelligent man who researched painstakingly in one of the best libraries in Greece, yet he's still not said exactly what it's all about."

"Come on, let's have our coffee, you sound like you need a break. Is it still too cold outside?"

She opened the glass door and discovered the temperature was acceptable, even though they were in their dressing gowns. It was still cool enough to see the steam rising from their cups, through which they looked out at the valley and the slowly sliding shadows that crept away from the sun. In the slight dampness of the early morning, the unmistakable smell of turned earth in the neighbour's garden was discernible through the comforting aroma of coffee.

"I've woken up absolutely determined to get on with this," said Day. "It's actually been good fun getting out my old Greek dictionary and doing a bit of translation again. I haven't done any since the biography of Elias last year."

"It's going to take a long time. Can we speed it up? Can I do some for you?"

"The best thing, I think, is if you read through the English version and see what you make of it. You'll see meanings that I'll overlook because I'm busy doing the translation. My plan is to work on it all morning, while the UK is waking up, and then make some calls to England. I want to find out more about Ophelia from people who knew her. I'm going to start with Alex."

Helen nodded, frowning. "What are you looking for, Martin? Are you going after Christos's treasure or are you trying to find Ophelia?"

"Both. Today I need to go back to the police too. I should tell Tsountas about the parcel and the book. Would you mind coming with me? It might make things easier, and anyway I'd like to hear what you think of him."

"If you want. He sounds rather unpleasant."

"Not really, he just made me angry. Anyway, we need him. I'll call him in a while and make an appointment. For now, back to the translation for me. How about you?"

"Shower, then I'll come and start work too."

"Exciting! How's it going with your novel? What's it about?"

"How should I know, Martin? I'm just the author!"

Day very nearly followed her to the shower. Instead he watched her go rather longingly and returned to the table and his laptop. His translations of the short preface and introduction were finished, and he was part way through the first chapter. He considered what he had found out so far.

As a boy growing up on the island, Christos heard older members of the community talking about something they called the Kállos, which he discovered was an ancient word for beauty. According to local legend a few people had seen the Kállos long ago, but nobody had set eyes on it in a generation. Like the best stories of lost treasure, of course, nobody knew what or where it was. This fascinated the young Christos.

He returned from university in Thessaloniki, where he had studied Ancient Greek History and Archaeology (not Art as the internet article had said), and become a teacher at the local secondary school. He retired just before his sixtieth birthday. He had been thinking about the Kállos for many years, although at first it was just a casual interest. Then he started talking to the old people in his community, asking what they knew about it and trying to separate fiction from fact. In his early fifties he came to believe that there was some truth in the story, at which point he obtained permission to use the library of the British School at Athens. For several years in succession he spent the school holidays there, studying reports of excavations and the accounts of early travellers, sleeping in the cheapest rented room he could find.

After gleaning all he could from the library he began a systematic search of Naxos and the neighbouring islands of the Lesser Cyclades. Following the clues he had amassed over the years, he tried to be methodical. Needing financial support to go further, he had written the book that Day now had before him.

At the time of writing the book, now well into his fifties, he had not found the Kállos. He had failed to convince anyone to support him, unsurprisingly to Day in view of his wary and mysterious writing style. Only later, according to the unposted letter, had he allegedly found it, and that discovery had gone with him to the grave.

Day opened the book again. There must be something in here, something everyone had missed. After the conversations with local people came the overview of Christos's work in the British School library, and after that the report of his search of the islands. The fourth and fifth chapters described possible topographical features of the location of the Kállos, and offered some suggestions as to what it might be. It was all Day could do not to read the last chapters immediately. Instead he opened the book again at the point he was working and translated without a break until he had finished all the transcripts. In the last one, the oldest woman in the village of Panagia on Iraklia island claimed that a hoard of ancient objects had been sealed up in a cave below a ridge and guarded by a mountain. Day rubbed his eyes with both hands and leaned back in the chair with a groan. Helen looked up from her work.

"Lunch time?" she asked.

Day nodded with relief, although it was not hunger he felt. They put some cheese, tomatoes and bread on small plates and took them outside with glasses of water. Day blinked at the sudden brightness; he had not looked up for several hours. He focused as far into the distance as he could to relax his eyes, and noticed the blue bee hives, in full sunlight, glowing like distant windows seen in the darkness of the night.

"You've been working for over three hours, you know. Found anything useful yet?"

"It's too early to tell. I've just finished the transcriptions. Next is the work he did in the library."

"Are you going to carry on this afternoon?"

"I don't think so, it's time to make a few calls," he replied, "starting with Alex."

"How's married life then, Alex?" began Day when his friend answered the phone.

"Martin! Good to hear from you. We're fine, thanks. How are you?"

"Great, thanks. Kate in London?"

"Sadly not, she's up in Warwick teaching all hours. It's just as I thought, both our jobs are pretty full on. She's coming home next weekend."

"Give her our love. Any feedback from the Museum on the book?"

"No word from the Director yet. I'll let you know when I hear something. Was that why you called?"

"No, something completely different, it's about Ophelia Blue. She's a friend of yours, isn't she?"

"Certainly. Ophelia from Cambridge. I saw her recently actually. We talked about you."

"Mmm, so she told me. Did she tell you she planned to come out to Naxos to see me?"

"What? No, nothing like that. She just asked where you were these days."

Day repeated the story of Ophelia's disappearance and her strange request for help, without actually mentioning Christos or the Kállos. He chose his words carefully as his former relationship with Ophelia was, he hoped, not common knowledge. Alex listened in silence. When he spoke he apologised for having given Day's contact details to Ophelia and for describing how Day had worked out the location of the tholos tomb known only to the late Nikos Elias.

"I feel bad, Martin. Perhaps I should have been more careful what I said."

"It's not a problem. She wanted my help and she's welcome to it. At the moment, at least, I don't think her disappearance is something to be extremely concerned about. My problem is, I need a bit more background knowledge if I'm to help her. I was hoping you could tell me more, especially about her work."

"I don't know her very well, Martin, we just bump into each other, like we did last month at the Conference of Aegean Studies. You know her subject is the archaeology of the Cyclades?"

"I certainly do. Ophelia taught on my undergrad degree course, although she wasn't much older than I was. It's her specific work in the last few months that might be useful to know about."

"She talked about 19th-century travellers' accounts of visits to ancient Greek sites, which was the subject of the conference. And she said that she's going to bring out a new edition of her book on Cycladic sculpture. She's hoping that Professor Renfrew might write a preface for her. She's always idolised the Great Man. That's all I can remember, I'm sorry."

"Don't worry. Did she talk about about her life outside work?"

"Yes, she'd been in touch with some charity that works with Syrian refugees in Turkey; she said she wanted to help them. She's a very nice, caring human being, Ophelia."

Day took this in, and for a moment said nothing.

"Yes," he agreed quietly. "Thanks, Alex. One last question, if you don't mind. Did she mention someone called Christos Nikolaidis?"

"Nikolaidis? I don't think so. Who is he?"

"A Greek amateur, wrote an interesting book. I thought Ophelia might have mentioned him."

"No, I'd have remembered that. What do you think Ophelia wanted, so badly she went all the way to Naxos to speak to you?"

"I'm still not entirely sure," he said on impulse. There was something else he wanted to tell Alex. "I have some good news, Alex. It's about Helen and me …"

Day came inside from the balcony and his eyes met Helen's as she looked up from her computer.

"All well?"

"Yes, I just spoke to Alex. He couldn't tell me much about Ophelia that we don't already know, and she didn't mention Christos to him at all. I told him about us. He said it calls for a visit from Kate and him in August."

"That's the best news. Do you have any more calls to make?"

"Yes, I'm going to try and speak to Ophelia's friend Mary next. Do you remember her surname? I know it was Mary someone."

"Merriman, I think. Mary Merriman. Rather a good name for a character, except I can't use it now."

"Mary Merriman," said Day, typing the name into his phone. "I'm really hoping she's a friend from the university or it will be much harder to find her. Ah, the Department of Ancient History. Got it! She's the Departmental Administrator. I'll call her on the balcony so I don't disturb you."

Mary Merriman, who answered the phone with efficiency and professional warmth, announced the name of the department and asked how she could be of help.

"Hello, this is Martin Day."

The woman on the other end was clearly taken by surprise, and equally clearly recognised his name.

"Martin? Sorry, I don't know you, of course, but Ophelia talked about you. What can I do for you, Mr Day?"

"Please, Martin is fine. I'm calling because Ophelia told me you were a good friend of hers. You knew she was coming to visit me?"

"Oh yes, of course, she was very excited to be going to Naxos again and looking forward to seeing you. Is something the matter?"

Despite putting it as gently as he could, he was painfully aware of Mary's emotional reaction when he gave her the news.

"What do you mean? She's disappeared? You don't know where she is?"

"There's no sign that she's come to harm, Mary. The police on Naxos are looking for her, we know she isn't in the hospital, and there's no record of her leaving the island. She might just need a bit of time to herself."

"That would be in character. Ophelia needs time alone. I know she doesn't share everything with me, she needs her privacy, we're very different. I wear my heart on my sleeve, you see, and Ophelia keeps herself to herself. I'm not saying she's cold, not at all, just a person who likes her own company and thoughts."

"She told me how much she values you, especially since she's been on her own," he said. "Would you mind if I asked you a few questions? It might help me to find her."

"Oh, of course, Martin! Anything to help Ophelia."

"She mentioned an adopted son…"

"Yes, his name is Raj Chaminda. He's about twenty-five now, of course, but they adopted him when he was ten or so years old. She and Tim. That's her husband, Tim Mitchell. They were so lovely together, and when little Raj came into their lives they were such a happy family. Tim's in America now, and Raj lives in London. I know, why don't I get Raj to call you? He adores his mother, maybe he could help you."

"Good idea, please do. Would you mind if we start at the beginning? When I first knew Ophelia there had been a boyfriend called Stephen…?"

"Yes, that's right, that was Stephen Lazenby. He and Ophelia are still friends. He lives in Cardiff, he works at the university. After she finished with Stephen there was …"

She stopped abruptly and Day winced.

"Yes, indeed. And after that, Mary, did she have any other close relationships before Tim?"

"Oh no. She and Tim were a whirlwind romance, he was quite a bit older than her, and she fell for him in a big way. I was new here and didn't know Ophelia well by then, but I saw it all happening. Tim was a life force."

"Yet they separated and he went to the States."

"Yes, he went to New York. He wasn't himself. Nervous breakdown, I'd say. He went to pieces."

"How long ago was that?"

"It must have been something like four years ago. He told her that he wasn't going to come back. You know how it is sometimes when someone has a mental problem, they want to cut their ties with anyone connected with their illness."

Day said that he was no expert on that, but that it sounded very sad. He tried to think of anything else that he needed to ask while she was on the phone.

"When you last saw Ophelia did she seem upset? Anything that you now think might be connected with her choosing to go off alone??"

"No," said Mary Merriman, her voice trembling again. "No, she seemed very happy, her usual self. Happier, even."

"Did she mention that her home was broken into?"

"No!" Mary coughed, then apologised. "This is so dreadful!"

"I'm really sorry. One last question. Did she tell you why she was coming to Naxos?"

"Only to see you. I thought that was what she was going for."

He heard a sniff and realised she was crying. He gave her his email and phone number, and said she was welcome to contact him any time.

"She trusted you, Martin," murmured Mary just before they hung up. "I know that. She went to you because she trusted you. Please find her."

12

Like many of the shops and businesses on the island, the police station was officially closed for several hours during the afternoon, but only to the public: the police force, of course, never rested. Day was given an appointment to see Inspector Tsountas at six o'clock in the evening when the station officially re-opened.

"That's not bad," said Day. "I expect we'll need a drink once we've finished with Tsountas."

Their reception at the police station at six o'clock was more civil than Day had come to expect, which could have been because they had an appointment, or, as Day liked to think, because Helen was with him. They were shown into the Chief of Police's office where Tsountas joined them after a few minutes. Day introduced Helen as Helen Aitchison, as she preferred. It had been many years since she had used the surname of her late husband, the Greek playboy Zissis Xenos. Besides, as she would sometimes say, nobody in England knows how to spell or pronounce Xenos. Unfortunately, in Greece the same could be said of Aitchison.

'Please take a seat," said Tsountas, courteously indicating the chairs in front of his desk and sitting opposite them. Steepling his fingers in front of his chin, he regarded them with tired, dark eyes. "How can I help you?"

"I've received a parcel from our missing friend Ophelia," said Day. "It was wrapped before she left England and posted from the post office in Chora so that it would arrive after she had gone."

"I see. What was in the parcel?"

Day described the book by Christos Nikolaidis, his letter, and Ophelia's own note. He held nothing back this time, and said enough to cover the content of the book and what seemed to be Ophelia's challenge. Inspector Tsountas gave it his complete attention, showing no sign of noticing that the case now involved a considerable amount of archaeology.

Helen took over as Day finished.

"Ophelia told us that her house in Cambridge was broken into twice and that she thought she was being followed. Martin forgot to tell you before. If somebody did this to her in England, they may have followed her to Naxos."

"In that case I shall contact the police in Cambridge and ask what they know of these break-ins. I have to tell you, though, that if your friend did not report them to the police, there may be little more I can do. Remember, we have seen no sign of violence up to now."

There was something uncaring in the policeman's voice that was beginning to make Day angry again. While he worked to suppress his irritation, Helen carried on.

"May I ask you something, Inspector? Would you be able to find out whether anyone gave Ophelia a lift from the hotel? Could you ask the bus drivers, the taxi companies? She couldn't have walked from Yiasemi Villas, it's too far. She must have got a ride. Could you find out?"

Tsountas gave her a rare smile and stood up heavily from his chair, indicating that the interview was over as far as he was concerned.

"We will make those enquiries also, Miss Aitchison, when I have the men available. Until then I urge you both not to worry. I am personally quite certain that your friend, if she has in fact left Naxos, has done so of her own accord and will soon prove to be quite safe and well. You can look forward to her return when she is ready. Good evening."

So saying, Tsountas extended his hand, shook theirs, and opened the door for them. Outside on the square, drawing deeply on the evening air, Day checked his phone for the time.

"I was right - a drink is needed, and the hour is respectable. Agreed?"

They walked slowly out of the square and towards the pavement that ran parallel to the sea, the popular Protopapathaki. They joined the people out for the evening *volta* and headed in the direction of the Portara, their objective Diogenes bar. As they sank into the cushioned bench at their usual table and Helen kissed him lightly on the cheek, Day felt the tension release its hold on him. Alexandros saw them coming and gave a relaxed wave that promised he would be with them shortly.

"Well, at least you've seen our friend Tsountas at his caring best, darling, so you can't think I'm imagining it."

"I never thought you were imagining it, but I see what you mean about him now. Of course, he's probably right. There's not much the police can do unless a crime has obviously been committed."

"Well at least you charmed him, as I knew you would. I hope he gets a move on with those enquiries. We can only hope that somebody remembers seeing her on the day she left, otherwise we have absolutely nowhere left to go with this. Other than to do what she came here to ask of me, I suppose."

"I agree," she said. "It does seem that she wants you to look for the Kállos, and what else can you do? Do you think she'll come back if you find it?"

That really was a question to which he had no answer.

After a gin and tonic at Diogenes they felt restored. An excited group of children had gathered to play in the little civic square near the bar, chasing each other round the flagpoles that stood waiting for new flags. As the sun slid gently beneath the horizon their voices became more shrill until one by one their parents took them home. The people who had gathered by the Portara to watch the sunset started to walk back past Diogenes.

"Would you like something to eat here, or shall we go home?" Day asked, placing his empty glass on the table.

"I don't mind. If we go home, I can fry some chicken, make a salad, …"

"Let's do that then. I'm quite keen to work on the translation tonight. We can't really make any progress until it's finished."

Day drove carefully back through the darkness of the central hills. A few security lights illuminated the cement works on a bend in the road, then the darkness reasserted its undisputed ownership of the rolling upland meadows. In each village the lights of street lamps and houses shone warmly, but in the uninhabited countryside Day drove only by the light of the headlamps. Not for the first time he was grateful that he knew the road well. He parked the Fiat outside their own, lightless house, the last building on the road to Apeiranthos. The fresh, cool air of the night welcomed them to Filoti.

After a simple meal of well-seasoned pan-fried chicken and salad, Helen brought a book and lay on the sofa to read while Day continued to translate. When he reached the second chapter he found the tone very different. Christos summarised the work he had done in the library of the British School in a crisp, economical style. He outlined the nature of the known Cycladic finds on Naxos and the smaller islands, explaining that this would be relevant to his later argument for the existence of the Kállos. There was a section on looters and illicit excavations which had led to the loss of important discoveries and the destruction of the context in which they had lain. As Day read on and his translation lengthened, he really appreciated Christos's desire to protect his discovery from being plundered.

Much of the information was familiar to Day, but one or two things were especially interesting, such as the discovery of nearly two hundred Bronze Age graves at Aphendika on Naxos in the 1970s. Day had not appreciated the scale of this discovery, although he did remember reading that these graves, which were in the form of flat slabs of schist or marble that resembled boxes, had contained 'grave goods'. In other words, precious items buried with the dead. It was certainly possible that there remained more such things to be found.

He worked solidly even after Helen declared she was heading to bed. She showed a brief interest in his translation, kissed his forehead, and encouraged him to keep at it. Only when he reached the end of the second chapter did he send the translations to her computer and closed his laptop with relief. The house was exceptionally silent now, only one small light still on. He poured himself a glass of wine and sat on the sofa where Helen had lain earlier. The silence and darkness in the room made him reflective, and he found himself thinking of Ophelia.

Whether it was due to his tiredness, the silence and darkness of the room, or the effect of the wine, he suddenly felt the need to examine his past relationship with Ophelia. He must do so with all the honesty he could find. He knew that he had to know her better to have any chance of helping her, but to do that he had to start at the beginning.

He had found her attractive the first time he attended one of her seminars, at the beginning of his third year. She was seven years older than him, though a world apart in maturity. He began to look forward to her classes and imagine himself with her. It was clearly an impossibility, which only enhanced his enjoyment of the idea. He was fairly sure that a relationship with one of the students was career suicide for a young member of academic staff. He had no way of knowing. Instead of approaching her directly, therefore, he indulged in languorous looks of adoration, warm smiles and impressively intelligent questions. He could see that she had noticed him.

Within a few weeks she returned a piece of work to him and asked him to come to her office to discuss it. It was Ophelia herself who made the first move. After commenting on his essay with an intelligence that thrilled him, and without changing her tone in the slightest, she suggested they meet for a drink. The way she laid a hand on his arm left him in no doubt. And so it began, two years of emotional turmoil. Ophelia told him about her break-up with Stephen Lazenby the previous year. She was not a woman to be content for long without a partner, and Day had presented himself at the right time. She laughed at his reservations about a staff-student liaison, especially after he had made his attraction to her so clear. Only later did she come to understand the depth of his inner reserve.

He must now look at their time together more honestly than he had ever done before. He had always allowed himself to dwell on the good things in their relationship: the passion, the romance, the excitement. The truth was that his twenty-year-old self had been carrying a great deal of baggage from his childhood, unresolved issues he barely understood, fear and resentment that lurked beneath a constitutional grief at the early death of his mother. He had tried to explain this to Helen once, but it had been poor Ophelia who had felt its effects at first hand. Two steps forward, one step back: he had been a passionate lover one night and a reticent youth the next. She had not always dealt with it well, and who could blame her? Their arguments had been fiery, and none of them were to do with ancient history.

Day sipped his wine. He would have liked to go to bed and forget the past, but he did not want to lie next to Helen with unresolved thoughts about Ophelia. He must finish this, and discover where it was leading.

His relationship with Ophelia had come crashing to an end during his last summer at Cambridge, leaving them both bruised and reeling. He thought it through in detail, every cruel word, every recrimination, every apology. She must have met Tim not long afterwards. Day grimaced. Tim Mitchell had acted quickly, and they were married before a year had passed. One thing was clear: Ophelia had not been hampered by any lingering feelings for himself.

He got up and took his glass to the kitchen sink, rinsing it in the near darkness and leaving it to drain. One thing about which he was now confident was that Ophelia had not come to Naxos to rekindle their passion. He could not give himself the satisfaction of even suspecting it, and it was something of a relief. Yet there had once been a deep connection between them, and whatever had caused her to seek him out now must be of considerable importance to her.

He switched off the wall lamp on the balcony that had been casting a faint glow into the room for the last few hours, and made his way to the bedroom by the light of the moon. He undressed quietly and watched Helen sleeping for a moment or two before slipping into bed next to her and gratefully stretching himself out against her.

13

"Good morning, darling," he whispered. Helen opened her eyes and looked at him sleepily.

"Good morning. Have we slept in?"

"I expect so. I love you."

"Mmm. Me too. Are you all right?"

He said nothing. She was right to tease him, he was not usually so direct in expressing his feelings, but after his reflections of last night he felt a kind of liberation, or empowerment, such as he could not remember ever feeling before. He decided there was no great need to talk about it, and no great need to get out of bed either.

Two hours later they sat at one of the tables closest to the sea at Taverna Ta Votsala, the only customers currently requiring the coffee-making skills of Vasilios. He brought them a tray containing their usual drinks and a slice of Maroula's cake for Helen, and leaned on the back of a nearby chair to chat. He did not need to ask how they were, because their happiness was plain to see.

"Your first guests are in the house, Martin," he said, gesturing towards the Elias House at the other end of the beach. "They arrived three days ago. There's a couple from Germany, and a man from Athens who is here on his own. They've eaten in our taverna every night, it's extremely good for business. I'm very grateful to you. Anything you want doing to the house, you only have to tell me and it will be done. If I can't do it myself, I will arrange for someone very good to fix it."

"You do more than enough already, Vasili."

"This time last year we hardly knew each other, and now we are friends and business partners!" exclaimed the Greek. "When we met, you were about to visit the Elias House for the first time, and then there were all those dreadful murders and you were the one who eventually found out what had happened! *Panagia mou*! Pater Giannis was talking about you only last week. What terrible things to have happened on our beautiful island."

"Actually, something strange has happened again," said Day. Vasilios Papathoma stared him directly in the eyes, beginning to fear the worst. He was getting to know his friend Martin Day.

"Please, sit down and I'll tell you. Maybe you can help."

Vasilios pulled up a chair from a nearby table and sat opposite them with a face full of concern. "I hope you're not going to tell me that you have found another dead person in the hills, or know somebody who has been stabbed to death in one of our hotels?" he said seriously.

"No, nothing like that. But an old friend of mine from England has disappeared, and she may still be somewhere on the island."

Day had not planned to talk to anyone about Ophelia, but something told him that the help of someone like Vasilios, who not only could be trusted but whose knowledge of Naxos was extensive, might be valuable. Saying nothing of Christos or his book, he told the story of Ophelia's arrival and disappearance. Helen said nothing, aware that Day was sharing only a select version of the increasingly complicated story.

"So it's possible, indeed likely, that she's still somewhere on Naxos. We all know there are plenty of casual rooms available on the island. We hope that she's just taking some time to be alone, and is safe and well. It's possible, of course, that she's in some kind of trouble, so the sooner we find her, the better."

"Why would the lady come to see you and then cause you to worry by going away without telling you? No, Martin, she wouldn't do that, especially a friend of yours. This is very dreadful indeed. We must find her. She must surely be ill, or in some difficulty! I will ask everyone I know, we will find her wherever she is. *Panagia mou*! What does she look like, this Ophelia?"

"I hope you're wrong, Vasili," said Day. "My guess is that she'll return when she's ready. All the same, it wouldn't hurt to ask your friends. She's in her forties, quite slim, and has long, auburn hair."

"Auburn hair?"

"*Kastanozantha mallia*," Day translated.

"Ah, very well, a beautiful woman with that hair colouring should not be too hard to find on a Greek island! Leave it to me! We will find her for you, this Ophelia."

"Poor Vasilios," said Helen, when they were back home in Filoti. "He did seem upset. Such a kind-hearted person. Why did you get him so worked up?"

"I didn't think it would affect him so much. As you say, he's a lovely man. The whole island will soon be on the alert for Ophelia. The thing is, we're just sitting at home working on the Kállos book. Time is passing. I need to be doing something more constructive."

"Do you have any more ideas?"

"I'm going to make some more phone calls. The first will be to her former boyfriend Stephen, who according to Mary is still a friend of hers. Then I'll speak to the husband, Tim. They should both be told about what's happened, I suppose. More importantly, I might learn something useful. By the way, did the translations come through to your computer?"

"Yes, I have three files from you. I'll read them this afternoon. I'll just put some lunch together - for some reason, I'm ravenous."

Day winked, and with a small laugh she walked away. Day took his laptop and phone to the bedroom and began to do some preliminary research into Stephen Lazenby.

There was virtually nothing to be found about the man's private life, but plenty about his professional achievements. He was fifty years old, and a serious academic with an international reputation. Day formed the impression that he was reliable, but perhaps rather unexciting. He did the sums and worked out that Lazenby had been twenty-seven to Ophelia's twenty-four when their relationship had started. They had been together just over two years, but had parted company when Lazenby moved to Wales. Judging by the dates given on the Cardiff University website, Lazenby had been offered a professorship to move from Cambridge and unsurprisingly he had accepted. He was now Deputy Vice-Chancellor.

Day found a number for the Deputy Vice-Chancellor's office and hung on till a woman's voice answered the phone.

"Professor Lazenby's office, may I help you?"

"Good morning. My name is Martin Day, I'm hoping to be able to speak briefly to Professor Lazenby. I'm an associate and friend of Dr Ophelia Blue. It's in connection with her that I'm calling."

"Would you hold on, please, while I see if Professor Lazenby can talk to you?"

Day said he would, surprised at the ease with which it was going. He only had a few minutes to wait.

"Stephen Lazenby. Is that Martin Day?"

"Yes, that's right. Thank you for talking to me. I'm calling about Ophelia Blue."

"Am I right in thinking that you …? Ophelia has mentioned a Martin …"

"Yes, that might have been me," said Day, suddenly realising that Stephen Lazenby might know more about him than he knew of Lazenby. "I'm afraid there's some cause for concern. Are you still in touch with Ophelia?"

"Yes, once or twice a year we write or call. The last time I spoke to her was at Christmas."

"She called me a couple of weeks ago and said that she was coming to see me. I was astonished. I hadn't heard from her at all in the last twenty years. She just said that she wanted my help with something, an academic matter, I assumed. I live in Greece, on the island of Naxos, and she came here to find me. Did you know anything about this?"

"No. That's news to me."

"My partner and I met Ophelia when she arrived here, and had a perfectly pleasant time talking together, but she didn't tell me why she had come to see me. We had an arrangement to meet the following evening, when she said she would tell me everything. She didn't show up. Her hotel room was empty and she had left no message. We don't know where she is."

"What do you mean? Has something happened to her?"

"Not that we know of. The police have made the usual checks and she's not in the hospital, nor has she officially left the island. She's simply disappeared."

He decided not to insult Lazenby's intelligence with platitudes, and waited to hear his response. The other man was taking his time to consider what he had just heard.

"So I assume you think that she's being purposefully elusive? Look, Martin, Ophelia and I have been friends for many years, but I'm not in her confidence. She's a very intelligent woman, and if she has done this deliberately, she will have her reasons. She's clear-sighted, responsible and passionate - as I'm sure you know as well as I - and I trust her to act for the best. However, if there's the slightest chance that she's in trouble, then we must help her."

"I completely agree. I won't let it rest, believe me, until I know that she's safe. I called you because I thought you should know what's happened, but also because I hoped you might remember something, something that Ophelia might have said, some clue about what has made her do this. I'll leave you my contact details, and if you think of anything please call me, at any time."

"Of course, I'll think about it."

"I don't suppose you have the number of Ophelia's husband in New York? I should phone him too."

There was silence at the other end of the line. He wondered what the problem was between Lazenby and Tim Mitchell.

"I'm afraid that won't be possible, Martin. He died three or four years ago."

It was Day's turn to be surprised. In a second he raced through what he could remember of their evening at Yiasemi Villas and was sure that Ophelia had not even hinted at this. Surely it was a most obvious thing to have told them that evening. Mary Merriman said nothing about it either.

"He's dead?"

"I see you didn't know, I thought she might have told you. The marriage ended suddenly, when Tim announced that he was leaving her. I don't know the details. He got himself a job in New York and left almost immediately. She heard nothing from him after that until she was informed of his death. He had committed suicide 'while the balance of his mind was disturbed', as they say. Ophelia kept his death out of the British papers and persuaded the university not to announce it either. There wasn't even an obituary in *The Times*."

"That must be why I didn't hear about it from her friend, Mary Merriman, at the university."

"I believe Mary hasn't been told," said Lazenby. "Ophelia's choice. She didn't want people talking about the way Tim died. Mary might not have been able to keep it to herself, you see."

"I see. I'm grateful to you, Stephen."

"If I think of anything you might need to know I'll get in touch. Please let me know what happens. Whatever you may think of Ophelia, this disappearance of hers is … serious."

Day closed his phone and sat back. For a while the grave implications in Stephen Lazenby's last words resonated in his mind.

"So rather than provide you with answers, your conversation with Stephen Lazenby has just posed more questions," said Helen. "How astonishing about the death of her husband."

"Yes, poor man, I can understand why Ophelia wanted to keep word his death from becoming public knowledge."

"Absolutely, although it can't have been easy. Do you think she would have told us, if we'd stayed longer that night?"

"No idea. She might have done, because we're unconnected to the rest of her life and quite a lot of time has passed now. Who knows?" Day sighed, putting some salad on his plate and adding an extra chunk of Kefalotyri cheese. "I just hope we have a chance to ask her one day."

After lunch he resumed work on Christos's book and Helen began to read the chapters that he had already translated. Hours passed, after which he was able to send her his version of the third chapter, in which Christos described his search of Naxos and the small islands. When Helen stopped to make tea and urged Day to take a break, he had to admit that, for the first time, he had started to feel excited about the search for the lost Kállos.

"I can sense Christos's conviction that there was something important to be found, and he truly believed he could find it. His approach was very professional for a man with no experience of this kind of thing. There's also much less talk in this chapter and a great deal more action. Much better!"

He drank his tea and went straight back to work. This was something Day enjoyed and was good at: long hours of meticulous bookwork, the accumulation of an enormous amount of information, holding it in his mind and turning it over until, with luck, he could see something important, something nobody else had seen. It could be maddening, exhausting and seemingly endless, but the rewards were great. Day liked nothing better than the moment when the light dawned in his mind, the luminous moment of understanding.

To his surprise and disappointment, Christos's fourth chapter, which was called 'Topographical Features of the Location of the Kállos', did not cause any such light to dawn. It was written in the form of a list. It seemed to be loosely compiled from the conversations with local people that he had transcribed earlier in the book, from which he had pulled out all the geographical references and tried to assess the relative importance of each, aiming to arrive at a working description of the location of the Kállos.

After a while Day's neck ached and his eyes felt dry. Out to the balcony he stood against the railing, allowing his eyes to relax as he focused on a small, isolated farmhouse far across the valley. A woman was sitting on her porch, bent over her lap as if preparing vegetables or perhaps sewing. Behind her, in a small yard, a child was playing on a makeshift swing hung from an old tree. Day stretched. Another hour and it would be time to call a halt and make a gin and tonic, but he couldn't face any more translation. He would spend the time trying to find out about Tim Mitchell.

He had only been doing this for half an hour when his phone rang. It was an unknown number with a London dialling code.

"Hello, Martin Day here."

"Hello. You don't know me, my name is Raj Chaminda. I'm Ophelia Blue's son. I've been given your number."

"Hello Raj, it's good to hear from you. Was it Mary Merriman who told you about me?"

"That's right. She says my mother came to see you and now she's disappeared. Is that true?"

"I'm afraid so. At least, she hasn't been seen for several days. The police don't think that anything bad has happened to her: she's not in the hospital and she doesn't even seem to have left the island. In fact, the police think that she'll return safe and well when she's ready. However, while I don't have any grounds for real concern, I'm trying to find her myself."

"I'm confused. I don't see my mother very often, only every month or so, but I had no idea she was thinking of anything more complicated than next week's lecture schedule." He paused. "Mary didn't say how you know my mother…"

"She was one of my tutors at university. Since then I've had no contact with her at all until recently."

"Mary told me that you live on a Greek island. Sorry, but what do you do?"

"I'm an archaeologist. Mostly I write books, sometimes I make TV programmes."

"Oh. You're *that* Martin Day? And my mother taught you?"

"She was only a few years older than me at the time…"

"Sorry, I didn't mean to be rude. Look, what can I do to help find her? I can't just sit here and wait around."

"I don't think there's anything you can really do. I'll call you if there's any news at all, in fact I'll call you every couple of days anyway if you like."

"Thanks, that would be good. And if you need me, if anything happens, I'll drop everything…"

"Of course. Text me your email address and I'll keep you completely up to date. And try not to worry, if you can…"

It sounded hollow, even as he said it.

Helen had heard Day's end of the call from indoors and came out to the balcony. He drew her down to sit with him and sighed into her hair.

"Ophelia's son?"

"Yes. Poor guy. If Ophelia has disappeared deliberately, how could she do that to him?"

"Mmm. She must have known how much this would hurt him. It doesn't seem like her, even though I hardly know her at all. It makes you wonder whether she's really chosen to leave without telling anybody. Would a mother do that?"

Day held her closer. "I don't know what to think. I've tried her mobile so many times, I've left messages asking her to let us know she's safe, and Raj must be doing the same. Surely she would put our minds at rest if she could?"

"I agree. This can't just be an academic treasure hunt, Martin, can it? Or if it is, and if her disappearance is really connected to Christos and his Kállos book, it's a very serious matter indeed, much more serious than we know yet."

Day gently let her go and rubbed his forehead with his hand. "Serious is the word Stephen Lazenby just used. He gave it a kind of special emphasis, if you know what I mean. He said Ophelia's disappearance was 'serious' in a way that sent a chill through me."

He smiled grimly and pulled himself together.

"I think I'll make us a gin." He felt as if the mere act of preparing the drinks would help him to put his thoughts in order. Glasses, ice, lemon. He worked slowly, cutting the lemon with precision but with an abstracted gaze. Only when the sharp citrus spray reached his nose did he take a deep breath and force his shoulders to drop.

Helen closed both their computers with an air of finality and moved the balcony table and chairs to make the most of the warm, late afternoon sun. The days were lengthening as April progressed and the heat was steadily increasing. A tiny breeze breathed against her face, welcome and gentle. Day arrived next to her, gave her a glass on which the condensation was starting to form, and sat down heavily.

"I read some interesting stuff about Tim Mitchell online," he said. "I'll tell you about it over dinner. Shall we go to eat with Thanasis?"

"Yes, we should get out of the house. You look like you need a good meal, Martin. I think you're losing weight. Frankly, you haven't got it to lose."

His laugh was cut short by the ringing of his phone, indoors on the chair. When he reached it, he recognised Raj Chaminda's number.

"Martin? Raj again. I've just booked a flight to Athens for tomorrow. I can't just stay here. I'll get a boat to Naxos and come and talk to you. I'm going to look for Mum myself. I just wanted to ask you for the name of a cheap hotel."

"Right. Okay. I'll meet you off the ferry, message me which one you're arriving on, and you can stay here with Helen and me. You won't need a hotel."

He said goodbye and put his phone down.

"That was Raj," he said to Helen. "He's coming to Naxos."

14

The generous-hearted Thanasis seemed to recognise that his favourite customers were not in the mood for banter that night. He even refrained from addressing Helen in his usual jovial manner as La Belle Hélène. Summoning his son Vangelis in a rather imperious manner which fell little short of clicking his fingers, he managed to seat Day and Helen, provide them with empty glasses, water and bread, and have their favourite local red wine in front of them in a remarkably short space of time.

"*Lipon*," he said then with a smile. "Shall I bring you a few small plates?"

Day nodded gratefully and reflected afresh what a wonderful country this was. He loved it when little dishes of savoury food were brought at the beginning of the meal and the choice could be left to the kitchen.

It was Vangelis who brought the *mezethes*, which he placed in front of them before standing back and introducing them: "Fried zucchini, village sausage, *politiki* salad. *Kali orexi.*"

Day poured a little wine for them both and looked at Helen. He felt the sad lack of a siesta and a shower, and as if dark clouds were gathering in his mind as his apprehension began to deepen again about Ophelia. Helen must be as tired as he was, but nobody would guess from her face. He marvelled, and so little did he hide his thoughts that she laughed.

"What are you thinking, Martin?"

"How good you look. Shall we tuck in?"

He passed her the bread basket first before helping himself to a set of cutlery, a serviette and a chunk of fresh bread. They ate slowly, more for comfort than hunger, enjoying the freshness of the crisp-fried courgette and the earthy richness of the small pieces of local sausage, cut through by the vinegary marinade on the salad.

"Mmm, I do like this salad," said Helen. "I may have asked you this before, but I don't remember the answer - why is it called '*politiki*'? It can't mean political, can it?"

"It's 'politiki' in the sense of 'from the polis', from the city. The city in question is the great Constantinople, now Istanbul, once the home of many Greeks. This salad can be prepared in all sorts of ways, according to how people remember it from the past, but it's always very tasty, very sharp."

"I really like it. It makes sense that it's from the east, it has an exotic flavour. This is just what we needed, Martin, I'm glad we came tonight. Ophelia's son's anxiety has transferred itself to us, and that translation seems to be eating you up."

"At least it's nearly finished. Tomorrow I'll tackle the last chapter, Christos's theories about what the Kállos might be, although I've

121

already had a look at it and he clearly had no idea at the time he was writing. All the same, I think he was right in some of his assumptions."

"What makes you say that?"

"Well, several important Cycladic sites including settlements, quarries and fortifications have been found on Naxos and the outlying islands in the last twenty years, none of which Christos could have known about. Christos was homing in on a couple of locations that fit the facts as we now know them. At least, that's my opinion."

"Does this explain why nobody picked up on it at the time?"

"I think so. It could also have been to do with his manner, people thought he was a bit crazy. He also never gave them any evidence to support his theories. But they didn't have the benefit of coming to this much later, knowing what we know now. Even in the couple of decades since the book was published, a great many discoveries have have been made. Some of the most important, in fact, were made by the man Ophelia particularly admired, Professor Renfrew. "

"I've heard of Professor Renfrew. Actually you've mentioned him quite a lot."

"He and a colleague from Cambridge ran a fantastic project uncovering Cycladic remains on the island of Keros. They proved that people were able to travel in boats from the main settlement on Keros to Naxos and the neighbouring islands, and did so regularly. Christos and his contemporaries wouldn't have been so aware of this."

Thanasis arrived to take their order for main course.

"May I recommend my wife's *yemista*? It is not just the traditional roasted vegetables, a wonderful dish though that is. We include aubergines and potatoes with the usual red peppers and tomatoes, but the stuffing ... this is made from onions, raisins, pine nuts and *trahanas* - I don't know the English for that... And, of course, our local Arseniko cheese. It is *telia*! Perfect!"

"Comfort food made by the wonderful Koula. Exactly what we need," said Helen.

"Yes, we'll have a portion of Koula's *yemista*, please, and a few little lamb chops, and some chips," said Day.

As soon as Thanasis had turned away to the kitchen, Helen looked up *trahanas* on her phone. "Apparently *trahanas* is made from cracked wheat, sheep's milk and yogurt."

"Mmm! I trust Koula completely," smiled Day, focusing on lamb chops and chips, and raised his glass.

"What did you find out about Tim Mitchell?"

"He was a few years older than Ophelia and published one or two interesting things a few years ago, ancient Greek civilisation and its place in the Mediterranean, rather general stuff. I found very little online about him after he left the UK, except his biography on the staff list of the college he joined in New York. I've formed a picture of him though - charismatic, popular, good-looking. I can't see what Ophelia saw in him."

This made her laugh, as he had meant it to do. He watched her.

"Well," she said, picking up her glass. "She was probably looking for a partner after losing you, and there was Tim, handsome, larger than life, someone who shared her interests and seemed to be going somewhere."

Day remained silent, unusually for him, then leaned back.

"He was everything I wasn't. He was going somewhere, ambitious, swept her off her feet…"

"Oh come off it, Martin. I met you soon after that and remember what you were like. You were charismatic, exciting, and you've always been popular. And, if you force me to say so, not bad looking either. You were just not ready to have the kind of relationship she wanted, and it looks like Tim Mitchell was."

Day sniffed. To dislike a dead man, one who had been so unhappy that he had taken his own life, was pretty shameful. Was it really jealousy? Then he remembered.

"Yet he walked away from her. Ended the marriage after twenty years and left her."

"Yes, and we'll probably never know the reason. It will remain their secret, Tim's and Ophelia's."

"Oh, secrets! They have their place, of course, but there are just too many of them cluttering up this entire muddle. Christos kept the secret of his wonderful Kállos, Ophelia kept the secret of Tim's suicide. The biggest secret of them all is where she is now."

"Well, it's no secret that our main course is arriving."

A generous portion of the *trahanas*-stuffed vegetables had been carefully arranged on a deep plate, which Thanasis placed before them with pride. He returned with a dish of tiny, tender lamb chops grilled to perfection, and the essential chips which he put within easy reach of Day with a smile.

"If you could eat nothing else on Naxos," he said, indicating the stuffed vegetables, "this dish would give you the essence of Greek home cooking. *Kali orexi*!"

He walked away to welcome some newly-arrived guests and offer them a table. Day took a little of the *yemista*, enjoying the aroma of baked cheese and savoury juices that arose from it. The crunchy, dark brown lids of the baked tomatoes, which had been topped with breadcrumbs and olive oil before being cooked in the oven, gave way with a pleasing amount of resistance to his fork. He took a first mouthful.

"Oh, that's good. You know me, Helen, not a huge fan of vegetables, but I might just be converted by this. I like the *trahanas* as a change from rice. More wine?" He poured a little more of the 'barrel' wine into their small glasses, helped himself to a couple of the delicate lamb chops and, finally, took a portion of chips.

That night Day worked late on the translation. The end was in sight and he thought he could finish it before he went to bed. Helen left him to it, his huge Greek-English dictionary at his elbow, squinting at Christos's little book and typing his translation into the computer. When he was done he sent the file to Helen, fetched himself a glass of cold water and stretched out on the sofa once again to think.

In his unposted letter, Christos had written that he had found the Kállos. Now that he had been through the book with care, especially in the light of more recent knowledge, Day believed him. If he hadn't read the letter, he might not have chosen to take Christos seriously any more than the experts at the time. The letter changed that. Clearly it had had the same effect on Ophelia. Day wondered again why she had chosen to give him this strange challenge, why she had thought of him after so many years. Was it only because Alex had told her about his reputation for unravelling mysteries, and that he lived on Naxos? Or was it because he was completely independent of the rest of her life? Perhaps she suspected that she was not the only person to have read Christos's letter, to believe that this beautiful treasure existed. Perhaps she thought that somebody else also knew about the Kállos, somebody who had twice broken into her home and even followed her in the street. Had she come to Day because he was the only person she could trust?

15

The next morning Day settled down on the balcony with his coffee to read his backlog of emails. There were several from his London agent, Maurice, who was naturally curious about his progress on the two jobs he had undertaken for the summer. A strong April sun beamed across the balcony from the east, and the scent of spring seemed to float in the air. Day sent Maurice a reassuring reply before returning immediately to the mystery of the Kállos. His thoughts were disrupted by an unwelcome noise, as if the Ruler of the Gods had hurled a thunderbolt into Day's morning from nearby Mount Zas.

"*Oriste!* Martin Day," he said into his phone, the source of the problem. The call was from an unknown Greek mobile.

"*Kalimera sas*, Kyrie Day," said a voice he instantly recognised. "This is Kyriakos Tsountas. I hope you are well?"

"*Kalimera*, Inspector. Do you have some news?"

"I'm afraid not, but I'm hoping to arrange an informal meeting with you for later this morning. In Apeiranthos, in fact. I believe you live not far from there? Would you and Miss Aitchison perhaps join me for coffee? The place near the public park, do you know it?"

Day mastered his surprise and a time was agreed. Putting down the phone, he wandered into the bedroom to find Helen.

"We've been summoned by the police - to coffee!" he said, watching as she pulled a light sweater over her head. "Tsountas has invited us to join him at a café in Apeiranthos at eleven."

"How strange. Why not ask us to meet him at the station?"

"He said there's no news of Ophelia. I suppose he'll tell us what this is about we get there."

Helen checked the time. "We don't have long. I can be ready in five minutes."

Day closed his computer, and soon they were driving north-east along the winding hill road. The village of Apeiranthos clung to the steep slope of Mount Fanari, the tallest peak after Mount Zas, and was built directly into the mountainside, so there was no wide *plateia* as would be usual in a Greek village. Instead the houses spread in lines along ridges backed in places by sheets of marble, an elongated but impressive settlement that shone white in the sun. Day had heard it said that the village had been the home of Cretan settlers in the tenth century, and the local dialect still resembled Cretan. Though no linguistic expert, he loved to sit at the café and listen to the locals as they talked. He doubted he would ever master the special language of mountainous Apeiranthos.

The road rose and twisted, and a pair of hoopoes flew in front of the car as they parked, a flurry of orange and white. He and Helen took a footpath that led steeply downhill, passed through a small municipal park, and disgorged visitors into a quiet main street. With café tables spilling out onto the pavement, this was one of the best places in Apeiranthos to sit and watch people going about their business.

Only two tables were occupied at the café. At one, a pair of old men sat playing the Greek backgammon game, *tavli*, with empty coffee cups and a sense of having all the time in the world. At the other, a pretty young woman sat alone looking at her phone. They chose a table in the warm sun between the two.

"One day I'd like to take you to the museum here," said Day, who had just signalled to the proprietor that they were waiting for friends. "The archaeological one - Apeiranthos has at least three museums, it's quite an amazing place. The archaeological museum is the best - although I'm biased, of course - and has a good story attached to it. Years ago the authorities declared a sort of amnesty, to encourage the locals to give up all the historical objects they'd kept in their family homes for generations, and this worked so well that they have a couple of thousand exhibits, some quite unique. There are even chunks of limestone carved with scenes of daily life in the Bronze Age - farming, fishing, that kind of thing. Petroglyphs, they're called, carvings on rock. I must take you to see them."

Helen, however, was dwelling on the more recent past, and with far less pleasure.

"I remember Zissis brought me here once. I think we visited the church…"

"I'm sure you did," murmured Day, thinking that her ex-husband had been rather more appreciative of the Virgin Mary than his wife. "Apeiranthos is a gem, we could walk through its narrow lanes for hours and I think you'd love it. I believe the streets are the original marble-paved mule tracks. I'd like to show you the Tower of Zevgoli too, the Venetian tower along there. And at the far end of this road you come to a walking track which I think was an ancient pathway created more than a thousand years ago."

"That's almost enough to make me take up hiking!" she smiled, although Day was unsure how seriously she meant it.

"The other thing about Apeiranthos is it was the birthplace of one of the two young men who scaled the steep side of the Acropolis of Athens during the War, and took the Nazi flag down from the flagpole. Have I ever told you about that?"

"Yes, you have done. Unforgettable, isn't it? And one of them came from this village?"

"Manolis Glezos was his name. He achieved folk hero status overnight. He went on to be a left-wing activist and politician."

"So he survived the flag adventure? Amazing. Is he still alive?"

"If so, he must be in his nineties. Sorry, I'm not sure. His brother, unfortunately, was shot by the Nazis; there's a library here in his name."

Before he could continue, they saw the unmistakable figure of Kyriakos Tsountas emerging from a small shop nearby with a new packet of cigarettes. He gave them a small wave as he came closer, a grin on his face.

"*Ti kanete?*" he said, shaking their hands and straightening up. "Thank you for coming. May I introduce my girlfriend, Angeliki Solomou? Angeliki - Helen - Martin."

Unnoticed by Day and Helen, the pretty woman from the nearby table had got up to join them, and the reason for the policeman's grin was now evident. Tsountas touched her gently on the arm and invited them all to sit down. Angeliki took the chair opposite Day, while Tsountas sat facing Helen.

"Coffee? What will you have?" he asked.

The proprietor took their orders and returned to the interior of the café. The two older men with the *tavli* board, who had been openly staring at Angeliki, now returned to their game.

"I thought we could talk more easily away from the police station," said Tsountas. "There are one or two items I want to share with you. I also remembered your very hospitable invitation, which I had to turn down, but since Angeliki has been able to visit me this weekend …"

"Of course. Good to meet you, Angeliki. Business or pleasure first, Inspector?"

"Kyriakos, please. Shall we begin with Ophelia? We can talk in front of Angeliki: she has already taken a personal interest in your missing friend."

"I'm concerned for her," said the girl. "I've told Kyriako that he must make every effort to find out what has happened to her!"

Tsountas grinned. "I'd come to the same conclusion all on my own. I spoke to the police in Cambridge and they did investigate the break-ins. The police examined the house after the second incident but unfortunately found no evidence and made no further progress. You will be pleased to know that we're now treating this as a missing person case, as it seems likely that there was some trouble for your friend in England before she came to Naxos."

"Did you discover how she left the hotel?"

"My men have been working on it, but I'm afraid they have had no success. All the registered taxi companies have been questioned, the staff at the hotel, car and motor-cycle hire businesses, bus drivers. We've asked again at the ferry port and all the ticket offices, and at the airport. Her description has been circulated, and with her striking colouring I'm surprised we haven't heard any report of her. I'm sorry, but for now that is everything. Have you learned anything new since we spoke, Martin?"

"Very little of use. I called two friends of Ophelia's in England, hoping they could tell me something about her that would suggest why she left. Her closest female friend told me that Ophelia and her ex-husband have an adopted son, and she got him to call me. He's arriving on Naxos tomorrow to look for her himself."

"Is he? Ask him to come and talk to me, please," said Tsountas. "Anything else?"

"I've translated the book that Ophelia sent me, the one I told you about. I thought I might find something to explain why she wanted me to have it, and Helen is reading it too. I want her reaction to it as a non-historian and she has insights into people that I don't have."

"And have you learned anything from it?"

Day shrugged. "The main thing is that I think Nikolaidis might have been right. There might really be something valuable to be found."

"We think Ophelia gave the book to Martin because she wanted him to look for it," put in Helen. "And then she left."

"I'm becoming concerned that whoever broke into her home might also be trying to find it," said Day.

"Indeed. I have already alerted the UK and Greek authorities, and spoken to the Press. If nothing else, taking official action will bring some reassurance to her son."

"If nothing else?" said Angeliki. "Don't you think you will find her, Kyriako?"

"I wouldn't take the course of action unless I believed it might be productive, *agapi mou*. I want this woman safely found as much as you do."

The Inspector lit a fresh cigarette and leaned back in his chair. He was, as before, dressed entirely in black, but his bearing was relaxed, his hand rested on Angeliki's, and his stern, bearded face wore a contented expression. Benevolent was the word that came to mind, and Day found it extraordinary. He supposed he must get used to calling this man Kyriakos, this inspector from Volos to whom he had initially taken an immediate dislike. He still feared that the former incarnation of Kyriakos Tsountas would reassert itself.

As the two women began to talk sociably of other things, Day drank his coffee quietly and watched Kyriakos as he smoked and gazed at his girlfriend with unmistakable happiness. He remembered something that the young inspector had said when they first met: *I am a most ambitious police officer, perhaps too ambitious. I have something to prove, and it is not that I am the next excavator of Greece.* Now here was Kyriakos on a supposedly crime-free Cycladic island, befriending an archaeologist, searching for another, and listening to tales of a mysterious ancient legend. What was responsible for the contentment on his face? Day had no doubt that the answer was the young woman opposite him. Smiling at Angeliki, Day joined in the conversation and asked her where she lived.

The girl glanced at Kyriakos, her expression suddenly wistful. Day noticed the colour of her eyes for the first time, a light greenish blue like shallow water over a sandy seabed, unusual in a Greek woman. She wore a lot of dark eye makeup, which Day thought unnecessary, but he recognised that on Angeliki it looked good. The oversized, multicoloured hoop earrings, too, were a statement of personal flair which suited her.

"I was born on Syros, but although it is very close to here I only visited Naxos occasionally when I was a child. I moved to the mainland when I was eighteen, and I have lived in Volos ever since."

"What do you do?" asked Helen.

"I'm a lab technician," she answered. "I do virus identification, blood testing, immunology. I'm hoping to find a position on Naxos."

"Before I came here, Angeliki and I were about to get engaged," said Kyriakos. "My promotion therefore involved a difficult decision for us both. It would have been foolish to turn it down, but it was hard to accept a separation. It has not been easy. It is difficult for either of us to leave our work, so this is the first time we have been able to be together since I arrived."

"This weekend we've decided," said Angeliki. "I will find a job on Naxos as soon as possible, and we will be together properly."

"I wish you both the best of luck," said Helen.

Tsountas put out his cigarette, excused himself and went into the café to find the bathroom. Angeliki watched him go then turned to Helen.

"Kyriako and I have known each other since I first arrived in Volos. He had a most difficult childhood, his father was really a very strange man. When I first met him, he had just joined the police. He had just broken free of his father."

"He told me something about that," murmured Day.

"He finds it difficult even now to forget those early struggles. He is not perhaps the kind of man who usually enters the police. But he is very determined, very driven to succeed. When I am here permanently, we will have the kind of family life that he missed as a child. Thank you for meeting us this morning. I hope we can meet again?"

Day listened as Helen expertly responded to this generous expression of friendship from the young Greek woman. He allowed himself to gaze at her, placing a sympathetic smile on his face, while privately wondering about the real Kyriakos Tsountas. Was he this girl's amiable but troubled fiancé, or the officious and rather feared Chief of Police? Or was it possible that he was both?

16

Day received a message from Raj with the details of his ferry to Naxos. He was in Athens and would be arriving on the *Worldchampion Jet* from Piraeus that docked mid-afternoon that same day. Day replied that he and Helen would meet the boat.

The *Worldchampion Jet* was the newest and fastest of the vessels that brought passengers from Athens. It also served such fashionable venues as the islands of Santorini and Mykonos, and was impressive in the extreme. Its huge bulk, in a livery of black and white, approached the harbour with a steadiness that suggested regal status. Giving vent to two massive blasts of the horn, the first long and the second short, it approached the quay and began its controlled pirouette, enabling it to present its vehicle ramp to the port. Passengers not planning to disembark at Naxos had assembled on the high deck at the back of the boat to watch the docking from a superior elevation.

As the rear of the vessel edged towards the quay, men in orange jackets on the land stood ready to fix the ropes to iron bollards. The ramp began to unfold itself like the arm of a crane, and as the distance closed between the ship and the shore, it lowered until it touched gently down. The view from the shore into the giant catamaran's interior was like gazing into the gaping mouth of a whale.

"Not exactly a rusty old ferry, is it?" Day muttered into Helen's ear over the noise of the people around them. As if in agreement, the *Worldchampion Jet* began the orderly disembarkation of its passengers at the imperious wave of its smartly dressed crewmen, and its Greek flag fluttered proudly from the superstructure.

It was not hard to guess which of the descending passengers might be Raj Chaminda. He was the only young man to disembark on his own, wearing a black leather jacket over a white T-shirt and jeans, and carrying a small bag. He looked round keenly almost as soon as he reached the quay, and when Day gave a wave he walked towards them.

"Raj? I'm Martin, good to see you. This is Helen. How was your journey?"

He took Raj's bag and they walked to the car through the crowded port. Raj looked tired but in control of himself, thanking them for their invitation to stay with them and for what they were doing to find his mother. In the back of the car, as they joined the congested roads that were a consequence of every boat's arrival, he told them about his sudden decision to come to Naxos, his negotiation with his boss for a few days' leave and his struggle to find an overnight room in Piraeus. He spoke with a slight east London accent, and despite his obvious anxiety he laughed easily. Day immediately liked him.

As they left Chora and took the road towards Filoti, Raj showed an interest in the island, asking questions about it and about why they lived there. As the road climbed towards Halki he looked keenly out of the window, awed by the scenery that Day now took for granted. At the house they showed him to the spare room and left him to shower and change. Half an hour later he joined them on the balcony looking refreshed in a clean cotton shirt.

"What can I get you to drink, Raj? Tea, coffee? Water? Wine?"

"I'll have whatever you're having, Martin. Thank you."

Day brought a cold white wine out to the balcony, with three glasses and a bottle of mineral water. He poured a little wine into each glass and raised his in welcome to their guest.

"This evening we've arranged to take you to the hotel where your mother was staying. We thought you'd like to see it, and we'll get something to eat there. Tomorrow you need to go and talk to the police, they want to see you. You can stay with us as long as you like. Treat this as your home and just let us know whatever you need."

"You're both very kind. How well did you know my mother?"

"She was one of my university tutors, as I think I told you on the phone. We also went out together for a while. This was before she met your father, Tim. Our relationship ended when I finished my degree and we lost contact then until she called me less than a fortnight ago."

"And that's when I met Ophelia for the first time," said Helen. "She asked us to her hotel where we had supper on her balcony. I liked her very much."

Raj nodded. Day found him rather impressive. Though in his late twenties he was mature and confident. He had short black hair and full eyebrows, and his moustache was trimmed neatly across his upper lip. A tidy beard hovered around the end of his chin. He was a young man in charge of his life, and he was certainly handling the situation well.

"Tell us a little about yourself, Raj," said Helen.

"Okay. I'm Nepali by birth, as you may have guessed. I lost my parents very young and spent years in various institutions until Ophelia and Tim came along. I was eleven when they adopted me. That was fifteen years ago now. Mum and Tim hadn't been married more than a couple of years then. They were a great team. You know, people like me tend to have a few issues and I was no different, but they got me through it all. You couldn't be insecure for long with them around."

"What were they like?" asked Helen, with genuine interest.

"Mum was massively supportive while I was growing up. She gave great hugs too. Tim had so much energy, he was always on some mission or other, some project, the next goal. He was very ambitious, professionally, and he was ambitious for me too. Mum was my bedrock and Tim was the bomb under my backside."

"Tim was a historian like Ophelia, wasn't he? Did they encourage you to do the same?"

"They never put any pressure on me at all. I had a gift for languages, and that was what they agreed I should do. I work in London now as a simultaneous interpreter. Mum and Tim had first-hand experience of parents who put pressure on their kids, and they told me they would never do that to me."

Day poured a little more wine into Helen's glass and offered to do the same for Raj. He declined politely and helped himself from the bottle of water.

"What kind of parental pressure had they experienced?" Helen asked.

"Well, Tim wanted to go to uni and do Classics and Ancient History, but in his family nobody had ever gone to college and they didn't like the sound of Classics. He made his own way, and I think it was a while before the family got used to it. As for Mum, her father was the famous art curator, Alastair Blue. Have you heard of him? He's been on TV. He's completely obsessed with the Pre-Raphaelites. He named her after Millais's painting of Ophelia in the Tate. Her sister, who sadly died as a baby, was called Isabella after another Millais painting. Mum told me he'd wanted to name one of the girls Proserpine - that's a painting by Rossetti - but his wife refused point blank. He expected Mum to become either an artist or an art historian like himself. Instead, like Tim, she chose Classics, and after that had very little to do with her father."

"Yet Ophelia loved the painted ceramics of Ancient Greece," said Day with a small smile. He wondered if she had ever told him about her difficult father; he hoped he would have remembered.

"I've got something to show you, Raj," he said, getting up. He fetched the book and Christos's letter, but left Ophelia's note in the bedroom.

"This arrived from your mother recently. "

Raj glanced at the book, put it on the table, and read the letter.

"I don't know Greek, I'm afraid. What's the book about? Who is this … Nikolaidis?"

Day told him, and added that he had just finished translating the book into English. "You can read my translation if you want, it's not too long. My current theory is that when he wrote the book Christos believed this lost treasure, the Kállos, might be on Iraklia. It's a small island off the south coast of Naxos."

"This letter, though - he's saying that he's seen this thing with his own eyes, isn't he? He must have known where it is."

"That's right, but the letter was written after the publication of the book. It's the only evidence that Christos found the Kállos, and it may be that only Ophelia, you, Helen and I know about it."

"How come Mum had it?"

"She bought this book for her rare book collection. The letter was inside."

"And she wanted you to help her find this thing? What do you think it is?"

"I don't know. Small marble figurines for use in a ritual ceremony, perhaps, or 'grave goods', objects that were buried with the dead."

"I see. Perhaps if we announced that you'd found it, she'd come back? It's worth a try, isn't it?"

"My instinct is to do this properly and try to actually find the Kállos, and then maybe announce it. Whatever lies behind your mother's disappearance, it must be serious, and she wouldn't want me to be dishonest with her."

Helen had not said anything for a while and now intervened. "Look, shall we go and get something to eat at Yiasemi Villas? It's about time and it's only a short drive. We can talk more when we get there."

The owner of Yiasemi Villas made a point of meeting them as soon as they arrived, because Helen had explained, when she made the table reservation, that Ophelia's son would be with them. When Raj heard that his mother's rooms were unoccupied, he accepted the offer to look inside. The little villa had been carefully cleaned in readiness for the next guest. Raj looked around and then lingered for a few minutes on the balcony.

"This is where you all sat and talked?"

"Yes."

The proprietor was waiting for them outside the villa and led them to the pool-bar. Day wondered fleetingly whether Ophelia had ever swum in the clear water of the swimming pool, which was empty and inviting, lit by underwater lights. They were shown to a quiet table in the restaurant, which was usually only used by the hotel guests. The white walls were decorated with original murals showing scenes of Naxos, and round the windows were a number of ornate antefix tiles from the roofs of traditional houses. The staff were friendly and everyone began to relax.

Day described his calls to Mary Merriman and Stephen Lazenby. The young man listened carefully without interrupting. When Day told him what Stephen Lazenby had said about the death of Tim Mitchell, he was expecting more of a reaction from Raj.

"Yes, I knew about Tim," the young man said frankly. "I wasn't sure whether I should tell you, but since you already know there's no harm. Tim killed himself and my mother desperately wanted nobody to know. I gave her my word. Did you hear it from Mum?"

"No, Stephen told me. Your mother spoke as if Tim were still alive. She told us that he'd been unwell and gone to New York for some space, and that she hadn't heard from him after that. I suppose they didn't divorce?"

"No."

"Ophelia told us that her home had been broken into a couple of times. Did you know about that?"

"No! She didn't tell me. Maybe it happened after our last phone call. Perhaps she didn't want to worry me. That would be so typical of her. She carries her own and everyone else's problems inside her, and protects the people she loves."

17

Day's phone rang just as he was dressing the next morning and he saw the caller was Vasilios. His first thought was that there must be a problem at the Elias House or the taverna.

"*Kalimera*, Vasili, *pos paei?*" he said. "Is something wrong?"

"Nothing's wrong, Martin, but you should come over right away. I have a local man here, a fisherman called Panos Dimou. I think he's seen your friend Ophelia. From the description it sounds like her and I think you should speak to him. He needs to get back to work as soon as possible."

"Right, I'll come straight away. Thanks, Vasili. Give him a coffee and ask him please to wait."

Still buttoning his shirt, Day left the bedroom and saw that Helen had heard and was closing the shutters.

"Raj?" he called. "There's a change of plan. We're going to speak to a man who thinks he's seen your mother. Five minutes at the car?"

There was just time to call Aristos.

"*Kalimera*, Aristo. Martin here. Quick question - would you mind taking a look at the Nikolaidis book for me? I'm going to need your help. Thanks, I really appreciate it. I'll probably drop it in to the museum tomorrow."

Putting his mobile in his pocket, he scooped his jacket off the back of a chair and joined Helen and Raj in the car.

Helen drove to Paralia Votsala more calmly than Day might have done. Raj too was on edge, shifting in his cramped seat in the back of the Fiat 500 more from nervous energy than discomfort. After an initial burst of excited speculation, they fell quiet. Halki was full of activity, but beyond, in the olive groves of the Tragea, a more sedate pace of life was in evidence. Helen took the serpentine road north through the hills, saving some ten minutes by using the rural route through Melanes and Engares. As they drove down towards the glittering sea the high land behind them cast a cool shadow over the long, narrow beach.

At the Taverna Ta Votsala, Vasilios introduced them to the fisherman who was waiting at one of the tables. He wore old jeans, a long-sleeved denim shirt and an unzipped grey gilet to which his keys were attached by a carabiner. On the table next to him was a cup of Greek coffee and his black fisherman's cap. He stood when he saw them and ran his gnarled fingers across his generous white moustache. With his head tilted to one side he regarded them from under heavy dark brows, and shook hands with them seriously. Vasilios took charge and asked the fisherman to repeat what he had seen. The conversation was in Greek, which Helen, who had an adequate knowledge of the language from her marriage to Zissis, managed to translate for Raj as they went along.

"I read in the paper this morning about the woman that's missing," said Panos. "I think I saw her a few days ago. I knew Vasilios was looking for her, so I came here. Better than talking to the police. So I came here. I was out there in the bay in my boat, coming home from fishing. I'd been at sea since first light. That's when the fishing is best. I had brought in the nets and was cleaning the fish when I heard another boat coming from the north, from up near Apollonas maybe. It was going fast, definitely not fishing. There was a passenger in it, a woman."

"Describe the woman, Pano," urged Vasilios.

"Beautiful, she was. Long hair, a red colour."

"Yes!" muttered Raj, when Helen translated. "What time was this?"

Day repeated the question in Greek for the fisherman. The sideways look that accompanied his answer may have been a mannerism or it may have conveyed a certain scorn.

"No watch," he said, showing his wrist and lifting his chin as if this was obvious. "About two hours after dawn, no later."

"And the boat was heading to Chora?" continued Raj.

Again, a sideways movement of the head and a shrug accompanied Panos's reply when Day translated. "Who can say where the boat was going?"

"Did you recognise it?" asked Day.

"No."

"If the boat came from the north of the island, Panos wouldn't know it," said Vasilios. "He's from the south. Do you think it was Ophelia, Martin?"

Day gave a slight shake of his head and turned back to Panos. "The woman with the red hair, how did she seem? Did you think she was in trouble?"

"She was sitting in the back of the boat looking at the sea. A passenger, as I said."

Day was aware of Raj's relief. He tried to think of anything else he should ask.

"Would you try to find out who owns that boat, Kyrie? What did it look like?"

"It was a fishing boat, white with a red cabin. A good engine, very good. I didn't see its name. I will ask in Chora, if you want."

"*Efharisto poli*," said Day, and Raj gave his thanks too, having learned that much by listening to the conversation. "Can I introduce my friend here? This is the son of the missing woman."

The fisherman's face registered confusion as he compared the red hair of the mother and the dark Nepali good looks of the son, but quickly a huge smile folded his face into weathered wrinkles, creased his eyes and revealed teeth browned by smoking. He shook Raj's hand with his head inclined to one side.

"*Kali epitichia!*" he said, and Helen translated: "I wish you success."

"We're very grateful to you, Kyrie," said Day. "Another coffee? Or an ouzo, perhaps?"

The fisherman politely declined and Vasilios walked with him to his car. Day sat down again and Raj, who was clearly elated, grinned at them both.

"She's okay, I'm sure she's okay! Thank goodness, what a relief! There must have been something about her in the local paper, mustn't there? Perhaps more people will remember seeing her. So, what's next, Martin?"

"You need to go and see the police, and while you're there you'd better tell them what Panos just told us. Then do exactly what you planned - show Ophelia's picture round the port and see if anybody remembers her. Surely *somebody* noticed her. Pick up a copy of *The Naxian* too, we should see what the article says." He paused. "You know, Raj, we can't be sure it was her in the boat, and even if it was, if she was leaving the island it will be hard to find out where she went."

"I know," said Raj and turned in his chair to look out to the empty sea. "I just feel better knowing she's okay."

"If it was her, though, she could have hired the boat in one of the quiet fishing villages in the north where it would easy not to attract attention, and been taken anywhere she wanted. That would suggest that everything that has happened was Ophelia's own choice."

"She could have gone to another island and taken a ferry from there to almost anywhere," said Helen.

"Yes, I know," said Day, and lowered his voice to avoid Raj overhearing; he had just begun to walk away. "Or she could be looking for the Kállos herself."

"That would mean she's playing a game with you," Helen replied equally quietly. "That would be very cruel. I don't believe she would do that."

Day glanced at Raj, but the younger man seemed not to have heard them. He was standing on the shingle, staring out to sea as if hoping to see a small boat with a red cabin. Realising he had missed something, he turned and smiled apologetically. "I'll look for the boat when I'm in the port later," he said, coming back.

"Good idea. Let's get going, you've a lot to do today."

Having dropped Raj in Chora, Day and Helen returned to Filoti. While searching online for Mary Merriman a few days ago, Day had noticed that Ophelia had a Research Assistant called James Sedge, who had taken up the post three years ago in a move to the UK from the City University of New York. Day hoped that in those three years Sedge had grown to know Ophelia well, because Day had begun to suspect that she was still keeping something important from him.

He dialled an office number in Jesus College. He was in luck; a voice announced itself as 'Sedge' before adding 'Head of Department's Office.'

"Good morning, I'm Martin Day. Dr James Sedge? I wonder if I could talk to you about Ophelia Blue."

"Martin?" the man sounded shocked. "Of course. Sorry, how can I help you?"

"You seem to know who I am."

"Yes, I do. We've been told that Ophelia is missing in Greece. I knew she was planning to visit you."

"She told you that?"

"I believe it was the Department Administrator. Is there any news?"

"I'm afraid not, but may I ask you a few questions? It might help me to work out what's happened to her. For instance, can you tell me what was she working on before she left for Greece?"

James sighed and there was a long pause before he spoke. "She was editing the papers from our recent conference, which was on historical accounts of ancient ruins. She wrote one of the papers herself, which is now online. It's on the Cambridge University website if you want to read it."

"What's the title?"

"*Looted Bronze Age sites in the Aegean as described by Nineteenth Century Travellers to Greece.*"

"Thanks. What else has she been working on in the last six months?"

"She was revising her book on the Keros Excavations. She planned to write a new introduction and conclusion using recent material."

"Okay. Anything else?" He hoped so, because so far he had not heard anything new.

"She was planning to write something about a Greek amateur archaeologist called Christos Nikolaidis. Ophelia has a collection of rare books connected to Cycladic history. She acquired a book by this man, she was pleased with it, there aren't many copies out there. Did she speak to you about it?"

Adopting a matter-of-fact tone to cover his excitement, and ignoring the question, Day asked if James could find Ophelia's notes on Nikolaidis.

"I'll do my best if you think it will help. We're all very concerned about her."

They exchanged email addresses and Day was about to end the call when James spoke again.

"I'm glad I've had a chance to talk to you, Martin. I know about your work, of course. I've seen some of your programmes, and I've read your book on Nikos Elias. It was stupid of me not to make the connection between you and Ophelia. She never mentioned that she'd seen you on her trips to Naxos, you see."

"Probably because we didn't meet. What trips to Naxos did she make?"

"She's spent a few weeks there each year for as long as I've known her. She always went alone, that's what she preferred to do. Didn't she tell you?"

While he waited to see whether James Sedge found anything to do with Christos Nikolaidis among Ophelia's papers, Day settled down to check the other things he had mentioned. Her conference paper was easy to bring up online, but Day read it with increasing disappointment. It was an interesting analysis of the serious problem of looting, but the only link to Christos was that they had both been concerned about the destructive plundering of antiquities.

He expected no greater success from her book on the excavations of Professor Lord Colin Renfrew, the great British archaeologist of Greece, on the nearby island of Keros. Day went to his bookcase, pulled out his signed copy and took it to the balcony where he threw himself wearily into a chair in the sun. He had forgotten that it had originally been her doctoral thesis, but he did remember that she had always been slightly obsessed with Keros, the spiritual home of the Cycladic civilisation. He was filled with sadness as he read Ophelia's chapter about the appalling plunder of Keros in the years before the excavation, a violation that had for ever diminished the world's knowledge of the Cycladic culture. He closed the book and, with a silent apology to its author, placed it on the table next to him. He was fairly sure that none of this would help him to find Ophelia.

He put his feet onto another chair and stared at the valley. Out there in the uncomplicated countryside, where nature existed in time but with no sense of future or past, and no knowledge of their complexity, there was some rest for the mind. The upland hills must have looked very much like this to the Cycladic people, those responsible for creating some of the most beautiful sculptures ever made. They had lived in well-organised communities and travelled across the sea between the islands of the Aegean in longships with no sail, rowed by as many as forty oarsmen. Evidence for these vessels was indisputable, because images of them had been found on pots dating from the period, and a small model boat had been unearthed from a Bronze Age grave on Naxos. Travel between the islands had been important for Bronze Age people. Their seafaring skills would have enabled them to find more than food: wives from other islands, marble and emery for their sculptures, and everything else that could be acquired through trade.

It was a civilisation that was doomed not to last. Their settlements became larger and more defensive, as if in fear of external attack. After 2000 BCE, only a few centuries after their most creative period, there was little left of their brilliance; the beautiful figurines so admired by Picasso, Modigliani and Henry Moore were no longer being made.

Some time later Day woke up and went to bed to continue his afternoon nap. He was unsuccessful. Instead, he found a map of the Cyclades in the bedside drawer and pored over it.

18

Raj came in through the unlocked front door and threw a copy of *The Naxian* onto the table.

POLICE SEARCH FOR MISSING WOMAN ON NAXOS: HAVE YOU SEEN HER?

Inspector Kyriakos Tsountas, Naxos Chief of Police following the retirement of Inspector T. Cristopoulos, put out an appeal today for anyone with information regarding the disappearance of a British visitor to the island.

Police are becoming concerned for the safety of Dr Ophelia Blue (47), who arrived on Naxos on 14th April. She was staying at Yiasemi Villas in Agios Prokopios, met local friends for dinner on the night of her arrival, and apparently left the hotel during the night or early the following morning. She has not been seen since.

The missing woman is of average height, slim, with distinctive long hair of a red-brown colour. It is possible that someone saw her as she left the hotel and travelled away from the Agios Prokopios area. There is no evidence that she has left the island. The public are asked to contact the police with any relevant information.

"I've walked all day!" said Raj, collapsing into a chair. "First I went to the police station to see Inspector Tsountas. He seems to know what he's doing, I found him quite reassuring actually. He's alerted the police across the entire Cyclades and the mainland, circulated Mum's description, and put an alert on all ports and airports. Then I walked all the way along the shore road to the port showing Mum's photograph to anyone who would talk to me. Most people were very sympathetic but couldn't help. Then I had some luck.

"I went on past the port to the Portara showing the picture, and I saw a bus which was leaving for Plaka, the one that goes past Yiasemi Villas. I bought a ticket at the kiosk and asked the driver to tell me when to get off for the hotel. I even asked the people on the bus if they'd seen Mum. The bus driver dropped me just past the hotel and the owner - I've forgotten her name now - she was very kind and gave me a free coffee in the bar. Several people asked if there was news. Then two women came up to me, one of them crying and the other telling her to speak to me. They had a copy of the newspaper. The woman who was crying had realised that she'd given Mum a lift from the hotel on the day she disappeared."

"What?"

"Yes. Her name is Soula and she cleans there part-time, early in the mornings, when the villas have to be turned round quickly. Mum had asked for her help. Soula agreed to take her to Apollonas, which is where Soula lives, after she finished work. It fits, doesn't it? In Apollonas Mum could have hired a man with a boat, and that could have been her that the fisherman saw."

"What else did this woman say?" asked Day, hoping he already knew the answer.

"Mum gave Soula a parcel and asked her to post it the next day in the post office in Chora."

"Brilliant! That's the parcel containing the book, which was posted so that it would only reach me once Ophelia had safely got away."

"The lady who owns Yiasemi Villas said she'd take Soula to the police station to tell the Inspector."

"I suppose Ophelia didn't tell Soula where she planned to go next?"

"No. But I'm just so relieved, Martin! Mum will come back when she's ready, when she's done whatever she needs to do. I needed some good news today, my boss has been on to me this afternoon. He needs me to go home. They're short of interpreters for a big EU event in London on Wednesday. I'll have to leave tomorrow, but I can always come back if I have to, it's easy to get a flight if you only need one seat. Or do you think I should stay?"

"No, you go, Raj, work is work. We'll keep in touch."

"You two are such good people! Right, I need a shower, then I'll book my tickets online and start packing. Can we all go to your friend Thanasis's place to eat tonight? I'd like to take you out to say thank you."

"That sounds good," said Helen, and added they would take Raj to the port for his ferry the next day, but her smile faded once he had gone to his room.

"What do you think, Martin?"

"On the face of it, Raj could be right. It does seem that Ophelia left deliberately, and that she's not in trouble. On the other hand, I'd love to know what the hell she's doing."

Helen got up and stood behind Day's chair, laid her hands on his shoulders, and then folded them across his chest. He covered them with his own.

"If anybody can get to the bottom of this, you can. Why don't you make us one of your special G&Ts?"

Day needed no further encouragement. He sliced the lemon and rubbed the rim of the glasses with it before dropping a sliver into each one. He cracked the ice tray to loosen the cubes and half filled each glass with ice. The gin made the ice splinter noisily and the fresh tonic splashed over it with a satisfying sound. He took the drinks out to Helen on the balcony, where she sat with her eyes shut, face raised to the gentle late-afternoon sun.

"So now we know what we have to do," he said. "We must find this lost treasure. Did I tell you I spoke to Aristo and he's agreed to take a look at the Kállos book for us? I'll drop it off to him tomorrow after we've taken Raj to the ferry. I'm hoping that his knowledge of the islands will help us to narrow down where to look.

"I have a proposal for you, Helen - do you fancy a little trip? There are two more people we should talk to, this time face to face. One is in Nafplio, the other in Athens."

Helen made a non-committal noise. "Who are they? What do you have in mind?"

"In Athens we can stay at my apartment. I haven't taken you there yet and you must see the old place. From there we can visit an old lady called Nina Angelopoulou. She's retired now, but she was the Secretary of the British School when Christos was using the library there. I'm pretty sure she actually knew him. Then in Nafplio there's a beautiful hotel I know, utterly wonderful with amazing views, you'll love it. Nafplio is one of my favourite towns in all Greece, I really want to go there with you. While we're there we'll talk to the bookseller from whom Ophelia bought her copy of Christos's book. His vendor sticker is inside the back cover."

"What do you think they can tell you?"

"I don't know yet, but I think it's important. If we aren't thorough, we might miss something crucial. I think we'll start with Nafplio, and then do Athens on the way back."

Helen lifted her glass and watched the condensation on the outside drip into her lap. She took a sip and smiled. The smile was caused by the citrus bite behind the cold gin, but it covered her lack of enthusiasm for Day's suggestion more than adequately.

"I do love a bookshop," she said, aiming her comment indirectly at the sunset.

19

Raj waved goodbye from the crowded passenger shelter at Naxos ferry port. As Day and Helen watched from the road, the ferry came into sight and made its well-practiced turn in the calm waters of the harbour. Sounding the horn to signal its approach and manoeuvre, it slowed, turned, and reversed to the quay, beginning to lower its ramp long before it touched dry land. Inside, beyond the white shirts of the crewmen and the blue dungarees of the engineers, foot passengers began jostling to escape. The sound of engines already throbbing in the ship's dark interior warned of the forthcoming competition between vehicles and pedestrians in the race to disembark. As usual, despite the thick, foul-smelling smoke of the reversing thrust, everything was accomplished with remarkable good humour. They could just make out Raj's head as he disappeared with the others into the spacious belly of the Blue Star *Naxos*.

"Let's go somewhere quieter," said Day. They set off for the Archaeological Museum of Naxos where Aristos Iraklidis had long been in charge.

"Good morning, I'm Martin Day, here to see the Curator, please?"

"The Curator is in his office, Kyrie Day, he's expecting you," said a young woman whom Day did not recognise, a new receptionist. "Do you know your way?"

Day said he did and thanked her. He knew the way very well indeed. He forced himself to take the wide, shallow steps from the entrance hall more slowly than usual, in fact at normal pace. When alone he would usually take the three flights to the top floor at speed, two at a time. It was no joke being forty, in his opinion, and he was not going to let himself go.

He knocked on the door of the Curator's office and pushed it open, showing Helen in ahead of him. It was her first visit to Aristos's lair. She saw a small room with a view over Venetian rooftops, bookcases on every wall and books on every surface. Day had warned her of the mess, but it took her breath away nevertheless. Perhaps because of it, she instantly liked this room. Aristos whisked a small pile of files off his best visitor's chair for her, and Day took Christos's book from his pocket and gave it to his friend before clearing a seat for himself.

"Thank you, Martin. It's even smaller than I remember," said the Curator. "I called a friend of mine in Thessaloniki just now, who told me how much this little volume would cost if you were able to locate a copy, which has been almost impossible for many years. It's a collector's piece, apparently. People seem to think that one day the Kállos will be found and the book's value will soar. I'm looking forward to re-reading it. How long do I have?"

"There's no rush, Aristo. We're going to the mainland for a few days, so perhaps we could meet sometime after Wednesday and you can tell me what you think."

Aristos Iraklidis regarded Day impassively, suddenly serious. "Am I right in thinking you really mean to look for this thing, Martin?"

"If you need to ask, my friend, you don't know me very well. I certainly do. It may not exist, and if it does I may not find it - but how can I resist the challenge? Besides, if I find the Kállos it might help Ophelia. It's the only thing I can do for her."

"With your help, Aristo, he might look in the right place," smiled Helen.

"I'll do what I can," said Aristos, putting the book on his desk and patting it absent-mindedly with his hand. "This little tome may yet reveal some secrets. I'll look at it tomorrow. Now, will you both join me for lunch?"

"I'm sorry, we can't, we're hoping to catch the next ferry to Piraeus."

"Ah, another time then. I've found a good new taverna which I'm sure you'll like." He stood and saw them out of his office. "Have a good trip. Call me when you get back."

After leaving the Museum they booked themselves on the next ferry at the ticket office on Papavasiliou and moved the Fiat to a free car park on the edge of town, walking back to the port with their bags. There was time for a coffee before the boat arrived, and Day remembered to text Irini, who looked after his Athens apartment, to tell her of their visit. Eventually they climbed the ramp to the boat with the other passengers, and Day felt the usual sinking feeling in his chest on leaving dry land. He was no lover of sea travel but it was part of life in the Cyclades and he had learned to manage it. He bought two bottles of water at the onboard café and struggled with them to their seats against the movement of the ferry as it prepared to leave. When it hit open water, he felt a stronger lurch in his stomach.

"Three and a half hours," he muttered. "Did you bring something to read? I may have to sleep for a while."

The ferry called at Paros first, not long after leaving Naxos. Day's eyes were already closed. Helen went up to the rear deck to watch the docking and disembarkation, and to admire the waterfront of Paros with its windmill, expanse of moored yachts and small boats, and the old town rising inland. She looked along the coastline to the left; the shoreline curved round the bay and eventually became a low peninsula that crumbled into the sea. She used to know people who lived over there, at the far end of Parikia town, and she tried to see their house. Before she managed to locate it, the ferry sounded its horn and set off back to sea with considerable clanking and a cloud of smoke.

The journey after Paros felt long, broken only by the passing beauty of other islands along the way. Helen dozed for a while against Day's shoulder. It seemed strange to leave Naxos so soon after they had arrived for the summer, but she would enjoy Athens. About Nafplio she was less sure. She had been there with Zissis shortly before their separation, and they had argued destructively. She would not have chosen to go there again had it not been for Martin. She was saved from too much introspection by the inevitability of sleep.

They were woken by the public announcement system advising passengers to prepare to disembark: they were approaching Piraeus. Out of the window she could see ferries and cruise ships, the high-rise buildings of the town, and the houses stretching along the shore. Piraeus, the mighty port of Athens; despite herself, Helen could not help but marvel at it. She had seen it in all weathers and seasons, by day and by night, and it was never still.

There was no time for further thought: the excited crowd was retrieving bags, gathering children and pushing towards the exits, and they must join it. The descending staircases to the car deck were invisible because so densely packed with passengers and baggage. It was no place for the frail or elderly; small children complained bitterly. Staff looked on from the side, unable to help, no longer really caring because on every trip the madness was the same. Eventually Helen realised that they had reached the lowest deck, and the crowd was now focused on reaching the luggage racks, grabbing their suitcases and being at the front of the rabble when the ramp was lowered.

"Humanity not at its best," shouted Day, hoping Helen could hear him. He kept close to her side to protect her from the press of the crowd and make sure they were not separated. The whole thing was a recipe for a panic attack, should anyone be prone to one, but their fellow travellers seemed to be robust. When the ramp went down and the light of the shore flooded the car deck, everyone began to move forwards. Vans, cars and lorries took the ramp to the quay at the same time as the foot passengers.

Day looked round keenly for the one face on the port that he would recognise. With relief he saw him, his regular taxi driver Nasos, whom he booked whenever he needed a taxi in Athens. The arrangement suited them both: Nasos had a regular client, Day had a reliable driver, albeit one who, in common with his colleagues, was perfectly able and willing to drive along the busy road without greatly needing to hold the steering wheel with either hand.

"Naso, *ti kanete?* Good to see you!"

Nasos took their bags in his big hands and stacked them in the boot of the yellow Athenian taxi. Day and Helen got into the back of the car with relief and closed the doors against the heat and the noise. Nasos joined the heavy traffic and took a clever back route to the road to Corinth which would eventually take them to Nafplio.

This was no ordinary car, this was an extension of its driver. From the taxi's rear view mirror hung three things: an air freshener, a blue lucky eye symbol, and an official licence. On the dashboard, Nasos had glued family photos. Strung from the sun visor was the largest item of all, an ornate silver cross which he would occasionally touch.

Nasos talked all the way out of Piraeus in English, displaying a certain pride in his ability to do so. He described in detail the latest adventures of his law-breaking cousin and the delights of his beautiful baby son without significantly changing his tone between the two. From time to time he operated the steering wheel with his knee while gesticulating with one hand and adjusting the radio with the other, but Day didn't greatly care. He had never felt at risk with Nasos, unless it was by association with the cousin.

Helen felt for his hand, but her eyes were fixed on the passing view from the window. The rambling extremities of Piraeus were thinning, the empty and deserted warehouses and the unmoving cranes that stood between the road and the sea were being left behind. Then the shipyards too were gone and the sea came almost up to the highway. The bulk of a small island lay just off the coast, and Helen smiled: Salamis. It was a name to savour, the scene of the historical victory about which British children learned at school. The greatly outnumbered Greek fleet had tricked and beaten the threatening Persians, a victory which had saved Athens from ruin. Some said that, but for the defeat of the Persians at Salamis, the flowering of Greek civilisation that followed would not have taken place, and the development of the Western World would have been different. For Day, Salamis was the site of an important piece of Greek history with cultural repercussions. Helen's response was emotional: it was the story of the great general Themistocles that she remembered, and his fierce argument that the Athenians must build a navy in order to defeat the mighty Xerxes and his Persians. Themistocles' argument was heard and the Athenians placed their faith in him. So the battle for Athens was won. It was the magnitude of Themistocles' gamble, and its effect on succeeding centuries, that Helen thought of when she saw Salamis.

She began to feel more cheerful and to look forward to being in Nafplio with Martin. The sky had cleared as they left behind Athens and its *nefos*, the strangely yellow-coloured halo of urban smog which was only really visible from outside the city. As the taxi slowed to negotiate the road system near Corinth, she leaned into Day to kiss him, and the chilling chasm of the Corinth Canal over which the road crossed was the first thing he saw when he opened his eyes afterwards.

"Welcome to the Peloponnese," he said happily.

Sometime around Corinth, Nasos ran out of conversation and put on the radio. The A7 motorway that ran the length of the Peloponnese from Corinth to Kalamata was modern and relatively empty, an apparent miracle after Piraeus, and incomparable to the busy motorways of the UK. They simply sped along. Helen thought of the lazy mountain road that she and Zissis had taken from Corinth to Nafplio, with its glimpses of the sea and the quiet lunch at Old Epidavros, and for a moment regretted the motorway. How much better, though, to be sharing this journey with Martin.

Nasos seemed to wake up as they approached Nafplio. Once again he began to chat, telling Helen with great pride about the historical importance of the area. They drove past the huge walls of Ancient Tiryns before continuing through the lemon groves towards Nafplio, Nasos boasting of his country's history all the way. Day was dreaming of taking her round Tiryns himself, to share his love of its Cyclopean walls and tell her the secrets of its ancient citadel. Then he would take her to Ancient Mycenae, which was less than twenty kilometres away. While at Mycenae they would call at a particular hotel called The Belle Hélène in the modern town outside the ancient site. Perhaps they would have lunch there. The name of the hotel would make her smile, being the nickname Thanasis gave her, but its old guest books would amaze her. They contained an astonishing list of visitors including

Jean-Paul Sartre, Agatha Christie, Lawrence Durrell and Virginia Woolf, and the original excavator of Mycenae, Heinrich Schliemann.

Nasos had moved on from the beauties of history to the beauties of modern Nafplio, and congratulated them on their choice of the Hotel Melissa. He parked at the foot of a steep path leading up to the Venetian castle, called the Fortress of Palamidi, that crowned the high ridge above the town. It was easier to walk up to the Hotel Melissa from here, he said, than take the car any closer. Nasos said his farewells, Day paid him and picked up both bags, and they headed up the hill to the hotel.

It was well worth the climb. Their room had a small balcony which overlooked the tiled roofs of the town, their warm terracotta cooled by the dark green of citrus trees and the fronds of palms. Beyond the town lay the sea and the mountains of the Argolid Peninsula, and, in the middle of the bay, a compact Venetian stronghold called the Bourtzi sat on a small island. Out of sight among the mountains to the right lay the modern towns of Nemea and Argos, names that would forever recall to Helen the heroes of myth, Hercules and Jason. To Day they meant only the excavation of the Temple of Nemean Zeus, and the large Mycenaean tomb very recently discovered in the area.

There was just time for a shower and change of clothes before their appointment with the bookseller. The way downhill to the town was steep, a series of stepped and cobbled paths that linked pedestrian lanes full of artisan shops and mature bougainvilleas. In the large *plateia*, noisy groups of small children were playing football, vendors were closing their businesses for the afternoon and visitors filled the café tables. Helen and Day crossed the square towards the historic building that housed the Archaeological Museum, beyond which lay the streets forgotten by tourism. In one of these was the shop of Dimitris Kakavas, purveyor of rare books and maps.

Dimitris Kakavas opened the door to them in person. He looked particularly pleased to see Day, whose hand he shook and retained as he drew them into the shop and towards his office at the back. Helen followed, smiling. The old man was short, with a covering of close-cropped white hair on a head that was otherwise almost bald. His eyebrows and stubble were the dark grey of his well-pressed shirt, and a pair of expensive titanium glasses sat on his wide, straight nose. In the office he turned to her with his large, dark eyes glittering.

"Kyria Day, please, take a seat," he said. Helen saw a fleeting smile cross Day's face as they all sat down. Noting the bookseller's use of the formal language, *katharevousa*, Day respectfully continued the conversation in the same manner.

"Thank you for seeing us, Kyrie Kakavas," he said. "You have a wonderful place here. The maps, they're magnificent. And I would love to have the time to look through the books. Is everything you have on display?"

"Ah no, the best, the oldest books are safely locked away. It would be irresponsible to leave some of the rarer books where they might be … vulnerable. When a client is interested in a particular item, I bring it here to show him. By appointment."

"They're a serious investment, aren't they, some of them?" laughed Day, fully aware of the cost of rare books in his subject.

"Indeed. To a collector, they are worth a great deal of money, but to a historian they are priceless. Some of the books in my possession are the only copy that remains in the world. It is my honour to take care of them until they pass to their next custodian."

"Do you sell mostly to private individuals, or to libraries and museums?" asked Helen.

"Mostly private collectors, Kyria, but there are universities that regularly use my services ... much depends on the book."

Dimitris Kakavas rubbed the back of his right ear with his index finger as if the wand of his spectacles was chafing. His glasses shifted erratically on his nose, causing him to blink in mild irritation.

'I understand, Kyrie Day, that you are not here to buy a book, but to ask me about one?"

"That's right. It's a book with an unusual history which I think you may have sold to a friend of mine. As I mentioned on the phone, the title is *To Κάλλος, ένας Κυκλαδικός χώρος* by Christos Nikolaidis."

The bookseller nodded thoughtfully and looked from Day to Helen and back to Day.

"Yes. I've only ever seen two copies of this book that you name. The first belonged to a friend. The other I sold some years ago to a lady from Cambridge University."

"Ophelia Blue?"

"That's correct. After you telephoned me yesterday I looked for the record of sale." He opened his desk drawer and brought out a sheet of paper which he handed to Day. "I remember arranging the delivery of this book. A colleague of mine in Athens took it to the client in person, as he was due to visit family in England. This was a great relief to me: the book was very expensive, as you can see."

Day was staring at the paper. The figure made his eyes water. No wonder Dimitris Kakavas had taken care to ensure the book's safe arrival. Day was astonished that Ophelia had been prepared to pay such a sum for Christos's book.

"Indeed," he murmured, and passed the paper to Helen. "Is it usual for you to deal in such a modern publication?"

"No, this was most unusual. How much do you know about Christos Nikolaidis, Kyrie Day? This is no ordinary book, you see. Perhaps I should explain. It might help you to understand the - er - price."

"I'd be grateful."

Dimitris Kakavas sat back in his chair, removed his spectacles, and rubbed the bridge of his nose before replacing them.

"The book was printed in 1999. You notice I say printed, not published. I don't know how many copies were made, but not many, because Nikolaidis had them made at his own expense. The copy I read at the time belonged to a friend of mine, and it was quite a few years afterwards that I came across another copy. The book had quickly acquired something of a reputation. I should say, perhaps, notoriety. In Greece our ancient heritage is very important to us, and this book had touched a nerve. I personally thought it was misguided, but others took a different view. I know of nobody who was indifferent to it."

Day nodded, and on impulse picked up the bill of sale from where Helen had replaced it on the table. He stared at the date, which initially he had not noticed.

"Ophelia bought the book *seventeen years ago*?"

"She did."

"You have a very good memory, Kyrie Kakavas."

"This was no ordinary sale," sniffed the bookseller. "I think you still don't understand. When it was printed, people thought that Nikolaidis was looking for a cave of marble figurines from the Cycladic era, a hoard of them, buried somewhere in the Lesser Cyclades. This was an assertion of the greatest importance and caused huge excitement."

"A hoard of figurines? I thought nobody knew what Nikolaidis was looking for."

"Oh yes, certainly, that was the rumour."

"But there's nothing in the book to suggest Cycladic figurines or any other specific item," Day insisted. "I've read every word myself."

"And you are correct," said the bookseller with shrug. "I have no idea how the rumour began and I myself have never believed it to be true. Nevertheless, many people did. It is the way with rumour, is it not? There were other stories. Some said that a rockfall, perhaps caused by an earthquake, had hidden the cave where the figurines lay. Others said that Nikolaidis had deliberately concealed the place, to keep the treasure for himself."

Day stared at the bookseller, who returned his gaze frankly, a smile beginning to crease his face and narrow his eyes.

"Do you begin to see why I remember this sale, Kyrie Day? Not only was the book valuable because of its rarity and its small print run. It was one of the most contentious books of its time in Greece."

"How did you come by the copy you sold to Ophelia?"

"It was part of the collection of a gentleman whose entire library I purchased after his death. That is often how I acquire my stock, regrettably."

"How would Ophelia have known about the copy, before she ordered it from you?"

The bookseller shrugged again. "I cannot remember now, Kyrie Day. I regularly send my catalogue to all the major universities … If you want something to be found, you must leave directions to it, you know."

"Of course. One last question, if I may. At the time, where did people believe the Kállos to be?"

"I have no idea, there were many rumours. Please understand, I find it difficult to see any truth in the story, but no doubt there are still people who do. That is why they will pay a great deal of money for the book."

"You've been very helpful, Kyrie Kakavas, thank you. By the way, were you aware there was a letter inside Ophelia's copy of the book?"

"Yes, I remember seeing a letter. I admit I took a look at it, but the handwriting was hard to read and it was in English. It looked personal, so I left it in the book. The lady had paid enough to have the letter too."

The light had faded by the time they left Kakavas's shop, and people were in the streets taking the evening stroll. They found a comfortable table at one of the tavernas that lined the pavement along the bay, a favourite route for those taking the *volta*. As they sat waiting to be served, an orange glow began to illuminate the historic Bourtzi, throwing a warm reflection on the surrounding water and plunging the mountains beyond further into obscurity. The city authorities had deemed that night had fallen.

Service was efficient in this professional tourist venue, and they were soon sipping small glasses of wine. Despite her bad memories of Nafplio, Helen had to admit that this was an idyllic place.

"I understand why you like Nafplio, Martin. It's historic, it's beautiful, and it's somehow intelligent. It's a real place, there's more to it than visitors usually see. I wish I could look round Mr Kakavas's shop in peace."

"So do I, and one day I'm going to buy one of his lovely old maps. This is a wonderful place, we must stay for longer next time. It was definitely worth coming today, though. Mr Kakavas told us several things we didn't know. I didn't realise just how much public interest Christos's book generated at the time. Passions always run high in Greece where ancient artefacts are concerned, of course."

"The date is important too. We were thinking that Ophelia found the book recently and immediately got in touch with you, but she bought it seventeen years ago. You know, Christos might still have been alive then."

"Yes, we need to re-think everything. But not tonight! I know a nice little place to eat, away from the main streets, then back to our lovely hotel. Hey, what's the matter?"

"Sorry," she said, shaking her head. "The last time I was here was with Zissis and we spent all the time arguing. That's when he told me he wanted a separation. Six weeks later it was over."

"Oh Helen, you didn't tell me," said Day. "Let me make up for it. We'll make new memories. I shall make it my mission."

20

The following morning, waking in the comfortable bed of the Hotel Melissa, Helen's bad memories of Nafplio had significantly receded. The sun was shining between the slats of the shutters, and yet no noise reached them from outside. They lay for a while enjoying the moment, summoning the energy to get up. Then the bell of the Catholic Church that she had noticed on their walk to the *plateia* began to ring and ring, a rich and inviting chime that seemed endless. It was soon joined by other, more distant church bells. Sunday in Greece had its own soundscape, full of invitations to contemplation and laden with promise.

There would not be a great deal of contemplation or reverence involved in their forthcoming bus journey to Athens, however. As some form of compensation for the trials ahead of them, they lingered over their hotel breakfast which was served on a high terrace overlooking the bay. The early morning warmth was enhanced by the protective walls of the hotel and the canvas canopy, and also by the colour theme of yellow and pale orange paintwork. Below them the old town stretched in one direction and the modern town in the other.

Beyond the glittering bay, the mountains of the Argolid Peninsula lay smoky blue under the bright morning sky.

They paid for their room and walked the short distance to the bus stop for the coach to Athens. The ride was good and the two hours passed smoothly. His eyes closed, Day spent some time recalling the visit to Nafplio, both the conversation with Dimitris Kakavas and the even more enjoyable hours with Helen. He was, he thought, about as happy as he was capable of being: in a relationship with a woman he loved, in a country which gave him everything he needed, and earning a living from the subject closest to his heart. He opened his eyes as the coach slowed to cross the Corinth Canal and manoeuvre the junction to take the motorway to Athens. Helen was quietly reading her book but looked up when she realised he was awake.

"We're at the Canal," she said. "It must have some story to tell, mustn't it? I don't know anything about how or when it was made. Do you?"

He grinned, and she knew he was about to tell her.

"It was opened in the 1890s, although the Germans sabotaged it in the war and American engineers had to clear up the mess. The existence of a shipway here had been a dream for many hundreds of years before it could be achieved. As early as the 7th century BCE people thought of cutting a route for boats through the isthmus, but they just didn't have the technology. Even worse, people died each time they tried it, so it was thought to be cursed. The Emperor Nero did better than most, and they say he even lifted a spade himself, but then he died too and the superstition became stronger. I've read that Nero's men made a monument to honour him in the shape of one of the Heroes, I think it's Hercules. I've never looked for it, but it's meant to be still near the canal somewhere."

"Interesting. It's an amazing feat of engineering. Herculean, indeed!"

"There are some really funny stories about the canal. I've heard that one attempt to create a passage through the isthmus was called off because the people thought that the sea on either side was at different levels, and if a canal was opened it would swamp the island of Aegina!"

Helen smiled, less at the anecdote than at Day's limitless fund of historical snippets.

"I'm looking forward to Athens," she said. "Are we going to your apartment first or to see Nina Angelopoulou?"

"The apartment. I said we'd be at Nina's house at half past two. Plenty of time."

From the Athens Central Bus Station they took a taxi to Day's apartment in Dinokratous street at the foot of the city's tallest hill, Lykavittos. In the taxi Day related, not for the first time, how his tiny flat had been left to him in the will of a couple who had known his father. They had bought it when house prices were low in Athens and Lykavittos was a poor outer suburb. Now the same area was one of the most prized and expensive in the city.

He was clearly excited as he unlocked the front door of the apartment building and opened the lift, holding it while she edged in. It was old, with a sliding cage door, barely large enough for two people and they had to squeeze together. He had the perfect opportunity to kiss her, saying, "Welcome to Athens."

As he put on a light and undid the shutters, the apartment revealed itself as an accurate reflection of its owner. Nearly half the walls were covered with bookcases, though most of the books themselves were now on Naxos. The kitchen was little more than a shelf and a sink, though both were made of a single piece of marble as was traditional in many of the older buildings of Athens.

"How do you cook in here?" she asked curiously.

"Infrequently," he said. "So many cheap tavernas in Athens if you know where to look. Which reminds me, I'm going to reserve a table for tonight, I don't want to get there and find we can't get in."

Helen went out to the balcony. It bore little resemblance to the one in Filoti: the view was of the street and the opposite apartment blocks, it was noisy, and a light city dust covered everything. A dead shrub in a pot of parched soil showed how long it had been since the owner had cared for it, and Irini had overlooked it. Yet there was a buzz about this place, a sense of the energy of the city, resilience and continuity. She was surprised to find that she liked it a great deal, and turned over the cushion on one of the plastic chairs to sit down and enjoy it.

The resonant sound of a monastery's call-to-prayer, its traditional chimes broadcast from somewhere nearby, began to dominate the distant tooting of the traffic on Vasilissis Sofias Avenue. Day shook his head as he took the red plastic chair next to Helen. The ringing of the monastery bell was not a sound he liked. He could only assume that the chimes, which were all on the same note and regular to a fraction of a second, were emitted electronically. They certainly carried a great distance. 123 - 123 - 1234567. Repeated time and again, they sounded particularly soulless to him. The pattern was what he noticed most. Three notes, another three, then a run of seven. He wondered whether the pattern represented words, but had no idea. 123 - 123 - 1234567... Eventually the bells stopped and he relaxed.

"So, do you like the flat? It was my home from the time I left London till my father died and I bought the Filoti house."

"I do like it, actually. I can imagine you living here. I suppose your daily exercise was running up Lykavittos hill at speed?"

Day laughed. "No need. I was young then."

Nina Angelopoulou, former Secretary of the British School at Athens, had been retired for more than twelve years and lived in an apartment in the Pangrati district. Day knew for a fact that it took just under thirty minutes to walk from his flat to Plateia Varnava, on the corner of which Nina lived. It was a lovely little square in Pangrati's safe and leafy streets, a square where he brought friends who were passing through from the UK to have dinner at one of the welcoming tavernas.

He timed it to the minute. Just before half past two they were at the ground floor entrance to the apartment block where Nina lived. He pressed the buzzer next to her name, which was clearly typed under a grey plastic film. The speaker crackled and a voice enquired briefly who was there.

"*O Martin Day eimai,*" replied Day politely in Greek.

"*Telia*! Come upstairs, Martin! Third floor."

The lady in her seventies who opened the door to them at the top of the stairs immediately drew Day into her arms and gave him the kind of hug normally reserved for family. Helen tried to hide her surprise.

"Martin! I'm so happy to see you again. And this is your wife? *Hairo poli*, Kyria! It is a pleasure to meet you. Your husband used to visit the library often in the year before I retired, and he even came to my retirement party. Come in, I will make coffee. Do you take it with sugar?"

Helen realised it was useless to correct the old lady on their marital status, and for the second time in two days she let it pass. The old lady seated them hospitably in her sitting room, easily reverting to the English language that she had used daily when she was Secretary of the British School. She then excused herself to prepare the coffee. Through the open door to the kitchen they watched her spoon the powder into her traditional brass *briki*, add water without needing to measure it, and place the little jug on the stove. She stooped to examine the gas flame, and only when satisfied did she return to her guests. She sat facing them and demanded, with the greatest politeness, to know Day's state of health and that of his family, what work he had done and was currently doing, and where he lived now. At one point in this she brought the coffee tray from the kitchen, having poured the thick, dark liquid into small cups for them all. As they sipped, one or two names were mentioned, mutual friends from Athens, and their wellbeing was discussed.

Only when this had been satisfactorily concluded and the coffee savoured with the respect due to it, did Nina allow a small pause before asking Day what it was that he had come to ask her. If she could be of any help to him, she said, she would be only too pleased.

"I'd like to ask what you remember of a man called Christos Nikolaidis," said Day. "I believe you knew him some years ago. He acknowledged your help specifically in the front of his book, *Το Κάλλος*."

"Christo," said Nina, shaking her head fondly. "Yes, I remember Christo." She had slipped easily into a familiar form of the name. "It's many years since I saw him. The poor man's dead now, I think?"

"I'm afraid so."

"Why do you want to know about him?"

"I've been asked to take a look at his work professionally," said Day, choosing his words carefully. "I could see that you knew him from the acknowledgement. The only other person he mentions at the School is the Director at the time - and I believe he has passed on too?"

"Yes, that was Michael Stanford, lovely man, he died a long time ago, he was poorly even when Christo knew him. You're right, I may be the only person left who really remembers poor Christo."

"What can you tell us about him?"

"He was a slightly strange man, Martin, and I don't mean to be unkind. He only really thought of one thing, and that sometimes makes a person rather withdrawn. He was obsessed with the subject he was researching. He spent probably two years visiting the School, appearing in the library without letting anybody know he was coming. We just got used to him floating in and out. He was always polite, and he had a nice smile, but he didn't usually start a conversation. He was short, and I remember he used to walk round with his head down. Maybe he was deep in thought, but I always felt it was so that he did not have to meet anyone's eyes."

She paused, guiltily.

"We had a nickname for him: we called him Odysseus. I don't remember who thought of it, but soon everybody was using it. Not to his face, of course. The name suited him. He roamed about the School with a look of being on an endless journey, pursuing his own course and sailing from one thing to the next. Just like Odysseus."

Odysseus, thought Day. A hero of Troy. Intellectually brilliant, full of guile and ingenuity. An interesting choice of nickname for a studious and introverted individual.

"I remember the book being published," Nina continued, "his little book with the exciting name. He tried so hard, poor Christo. He gave Michael Stanford a copy, and one to the School library. I'm afraid nobody thought there was anything in it. We didn't doubt that he believed it sincerely himself, but we didn't think he was right. Even he had to admit that he couldn't find the thing and didn't even know what it was."

Nina looked at Day but her eyes were slightly glazed; she was looking back to the past, seeing not Day's face but that of Christos Nikolaidis.

"I remember he often spoke about Iraklia, Martin, the island in the Cyclades. He grew up around there, I think. I'm sorry, but I can't think of anything else to tell you."

"Don't worry, you've already given me a very clear picture. Did Christos have any particular friends in Athens?"

"No, I told you."

"Where did he stay when he was using the School library?"

"Some room, a cheap one. He didn't have much money. Sometimes the Director let him stay for free in the visitors' accommodation at the School."

"One last question, Nina, if I may," said Day, not entirely sure why he had thought of it. "I understand his theories didn't seem very credible, but would you say Christos was a clever man?"

The old lady smiled before she answered, and when she did it was with a benign certainty.

"Oh yes, I think so, Martin. Extremely clever."

A senior waiter met Helen and Day at the top of the stairs and led them to a table for two on the rooftop dining terrace. He returned quickly with menus, wine list and the details of the evening's specials. Before he left he gave Helen a look of open admiration and a broad smile.

"Looks like you've made another conquest," murmured Day, "and I'm not in the least surprised. So, what do you think of this place?"

He had booked a table at a restaurant known as Sto Nao, one of the oldest tavernas in Plaka at the foot of the hill of the Acropolis. He still remembered eating here to celebrate the first cheque he had received from his writing after moving to Athens.

"It's perfect, Martin. You look over there and see Lykavittos hill, and on this side the Acropolis is so close we could almost reach out and touch it. This must be a popular place."

"It is, and quite old. It's been in business over a hundred years, so they say. All sorts of famous people have eaten here. That's why I thought I'd better book tonight. The food's fine, but just being here is the real treat, isn't it? When it gets a bit darker the Acropolis and the little church at the top of Lykavittos will be lit up."

"Martin, what are you doing … ?"

"I'm going to take a picture of you. If the tourists can do it, so can I. Perfect timing - the lights behind you have just been turned on! The golden Acropolis and the golden lady!"

The photograph, taken swiftly on his phone, would become one of Day's favourite images of Helen, though he had no idea of it at the time. She looked happy and relaxed, and wore a cream dress with a fine gold necklace. Behind her, the sheer rock face that underpinned the Acropolis and the walls that ran along the north-east face of the hill were subtly uplit in a warm orange light. At one end of the wall rose the flagpole from which the two young men, one of them from Naxos, had bravely removed the Nazi flag in 1941. Beauty, history and heroism in a single photograph.

"What would you like to eat?" Helen asked, taking a discreet look at the food on the other tables before studying the menu. "How about a selection of small *orektika* tonight?"

Day readily agreed; *orektika*, or appetisers, were a very good way to taste as many delicious things as possible in Greece.

"You can choose whatever you fancy for us, as long as you order me some chips."

"Naturally," she said, and shot a smile at the waiter which had him instantly at their side. After a polite exchange of banter, during which Helen could feel the fluency of her Greek returning satisfactorily, the waiter raised his pencil slightly above his notebook and asked what they would like to drink.

Having already scanned the wine menu, Day asked for a bottle of Xinomavro red wine. It was not the cheapest bottle on the list, but it felt like a particularly special night. He had a strange sense of impending success.

"And to eat?" asked the waiter, enjoying himself.

"Some dishes to share, please," said Helen. "We'll have a Feta *ravasaki*, some of the zucchini balls, the grilled Anavra sausages, fried calamari and a rocket salad. Oh, and a portion of fried potatoes. Thank you."

The man bowed and turned away, clicking his fingers towards a younger waiter and lifting his chin imperiously. He passed the food order to him and almost ran down the stairs leading to the ground floor, returning with the expensive bottle of Xinomavro which he twisted in front of Day.

When the wine was in their glasses, most of the food on the table and the chips at his right hand, Day was extremely happy. He raised his glass in a toast.

"To another wonderful evening in Greece," he said.

"And to Athens."

They helped themselves from the small plates of carefully cooked appetisers, more than content to eat lightly. The Feta dish was exceptional: a parcel of filo pastry with the baked cheese inside, topped with Greek honey and sesame. The name *ravasaki* literally meant love-letter, as Day enjoyed telling her. The little sausages were appealingly chewy and full of flavour, and the courgette balls were freshly fried, crisp on the outside but soft and rich inside, with a smooth creamy sauce for dipping. Day naturally derived a great deal of pleasure from the chips, which were excellent, but he had to agree that the best dish of all was the salad. The fiery rocket leaves were soothed by sun-dried tomatoes, pieces of fresh fig, pine nuts, cherry tomatoes and Graviera cheese.

The waiter appeared at Day's side to check that they were enjoying the meal, although it was to Helen that he addressed the question. Satisfied with her reply, he turned to Day.

"The wine is good?"

"The wine is very good indeed."

With small exchanges like this, both management and customers succeeded in increasing their enjoyment of the evening in a way disproportionate to the words. The last evening of their short trip was most definitely a success.

21

It was with huge pleasure that Day followed Helen up the steps at the side of the Curator's house. On stepping onto the shady terrace where the vine-covered pergola gave onto a view of the garden, he experienced once again the feeling of being in a kind of Arcadia.

"Any moment now a faun will step out from the olive grove," he thought to himself.

"Ah, it's Professor Day!" teased the Curator.

They all chatted for a few moments before Aristos took Helen to see the heavily fruiting apricot tree and the clusters of young pistachios. He loved her interest in his various crops and was particularly proud of his grapes, which kind friends with a small vineyard took annually to add to their harvest, giving him a few bottles of the resulting wine.

Rania and Day went to sit in the comfortable, white-cushioned chairs by the bougainvillea. Purple-leaved tradescantia covered the soil in front of them and led the eye across the decorative part of the garden to a stately date palm and a group of flowering oleander bushes. Day knew that this was Rania's creation.

"We saw Deppi and Nick at the weekend, while you and Helen were away," she began, with a discreet sideways glance at Day. "Everyone is well, and the baby is growing to the doctor's satisfaction. Only ten weeks now till the birth."

"That's good," said Day. "The time has gone quickly."

"Can I ask you something, Martin *mou*? How did you feel when you heard that my niece was expecting a baby?"

Day smiled down at his hands. Rania was one of the cleverest and kindest women he had ever met. She understood people without judging them. She knew that for a while he had been captivated by Deppi, whose motherly rapport with Nestoras had shown him a relationship of which his own mother's early death had deprived him. Rania had understood. She had trusted him to deal with his feelings in private, but she had also known that he was struggling. He owed her an honest answer.

"It was a huge surprise, but truly I was delighted. Sounds odd, I know. Delight for them, but also for myself."

"You were free?"

Day smiled at the Curator's wife. "You understand exactly, as always."

"And now, you have Helen."

Day looked across the garden to the Curator's small olive grove where Aristos was explaining something with expansive gestures. Helen's hand was gently playing with the leaves of the nearest tree. Day would have liked to know how long Rania had been thinking that he and Helen should be together, but had no intention of asking. Rania deftly changed course to a subject he was always happy to talk about.

"What is Helen doing at the moment?"

"She's working on a new book. It's still at an early stage. She says that writing a novel falls into three parts, the planning, the writing and the real work, and that the writing takes the least time."

"And which part does she enjoy the most?"

"Good question, they all seem to drive her mad at some point. At the moment neither of us can settle to anything, though - we're trying to get to the truth about a man called Christos Nikolaidis."

"Yes, Aristos has told me quite a lot about that," she said, watching her husband and Helen returning from the garden. "He says that when he read the book before, he didn't have much time for the man's ideas. Now he's been looking at it from your point of view, Martin, like a detective."

Helen and Aristos had joined them, and the Curator chuckled at his wife's last words.

"Shall we get down to work, then? Let's go in the house where we can spread out the map and I expect you'll need to see your screens. Pity, the afternoon is beautiful."

They were soon round the dining table in the cool of the old house. Helen and Day opened their laptops and Aristos brought out the book.

"So, Aristo, what did you make of it?"

"I thought the quality of his research was good, and I can see that he tried to approach the legend in an objective way. I still don't think the Kállos exists, but that's just my personal opinion. Why don't you start us off, Martin?"

Day handed over the letter addressed to the Director of the British School, which he had not given to him with the book.

"Have a look at this. It's a letter written by Christos that was inside the book when Ophelia bought it. It was addressed but never posted. Christos writes that he found the Kállos - *after* the book was printed."

"So you believe it exists?"

"I don't know. There's still no evidence, we only have the claim in the letter. We still have to do what he presumably did and find out for ourselves."

Aristos nodded. "I presume you've been working on that?"

"We have. We've both gone through the book carefully and pulled out as many actual facts as we can find in it. If it does exist, I think the Kállos is hidden either on Naxos or on one of the smaller islands to the south. Of these I've discounted several already, particularly Keros, because the international archaeological community would have been keen on Christos's ideas if they had thought there was any possibility of another discovery to be made there. The Kállos may well have originated on Keros, of course, where the main Cycladic centre was, but I don't think that's where they ended up.

"We looked at the geographical features mentioned in the legend, and we think they could only describe two places: somewhere along the south coast of Naxos, or the island of Iraklia. Can I show you on the map? Here's the excavated Cycladic settlement on Keros, where the hoard of figurines was found a few years ago. Now we know that the people of that time had big rowing boats, and that they were forced to stay close to shore or in the shelter of land, so I looked for routes they might have taken from Keros."

He placed his finger on the map and from Keros he traced one imaginary sea route west-north-west to Naxos, and then another due west to Iraklia.

"Either of these would make a plausible route for a Cycladic boat. The arguments for Naxos are that it was the easier destination to reach, and we already know there was some Cycladic activity going on there: quarrying and small settlements. However, Christos mentions Iraklia more than any other location, and we spoke to someone who knew him personally who said that he often mentioned it. So, bear all that in mind and Helen can tell you the rest."

Helen consulted her laptop and found the place she needed.

"We extracted all the references to a possible location mentioned by Christos's informants at the beginning of the book," said Helen, "and matched our results with his. They were quite similar, close enough to make us feel we were on the right track. You have to use your imagination a bit, but we think we've ended up with something interesting. I'll give you a quick summary, since it's all new to Rania.

"Two people said it was 'buried beneath a rockfall'. One of these said that it was 'safe from the sea and the destructive force of the winds', which suggests it was quite close to the shore. Another person talked about 'a cave by a mountain'. This all suggests something buried, probably in a cave, close to the sea, perhaps near a rockfall and a mountain."

"That could be almost anywhere the Cyclades," murmured Rania.

"True," said Helen, "but there is more. An old woman in the village of Panagia on Iraklia, which is interesting, spoke about a hoard of ancient objects hidden in a cave that had been re-sealed, which means the cave idea is mentioned for a second time and now we have a connection with Iraklia. The idea of 'below a ridge', and 'within sight of a mountain', crops up again too in her story.

"The fourth interview, however, is interesting because the man's actual words were 'it belongs to *Naxos*'. He said it was buried deep in the ground and was guarded by a 'fierce old woman'."

"I discounted that witness on the grounds he was crazy," smiled Aristos.

"Fair enough! Then there's a woman in her nineties who had been told the legend as a child and said that the Kállos was something of the greatest beauty, a 'sea-woman' or mermaid. There's the connection to the sea again, from the mermaid idea.

"It gets worse, Aristo. Christos spoke to an old man who was working in his threshing circle with his donkey: you couldn't make it up! This man claimed to have seen the Kállos with his own eyes when he was young; he refused to say more, except that 'only a fit young man had any hope of finding it'. It could be just boasting or it might suggest a place with particularly difficult access."

"I should think so, if it's buried in a cave beneath a rockfall!" laughed Rania. "How old was Christos at the time of the interviews, by the way?"

"Fifty? I'm not sure. You wouldn't call him a fit young man, for certain. Now bear with me, some interesting details come out now.

"One of the conversations was so significant that Christos gave his interviewee a name, 'Kyria Alpha'. This woman showed him a notebook in which her grandmother had written down her childhood memories. They included being taken to see the Kállos by her father.

The Kállos didn't seem beautiful to her at all, it had deep lines cut into it and she found it frightening because it looked like 'a dead thing from the sea'. The little girl was wet, cold and exhausted by the time she saw it, suggesting a long walk perhaps. The father covered the object up - could this mean he buried it? - and they sat together looking out to sea before going home."

"Now that does seem grounded in some sort of reality," said Rania. "Where did the little girl live, does it say?"

"Christos asked Kyria Alpha but she didn't know where her grandmother grew up. She herself lived in the tiny village of Kanaki on Naxos. It's a small fishing community east of Panormos on the south coast."

"That suggests not Iraklia but Naxos, then, doesn't it?"

"I suppose so."

"Where is this notebook now?" asked Aristos.

"Christos left it with Kyria Alpha. It's lost. Yes, it's such a disappointment. Now, the last clue - an interesting one - is something Christos remembered hearing when he was young. It was the story of two thieves who broke into an old grave on Naxos and buried the loot somewhere on Iraklia planning to go back for it later. The robbers met some awful fate and never returned, but according to the story the hiding place was marked by scratches on a rock."

"Naxos again," noted Rania.

"And also Iraklia," said Day. "We're left with somewhere below ground, close to the sea, possibly in a cave, and close to a ridge or rockfall. It may also have been moved at some point, which could explain why it hasn't been seen for over a generation. There are various other minor clues, and it could apply to either Naxos or Iraklia."

Aristos patted the map reflectively and they waited for his response.

"I'm sorry, my friends, you've worked very hard on this, but it seems very … insubstantial. The Kállos became a legend, and we know what that means. The story was changed every time it was told, elaborated by people whose purpose was to delight or frighten children, or to spread cautionary tales about robbers. Any truth there may have been originally will have been obscured. And there may never have been any truth in it at all."

Everyone turned to look at Day, who sat back in his chair with a sigh.

"You're right, Aristo, and but for Ophelia I would have nothing to do with this. But I must go on."

Aristos said that he completely understood, and decided not to say that his reservations about the existence of the Kállos were nothing compared to those about finding Ophelia. He asked what Day thought about Nikolaidis's searches.

"I think he showed great determination and common sense, and he was thorough. On Naxos he looked at the archaeological sites at Spedos and Panormos, and a great many other places too. On the smaller islands he drew a blank on Koufonissia and Schinousa, but he stayed for a long time on Iraklia in the Panagia area in the central hills. He describes a path from Panagia village to the Cave of Agios Ioannis, and how he spent several days exploring round there. In my opinion, this is where we should start: on Iraklia."

"I agree," said the Curator, to everyone's surprise. "It was Iraklia that seemed to me the least unlikely place. If you're going to do this, that's where I'd suggest."

"I'll make some coffee," said Rania, getting up. The mood had changed.

"Right, shall we get down to details?" Aristos asked, with more conviction than he felt. "Let's look at the map again."

Aristos's knowledge of the islands was invaluable as they searched for specific locations on Iraklia that might match the features Helen had listed. With the help of the freshly-made coffee they approached the task with enthusiasm.

"Like Naxos, Iraklia has been inhabited from antiquity. There's an Early Cycladic settlement on the site of Agios Mamas, which is near Panagia where Nikolaidis was searching. For a mountain you have Mount Papas, and there's even an immense cave, the Cave of Agios Ioannis, or St John, which is believed to be just part of a vast system of caves running beneath the island."

"That sounds encouraging, Aristo," said Helen, "a cave is so strongly indicated in the descriptions. That particular cave is quite a long way from the sea, though. Would it have been closer to the shore in that period?"

"I'd have to check on that. There's something else. The petroglyphs that Iraklia is famous for. You know about them, Martin, don't you?"

"Yes, the prehistoric stones with spirals cut into them, found all over Iraklia. Do you think that's what could be meant by 'scratches on a rock'?"

He gave Day a brief look as if to a promising student.

"I think we deserve a glass of wine," he said. "Let's continue outside."

The warmth of the late afternoon was welcome. As they waited for Aristos to bring the wine, Day checked his mobile and discovered a missed call from an hour before. It was from James Sedge, who had left a voice message. Day excused himself and walked into the garden to listen to it. Leaning against the wall which bounded the little vineyard, he saw the Curator place four glasses on his marble table and begin to open the wine. Smiling, Day put the phone to his ear and listened to the recorded message.

Having listened to it twice, Day returned to the terrace and sat down next to Helen.

"We drank some of this with Nick and Deppi on Saturday," Aristos was saying. "It's from Syros, not far from where Deppi's brother lives. I found a few bottles in Chora yesterday. *Stin yia sas!*"

The wine was delicate and distinctive, worthy of Aristos's enthusiasm. Day commented on it, but when Helen asked what the matter was he realised that his distracted air had not gone unnoticed. They were all looking at him.

"Sorry, I didn't realise … It's the voice message I've just listened to. I don't quite know what to make of it. It's from James Sedge, Ophelia's research assistant in Cambridge. It's rather odd."

"Odd in what way?" asked Helen, not unreasonably.

"I'll play it to you. I talked to him just a few days ago and asked him for anything he could tell me about Ophelia's work. He didn't seem to know a great deal, or to be very interested. Here's what he says now."

He put the message on speaker.

'Hi Martin, it's James. I took a look round, like you asked, but I didn't find anything about Nikolaidis in Ophelia's files and I can't get into her computer. Then I did a bit of ferreting and found a few interesting things. I want to come out to Naxos and talk to you in person. We should definitely check out the island of Iraklia, I'll explain when I see you. And there's something else - Ophelia met Nikolaidis in person, did you know that? Give me a call back, will you?"

"Why does he want to come to Naxos?" asked Helen. "And how does he know that Ophelia met Christos *nearly two decades ago*? Did she tell him?"

"He certainly seems to know a great deal more than he told me on the phone," said Day. "I'm worried that he mentions Iraklia, it suggests he's somehow on the same track as we are. When we spoke he seemed hardly to know Christos's name. I have a bad feeling about him."

Nobody ventured a comment. Day took a generous sip from his glass and allowed the wine to sit in his mouth, its richness teasing his tastebuds and calming his nerves. When he swallowed, it was with a sudden decision.

"I don't want him here. I can't explain why, I just don't want him here."

22

Day did not reply to James Sedge and heard no more from him. Two days later he and Helen went to Iraklia following the trail of the Kállos.

The *Express Skopelitis* was the only ship of the Small Cyclades Lines that linked the smaller islands of the Lesser Cyclades with the larger islands of Naxos and Amorgos. It carried about 300 passengers at most, and only a dozen vehicles, and had been in action since the 1980s. When the sea was calm, the *Express Skopelitis* had charm and history, and carried nostalgia in its bows. In heavy seas it was probably better to watch it from the shore, in Day's opinion. All the same, the small ferry was a legend in these islands, it sailed in all weathers, responded to any emergency, and kept the islanders supplied and connected. One family, indeed a single man, had originally created this service with a small boat that had been barely powerful enough for the big seas it encountered. The family business had grown and was now a by-word for social connectivity in the Lesser Cyclades.

The boat's approach to Naxos was one of the iconic sights of the port, and Day stood with Helen among a small group of expectant passengers. It presented its stern to the concrete jetty and began to lower its ramp, revealing a blue car deck and chains and pipes painted yellow. A single van stood ready to board, and the foot-passengers followed it inside with their bags and boxes. Before the ramp was fully raised again, the *Express Skopelitis* was off, heading for the open sea and its next stop, Iraklia. It was two in the afternoon, and the crossing would take an hour and a half. Day and Helen settled on the slatted benches that ran the length of the forward deck, and waited to see what the sea would be like once they left the protective bulk of Naxos.

It was not long before the swell of the open sea hit the sides of the *Express Skopelitis*, and much of the first half hour seemed to be spent tilted over to port. Even in reasonable weather the wind buffeted the boats that passed the beaches and outcrops of Naxos's popular west coast. Day resolved to ignore his discomfort and focus on other things. First he asked Helen what accommodation she had booked for that night.

"I booked a room for us in Agios Georgios. It's only a short walk from where the ferry docks, and I liked the owner. Her name's Anna, she sounded very friendly."

"Perfect. Any idea where we could eat later?"

Helen smiled, realising that Day's interest was a way to distract himself from the sea crossing.

"There's a taverna in Agios Georgios that we might try. There aren't many places in Agios Georgios but this one looks really nice. Not surprisingly, their fish is meant to be excellent."

They began to talk about the search they had planned for the following day, but soon found that talking against the wind was too difficult. They learned to anticipate the regular rolling of the ferry and compensate by leaning into the swell and pressing one foot hard onto the wooden deck with each swing of the boat. Progress was slow because the

Express Skopelitis had a top speed of twelve knots and had to move forward in a zigzag pattern, turning alternately into the wind and then ahead again.

The sea conditions worsened when they turned to follow the southern coastline of Naxos. The view to their left became a landscape of wave-resistant rocks and secret bays. Not many people lived here on the south coast, and the inland roads through the mountains were few and challenging. Tourists were brought here by boat in the summer, to swim in one of the tiny bays and enjoy the safe shallow waters and pristine beaches. The *Express Skopelitis* stoically endured the more independent waters of the open sea, its engine noise increasing and its passengers having to shout or give up on conversation completely. Despite his discomfort, Day found the energy to wonder whether the forty oarsmen of the ancient Cycladic boats had followed this very route. Surely they must have done, and in considerably greater peril.

"Tomorrow we may even find the ancient Kállos," he said, gazing out beyond the ferry's wake to the Cycladic skyline. "And this afternoon, there's something I want to show you."

Helen nodded but only squeezed his hand in reply.

Finally Naxos fell away behind them. They approached their destination, Iraklia, following its eastern coast until they reached the sheltered harbour of Agios Georgios. The *Express Skopelitis* made a professional manoeuvre to land its descending ramp lightly on the old jetty, where a crewman jumped down to secure the rope.

Day and Helen were the only passengers to leave the ferry at Agios Georgios and the boat hardly paused before heading back to sea. Day dropped his small bag at his feet to admire the bay. The water was turquoise and tranquil, edged by a thin line of pale sand in front of a row of large tamarisk trees. Square white Cycladic houses, most with light blue shutters, stood at various angles on the gentle sides of the hill. Prominent in the middle of the little town, a white church with a blue dome looked down benignly. Among the houses were palm trees and pines, and vestiges of the wild shrubs and flowers that had always grown there. The purple-grey Cycladic mountain made a perfect backdrop.

It was easy to find Anna's House (Room To Let), and Anna turned out to be a confident young woman who told them, among a great many other things, that her husband drove the island's taxi in the summer and whitewashed people's houses in the winter. She gave them a bottle of cold water from her fridge and a plate of homemade honey and nut pastries before taking their bags and showing them to their room. Small, clean and white, it was ideal.

After drinking some water, changing their shoes and, in Helen's case, fortifying herself with a pastry, they sauntered back towards the harbour. It was already half past four. They had booked the overnight stay because the *Express Skopelitis* only sailed between Naxos and Iraklia once each day, and they would return to Naxos the following afternoon. The area they had come to explore would have to wait until the next morning, but there was enough time for a pleasant walk to the place that Day had long wanted to see. It faced straight out to sea and was of historical interest to him, but was not going to be the hiding place of the Kállos.

They began with an enjoyable fifteen minute stroll to Livadi, considered by many people to be Iraklia's best beach. From a headland they encountered a breathtaking view of Naxos in the north, Schinousa island to the east, and the beautiful and deserted beach of Livadi directly below them. The sea shone darkly in the afternoon sun.

"You see that hill over there? That's it, the hill of Kastro," said Day. "I've read about it but never been here to check it out. It's been inhabited pretty much continuously since prehistoric times. Most of the ruins you can see up there are modern, but beneath them lies the really distant past. Let's go up and take a closer look."

He took her hand and they climbed the gently sloping flank of the hill. A long wall ran horizontally across the slope beneath the ruins of a group of houses, and Day excitedly pointed out the large boulders at the base of the wall. These, he said, were the remains of prehistoric fortifications.

"What does 'prehistory' mean, exactly?" she asked.

"It's the period of human existence before we have any written records. In fact, prehistory is what archaeologists study, using material objects alone to discover more about that period of the past. It's an enormous span of time, many thousands of years. Historians used to think we would never understand that era and it wasn't even a recognised field of study until the nineteenth century. Up to that point people largely believed the biblical flood myth and it was assumed that humans had only existed on the planet for a few thousand years. Our way of looking at the distant past only changed when advances in geology, followed by Darwin's *Origin of Species*, opened up new ways of thinking. We began to look at places like Stonehenge in a different way and create some kind of realistic timeline for prehistory. This was all before carbon dating, of course. It's been a fascinating journey of discovery."

"And the Cycladic Era, where does that fit in?"

"It's also part of prehistory, in the Bronze Age. After the Stone Age and before the Iron Age. The Bronze Age developed here in the Cyclades very early, and in a unique way, and the name Cycladic Era means that civilisation. We subdivide it to keep track of how things developed. Early Cycladic 1, Early Cycladic 2 (also called the Keros period), ..."

"Hold on! I need to absorb it a bit at a time," she laughed. Living with an archaeologist certainly had its challenges, but she loved it. Martin was really happy, his forehead slightly red from the sun, standing on a hill on an Aegean island looking at boulders and seeing people of the distant past alive in his imagination.

As they wandered among the ruined settlement of Kastro, he helped her to see the different levels of antiquity beneath the crumbling modern walls until it all made sense. Neither the landscape nor the way of life changed quickly here. People had lived on Iraklia for thousands of years and had built on the same areas of land, the same vantage points, using some of the same materials from earlier houses and walls. She could see, when they were pointed out to her, the remains of vaults and cisterns, and much more recent stone threshing floors. This place had been inhabited continuously until about a hundred years ago. Now the abandoned village was left to the wind and the weather, and its own spectacular silence.

"The whole of the Cyclades is like the birthplace of our civilisation," said Day wistfully, "Tomorrow, when we go into the mountainous heart of this island … there will be more." He gave a deep sigh of pleasure and held out his hand for hers. "We should be starting back. The sun's getting low."

As they walked back to Agios Georgios he talked all the way, building pictures in her imagination of the development of the human mind, the growth of civilisation. He explained the fascination that he felt in the study of prehistory when he considered, often alone in the dark with a glass of wine, why and how we became the people we are today. Why and how, indeed, modern cultures are so diverse across our planet, despite us all having started from the same prehistoric beginning.

As they walked through Agios Georgios towards Anna's house, and the exhilaration of visiting Kastro began to fade, Day grew quiet.

He felt a growing melancholy that he could not account for. His enthusiasm and optimism were seeping out of him, like a sky filling with unexpected cloud.

"You just need something to eat," said Helen, slipping her arm from his as they opened the door to their accommodation. "Thank you, that was a wonderful afternoon. You'll feel better after a shower, and then we'll go to the taverna."

After washing away the salt of the sea crossing and the dust of the afternoon, they joined the evening *volta* along the shore before going in search of the fish taverna. They found it easily in a quiet street, a blackboard on the wall announcing freshly-caught seafood. A homemade sign over the door said Psarotaverna Estiatorio 'Asterias'.

It was still rather early for dinner in Greece. Fortunately this seemed not to matter to the welcoming owner of the taverna. He led them up a flight of painted stone steps to a first floor dining terrace where seven or eight unoccupied tables stood beneath a delicate pergola with white canvas curtains at the corners. It was a simple and pleasant area which for the moment they had all to themselves. They chose a small table which gave them a view of white houses, more flights of steps, and the ubiquitous blue paintwork on shutters, pipes and flowerpots.

No sooner had they sat down than they were invited to the kitchen to choose their food. Three women were busy among the stainless steel surfaces, gleaming gas hobs and deep ovens. It was a surprisingly modern scene in contrast to the traditional house. Fresh fish and seafood were displayed on ice in a glass-fronted cabinet, and the hot food was steaming in vast aluminium trays. There was a gently bubbling pan of artichokes in some tempting sauce, roasted chicken legs on a bed of *orzo* pasta, aubergines cooked with tomatoes and cheese, and a tray of beef and potatoes topped with fresh green herbs. More dishes seemed to be still cooking. The owner pointed out the array of salads and reminded them of the ways in which any of the fresh fish could be prepared, then looked at them expectantly for their answer.

"*Perimenetay!*" called the oldest woman, waving at her husband and uncovering another tray of food that she had just brought out of an oven. When the fragrant steam dispersed they saw fine strands of spaghetti topped with mussels and cockles in their shells and generous pieces of lobster.

"Speciality of the Asterias!" said the lady proudly, brushing off her English in preparation for the season.

They ordered the lobster spaghetti, a portion of chips to complete Day's happiness, and a salad which they were told was a particularly good Asterias creation. Then, sipping a local white wine that had arrived at their table in a blue metal jug, they waited contentedly, still the only diners on the rooftop.

"What a treat!" mused Day, feeling completely restored as the first sip of wine hit his tastebuds. "To be sitting here on a little Cycladic island, at a fish taverna, with you... what could be better?"

"Does it make up for all the irritations of this wild goose chase?"

Before he could reply, the lobster spaghetti arrived. Putting it on the table, the owner told them proudly that people came from all the surrounding islands to eat at Asterias because the seafood was the best in the Cyclades. The lobster had been caught by his eldest son, whose boat they could see in the harbour, it was called '*O Asterias*'. He put the salad next to Helen and the chips next to Day. It may, of course, have been accidental. He then returned downstairs, leaving them chuckling.

"Lovely man!" said Helen. "Asterias means starfish, doesn't it?"

"Yes. I'd be rich if I had a pound for every *psarotaverna* in Greece called Asterias. I've eaten at quite a few of them. That salad looks good, doesn't it? Kopanisti cheese instead of Feta, and there are caper leaves in there, and those little rusks that look like miniature Cretan *dakos*. Excellent!"

He refilled their glasses and they began to eat. The lobster spaghetti lived up to its reputation, and not until they had done full justice to the tender pasta, fresh shellfish and tasty, well-cooked pieces of lobster did they talk of anything other than Iraklia, the meal and the night.

"I feel we're on the brink of something important," said Day, pouring the last of the wine into Helen's glass. "Tomorrow when we go to Panagia we'll try to do everything just as Christos did, according to his own words in the book. Panagia is about four kilometres away from here in the centre of Iraklia - the whole island is only seven kilometres long - and I think we should get Anna's husband to drive us there. He does own the local taxi, after all. We'll take all our things with us and go straight to the ferry afterwards; that will give us more time. The ferry goes at three tomorrow afternoon, doesn't it?"

"Yes. But we can't ask the taxi to wait about for that long."

Day waved aside her concerns. He could think of nothing beyond the history and the challenge, and would happily pay someone to enjoy a few cups of coffee or a bite of lunch to make a breakthrough possible.

"We'll follow the path that Christos talks about to the famous Cave of St John, or Agios Ioannis. Apparently it's now a well-marked hiking trail, unlike in his day, when it would have been rough terrain. The big cave is about an hour's walk along it, and it's mostly steep. We won't need to go all the way because nothing of significance is going to be lying in a well-visited cave. We must look out for somewhere that caught Christos's attention between the village and the cave, though I have no idea what it could be. Christos might have made some kind of marker to help him find his place again, given how barren and uniform it is up in the hills. I sincerely hope so, anyway. Do you remember those scratches on a rock that were mentioned? It could be that kind of thing." He looked at her anxiously. "I'm afraid it may be quite a challenging uphill climb."

"I don't mind that. It will be worth it if we find something. If the Kállos does exist, Martin, what's the most likely thing it might be?"

"It would be wonderful if it was a hoard of beautiful figurines, but it's more likely to be a few pots. The little girl who saw deep lines cut into patterns may have seen pottery vessels with incised decorations."

"Wouldn't she just say they were pots?"

"Of course, you're right. I don't know, then. It's so odd that the legend doesn't ever include what the Kállos actually is - wouldn't you think it would be natural to talk about it? Perhaps it was difficult to describe, or frightening in some way, or even too sacred to put into words."

He spoke wistfully and Helen was unconvinced. "How many Cycladic figurines have been found on Iraklia so far?"

"I haven't heard of any at all on this island. The most remarkable ancient remains here are the flat stones carved with spiral patterns that Aristos mentioned. They were made about three thousand years ago, in the early Bronze Age. There are a lot of them, about two dozen, some in museums and some still in the open. Their local name is *bousoules*, which means compasses, like the orientation device, so we think they might be a location marker indicating a burial site or an important settlement. The spiral, of course, is an old and potent symbol that turns up all over the world on the sites of prehistoric settlements."

"Do you remember the man who talked about the scratches on a rock? If he used the actual word *bousoules*, Christos might have changed it to hide the specific link to Iraklia."

Day stared at her. "Really, sometimes you have such flashes of genius!"

She laughed. "There's also a verb *bousoulo* in Greek that means to crawl, like to crawl on all fours. I don't suppose that's very helpful, though."

"That's hilarious, I love the idea that the Kállos has to be approached reverently on all fours! It's rather fitting when you think of the original meaning of the word kállos."

"I thought it meant beauty."

"It does, but when it first appears in the 7th century BCE it only means physical beauty. Its meaning changed later when the philosophers got hold of it, and it came to signify the beauty of the soul too."

He rested his elbows on the table in front of him, clasped his hands and looked at her as if he would be more than happy to crawl on all fours if required. Helen finished the little wine left in her glass and sighed.

"The spiral is a wonderful symbol. It suggests the circle of life, love everlasting. I've always thought of it as particularly Greek."

Day stared at her, his expression unreadable. He hadn't really noticed that the little taverna had filled up. All he could see was Helen and the soft lights from the houses of Agios Georgios behind her. Beyond that there was nothing but the utter darkness of the night. He was consumed by two completely compatible obsessions: the antiquity of the Cyclades and the woman opposite him.

"Would you like to go home with me now, Miss Aitchison?" he asked quietly.

23

Panagia was a traditional, one-street village in the middle of the high agricultural land that dominated the centre of Iraklia. It was a community still unspoilt by modern life, where cobbled lanes ran between traditional white-washed houses, where there were communal baking ovens and idiosyncratic clay pots used instead of normal chimney stacks. Anna's husband, Kostas, had been happy to take them to Panagia and pass a few hours in the café there with his friends before taking them to the port in time for the *Express Skopelitis* at three o'clock.

Shrugging a small rucksack onto his back and retrieving his sunglasses from his shirt pocket, Day squinted into the sunshine. The mountain air was clean and warm, and filled him with energy.

"I'm looking forward to this," he announced. "The trail that we want starts at the Church of the Virgin Mary, which has to be that church over there. Then it's all uphill, I'm afraid."

"I don't think I've ever seen you so enthusiastic about physical exercise, Martin."

"It helps if antiquity is involved. Here we are! Trail 3, Path to the Cave of Agios Ioannis. Let's go!"

They set off westwards from the church and the rocky path began to steepen almost at once. For a while there was room to walk side by side and talk, but further along they went single file and saved their breath. It was enough to take in their surroundings and revel in the view. The landscape was timeless, from the bent shrubs and prickly vegetation to the panoramic views across the island and the sea. Cycladic man must surely have walked here and felt the same sun on his neck. Day strode on up the trail, bare-headed and carefree, a man in his element. The reddish-coloured path, adequately marked with wooden signposts and stone cairns, was now flanked by a stone wall, and after half an hour they reached the highest point of their climb. The path disappeared through a narrow opening in the rock at the summit; on the other side they were rewarded with a vista across the western plain of Iraklia to the distant island of Ios, isolated in the shining sea.

The path descended downhill to an open area of level ground surrounded by a low drystone wall. It seemed to be a place where walkers could pause to take in their surroundings. A sign saying s*pilia*, or cave, pointed off from one corner of this refuge. Piles of small rocks had been built by people coming here over the past many years, each placing a stone on top of the rest until in some cases the precarious tower stood as high as a man. These mounds felt personal, organic, a testimony to the people who had made them.

"What an astonishing place," said Day, wandering round curiously.

"It's quite moving, isn't it, with all these piles of rocks?" she replied.

She hadn't expected an answer, but after several minutes something about Day's silence struck her as odd. He was standing with his back to her by the low stone wall where the path to the cave began its steep descent. She walked over to see what he was looking at. He was staring at a flat stone marked with a curious design. It was clearly recent. It looked like a child had drawn the heads of three hens, their combs and wattles depicted in red, two heads on the top and one underneath forming a triangular pattern. Round this was a red line in the shape of a shield, and beneath it all was an arrow that pointed to the left.

"Do you recognise that?" Day asked.

"No. What is it?"

"I think it's the crest of Jesus College, Cambridge. My God, Helen, Ophelia has been here! This is our college crest. Three black and red cockerels' heads."

He brushed his finger gently across the image on the stone. His finger came away stained in red.

"Lipstick! There's only one explanation: Ophelia has left this for me. When the fisherman saw her going past in a boat she was on her way to Iraklia. She followed this same path and stood right here."

Helen said nothing, trying to find some less unlikely explanation for the little drawing in pen and lipstick, but there was nothing else that made more sense.

"Okay, if Ophelia was here we must be on the right track. It seems she was sure that you'd come here and wanted to stop you taking a wrong turn. The arrow is to keep you on the right path."

"She wanted to make sure we didn't go down to the big cave." He turned round and leaned against the wall facing Helen. "Well, I thought it would be Christos who left us a sign. Instead, it seems it was Ophelia."

"It means she's alive and well, Martin."

He looked round thoughtfully, as if hoping to see Ophelia herself among the undulations of the hill, but they were very much alone.

"I wonder when she did this. Is she still here on Iraklia?"

"We can't possibly know, Martin. All we can do now is follow her arrow. Come on! It's the only way to find her, if she wants to be found."

They headed across the rocky hillside as the arrow instructed. This was no longer a walking trail. It was steep and sometimes precarious, but it was undeniably a path, used by goats if not people. After twenty minutes they felt they had lost their way and hesitated until they spotted red marks on a distant rock; the red colour stood out in that expanse of grey and dull green. From then on, whenever the choice of direction was uncertain, they found one of the signs scrawled on a stone. The crests had become just a scribble of three black marks inside a red circle.

"No room for doubt now," said Day, "Ophelia is leading us to the Kállos. Do you remember what Dimitris Kakavas, the bookseller, said? *If you want something to be found, you have to leave directions to it.* That's what Ophelia is doing."

The scanty path became progressively narrower and less distinct until it finally ended in a clump of tall aloes. The ground fell away sharply, leaving them and the aloes on the edge of a two metre drop overlooking an expanse of *maquis* that ended in the wide Aegean. There was evidence of a small landslide having taken place at sometime in the past, and the ground was slippery like scree. At the sight of the rockfall, Day became excited.

"Which way now?" said Helen. There was no sign of a black and red marker, and they seemed to be at the end of the trail.

"Why don't you wait here and I'll take a look around? Back in a few minutes."

Heedless of her request to be careful he headed off, skirting the edge of the drop. Helen was reminded of the time when he had organised a search party to look for a Mycenaean burial site, combing the ground for the smallest clue across a rough stretch of hillside on Naxos. She watched him walk below the ridge she was standing on and then disappear from view completely.

When he reappeared and climbed up to join her he was sweating from the climb.

"This must be the place, Helen!" he said. "There's another of Ophelia's markers right below here, in front of a massive pile of rocks. There's no way you and I could shift it, and nor could Ophelia. There are a lot of large stones, packed with smaller debris and grit, and it's been overgrown with tough vegetation that looks years old. There's something about the pile of rocks that looks manmade: no natural landslide would have piled them up like that. And another thing, all the rocks are right up against the overhang, but there are virtually none further down the slope. I've taken some pictures on my phone. We're going to have to get some help."

"What are you thinking, Martin?"

He shrugged, but answered confidently.

"My guess is there's a cave right beneath where we're standing now, and it's been deliberately closed up a long time ago using all the rocks in the immediate area. It really could be the place Christos found, Helen. This actually could be the place!"

They caught the *Express Skopelitis* with no difficulty thanks to Kostas, and had a rather smoother crossing back to Naxos in a calmer sea. Just after five o'clock they stepped onto the quay at Chora and walked straight to the police station. Windswept and dusty, carrying their overnight bags, they asked at the reception desk for Inspector Tsountas. The officer did not hide his surprise at their appearance and forgot to ask what the visit was about before going into the inspector's office and shutting the door behind him.

The inspector emerged almost at once. At the sight of him, Day felt tired. He was not up for an argument. He hoped that the man in front of him now was the Kyriakos of the morning with Angeliki, rather than the one who seemed to have a great deal to prove.

"You'd better come in," said Kyriakos, and led the way back into his office. Inside his tone became less formal. "Is something the matter?"

Day described the trip to Iraklia and the signs he believed that Ophelia had left him. Kyriakos frowned but listened carefully, which was all Day required at this point. He showed him the photographs on his phone and added, in a tone reminiscent of one of his television documentaries, that he thought it likely that behind the rocks and vegetation lay the discovery of which Christos Nikolaidis had written nearly twenty years ago. He delivered the final flourish by saying that if only they could unearth the discovery, Ophelia might be found.

Kyriakos raised his eyebrows and pushed himself back in his chair.

"Firstly, Martin, you should have consulted me before going to Iraklia on this expedition. It directly concerns the investigation into the disappearance of Miss Blue, and as such is police business."

Day hid a small smile. This was simply an assertion of authority before Kyriakos did what was required of him.

"You're right, of course, Kyriako. So I'm turning it all over to you. There's no possibility that we could move the debris on our own anyway. With your authority, you can arrange men and equipment and do the job properly. I'll take you right there by the most direct route." He gave Kyriakos his most winning smile. "You'll be making an extremely significant historical discovery, and probably solve your missing person case too."

The policeman tapped the desk in front of him with his nails, looking thoughtfully at Day. Kyriakos Tsountas had had no serious case for a very long time and was keen to undertake an active investigation. He nodded.

"Very well. Normally we wouldn't take a civilian with us, but as you know the location, Martin, we'll need you there. You can also oversee the discovery of the contents of the cave, if that's what it is, since you're a specialist. Be at the police jetty tomorrow morning at ten o'clock. Sea state permitting, we'll take the police launch. I'll arrange men, digging equipment and a police photographer."

Day grinned and his gratitude was genuine. It was entirely possible that, the very next day, he would find out the true nature of the legendary Kállos.

They sat in Diogenes bar, still dishevelled and salty from the long day and the sea crossing. Nobody at Diogenes cared. Alexandros served them with the same mixture of respect and amusement as always, and brought to their table two of the most welcome gin and tonics that Day could recall. After quenching his thirst, he tucked into the salty snacks that came with the drinks.

"What an amazing bit of success! I had a good feeling about today, but who would have guessed that Ophelia would be there ahead of us? I actually feel a bit overcome by her confidence in me. You and I both know it was guesswork that took us to Iraklia."

"Educated guesswork, Martin. And it was Ophelia who educated you." She took a sip from her glass and put it back on the table thoughtfully. "You must have known each other very well."

"I don't know about that," murmured Day. "I've never been very good at that kind of thing. Maybe she knew me better than I knew her. Or it's just a mindset that we both share and she knew how I would think. If she had really trusted me, she would have stayed and worked with me, instead of leaving me this ridiculously roundabout challenge. We would have found the Kállos so much more quickly together. I don't understand why she did it this way."

Helen had no answer, and thought they would never have one, but there was no point in damping Day's elation.

"Let's come back to that question later," she said. "The main thing now is to find out what's in the cave."

"Of course, you're right. Ophelia probably knows what she's doing. Shall we have another drink?"

24

Kyriakos Tsountas had put in many hours of work. He had ordered the police launch, instructed a group of officers on their responsibilities and involved the 'police photographer', a local man with a good camera whom his predecessor had recommended. He had given his immediate subordinate, Skouros, the task of ensuring they took the appropriate equipment to move the rocks, and obtained official permission to involve a civilian in the operation. When he finally returned to his modest apartment in Chora, he permitted himself a small ouzo.

He was relieved to have an operation to conduct at last. For the first time since his arrival on Naxos he had something to get his teeth into. In Volos there had been no shortage of action - raids on warehouses, searches of cargo vessels, hunts for illegal imports. He had felt energised and validated until that business with the American ship and his transfer here. The seniority of his new role hardly compensated for the absence of proper police work. To make matters worse, he longed for Angeliki all the time but felt guilty that she was trying to move to Naxos, giving up her good job in Volos to be with him. Their future was surely not on this peaceful, crime-free island. In a few years he would ask for a transfer back to the mainland, maybe to Athens if he could. Meanwhile, an operation like this one of Martin Day's was the best he could hope for.

He began to feel downhearted at the thought of years on the fringes of the Helladic Police and the possible delay to the start of his married life with Angeliki. He stared round his apartment disconsolately, drinking the ouzo without thinking. He was just regretting the fact that he had nothing in the house to eat when the sound of his phone gave him a jolt. It was Skouros, reporting on the completion of arrangements for the next morning. Somewhat cheered, Kyriakos pulled on his black leather jacket and left the apartment. He strode to his usual taverna where he ordered a generous plate of lamb with artichokes, feeling considerably more positive.

The next day was fine and the sea calm. Unwilling to go to the lengths of involving the Hellenic Coast Guard, Kyriakos had commandeered the 'police launch' which served Naxos, Paros, Amorgos and Ios, owned and skippered by a member of the Paros police force. This fine vessel, though rarely called upon for official duties, served the islands well in times when crime crossed from one island to another, as was occasionally the case. It was a retired coastal patrol boat by the name of *Poseidon*, and was a spacious rather than speedy craft. It was waiting at the designated mooring when he arrived in the trio of police vehicles that carried his team for the expedition.

Day and the photographer joined them shortly afterwards, and the boat set off from the harbour with its full complement of equipment and personnel. The skipper steered a course closer to the coastline than that taken by the *Express Skopelitis*, so the crossing took slightly longer but was less challenging. Day sheltered in the cabin with Kyriakos and the photographer, a fifty-year old local man called Michalis who was quietly enthusiastic and struck Day as very sensible.

At Agios Georgios the boat was unloaded and the equipment assembled on the jetty. A group of locals had gathered to watch the unusual events taking place at the port. One by one the policemen picked up a tool: a pick, a crowbar or a shovel. The last men to volunteer were left with the heaviest items. An old truck stood ready to take them all to Panagia, and the local taxi, driven by Kostas himself, waited with it to take Kyriakos, Day and Michalis.

The party that set off up the trail at Panagia towards the Cave of Agios Ioannis considerably outnumbered the people sitting at the local *kafenion*. Their progress was quietly efficient and nobody said much. At the open space on the other side of the summit, Day pointed out Ophelia's first marker and led the way to where the path ended at the aloes above the cave. Once they had scrambled down, Michalis took pictures of the blocked entrance before Skouros instructed the men to start clearing it.

Day remained as close to the action as he was allowed. It was an arduous and time-consuming job, since he had insisted that care must be taken not to disturb any evidence. This could be an important archaeological site, he said, where the smallest detail could add immeasurably to their knowledge of the meaning of the discovery.

"The context gives legal authenticity and archaeological significance to a find," he told Kyriakos, dimly aware of making a direct quote from something he had learned at university. "Not unlike a crime scene, I expect."

Kyriakos grinned and resumed issuing instructions. In his excitement he spoke so quickly that Day had trouble understanding him. Michalis was taking photographs and Day was only a step behind him when one of the policemen shouted that they were through. Kyriakos called an immediate halt and beckoned Day forward.

There was no doubt this was the entrance to a cave. Only a small aperture had been revealed and it was completely dark inside, but the air that came from the hole was stale and cold, trapped for years under the ground. Kyriakos passed Day his powerful torch and offered him the first look into the interior.

Afterwards Day said that, whatever he might have been expecting to see, it had certainly not been a skeleton.

They made an opening large enough to allow access to the forensic team that would be needed to examine the body, and officers were placed on guard. Kyriakos and Day, peering in from the opening to the cave, assessed the contents from their different professional standpoints. Rather than the heap of ancient artefacts he had expected, Day looked critically at the figure lying on the uneven ground. Nothing at all remained except the skeleton of an adult which must have been there for some time but was by no means ancient. It lay face upwards at the far end of the cave, about fifteen feet inside, the skull against the back wall. He staggered away and left the police to their work.

After a while Kyriakos walked over to him, barking instructions to his men as he came. Trailing behind him was Michalis the photographer, white faced.

Day's horrified expression had already started to change to one of anger.

"I don't understand. Who the hell is that in there? What's going on?" he said. Kyriakos ignored him.

"Martin, Michalis - this officer will escort you back to Panagia. Take the taxi to the port and send it back for me. Wait for me on the boat. I'll be about an hour, no more. The scene of crime officer is on her way from Naxos with the Coast Guard. We'll return to the station in Chora, and then you can go home. It's been very difficult, I understand that. We'll talk more on the boat."

On the walk back to Panagia, Day and the photographer spoke briefly about what had happened, then fell silent. From Panagia, Kostas drove them to the launch where the boat captain was surprised to see only two of the party returning. Then they waited for over an hour for Kyriakos and the others.

Day's low-spirited contemplation was disrupted by the arrival of the police team. The old truck and the taxi drove away as the launch turned in the bay and headed back to open water. He watched the northern tip of Iraklia slowly recede, knowing that round the western shore there was a cave containing a skeleton that had been immured there for maybe several decades. Who knew how long it took for someone's body to lose all its flesh, its clothes, its hair? Kyriakos, however, proved surprisingly knowledgeable.

"I made an amateur study of forensics some years ago," he admitted. "I don't like not knowing things. I was working on a murder case … Anyway, there are some features of our victim that we can be quite sure of, …"

"Let me guess," said Day moodily. "It's a man, old rather than young, and he's been there for twenty years."

"Yes, I'd say so. What kind of guess was that? It seems a bit out of your area of expertise."

"Sorry, Kyriako. I know very little about bodies, but it's my guess that we've just discovered what's left of poor Christos Nikolaidis, who went missing some twenty years ago and was presumed to have drowned. His body was never found."

"The man who wrote the book about the ancient treasure you thought would be inside that cave?"

"Yes. It seems he didn't drown after all. That always seemed strange to me, because people said he was an excellent swimmer. Perhaps he went into the cave to find his precious Kállos and became trapped. I have no idea. What are the chances of finding out what happened, Kyriako? Forensically, I mean?"

"Quite poor, I'm afraid. The gender and approximate age of the dead man should be straightforward, but it will be harder to establish when and how he died. As for the identity, it's possible that we'll be lucky...." He reached into his jacket pocket. "I found these among the rocks inside the cave ..."

He brought out an evidence bag containing a pair of glasses, black-rimmed, cheap and broken. Day could not recall whether or not Christos had worn glasses, but he should be able to find out. He held the bag thoughtfully before handing it back to Kyriakos.

"Even if we can't prove beyond doubt that the body is that of your historian, Martin, we should be able to establish that it *could* have been him. The same applies to how he died: I expect the pathologist will offer several possibilities. I noticed signs of blunt force trauma to the back of the skull, although it was hard to see the extent of the damage with the skeleton on its back. It suggests he could have fallen and banged his head on a rock, or he could have been hit with something."

219

Day nodded. "And then somehow the cave was sealed up with the poor man still inside."

The sea crossing back to Naxos seemed to take a long time despite the unusual calm of the sea. It was early afternoon; everyone was tired and spirits were low. The talk on the boat was of the identity of the skeleton in the cave, but speculation finally turned to silence.

Back in Naxos Police Station things were slightly better for everyone but Day, who alone had nothing to occupy his mind after he had given his official statement. All round him there were reports to write and calls to make to various authorities. Kyriakos was informed that the body would be taken to Syros within a few hours, to be examined by the pathologist the following day.

"There's nothing more you can do here, Martin," he said eventually, finding Day sitting wearily in the reception. "You can go home now. I'll call you in a few days, when I have some information. Please say nothing of what's happened today to anyone, other than Helen, of course. I appreciate you were hoping that Miss Blue would return as a result of opening the cave, but it's unlikely to help your friend if this particular story gets in the newspapers, and might hinder the investigation."

When Day left the police station there was a noticeable coolness in the air. The sky was no longer bright and a mistiness filled it like a portent of change. He had seen this before and guessed more bad weather was on its way, the easy sea crossing having been the calm before the storm. Weather changed quickly in the islands.

The drive to Filoti had a cheering effect on him, as with each village through the hills he sensed the approaching comfort of home. The light was fading and the wind had risen. No sooner had he closed the front door than large drops of rain began to thud on the canopy over the balcony and confuse the view of the valley outside the windows. Day lay on the bed with a snack of cheese, ham and salty biscuits telling Helen what had happened. When the plate was empty he fell asleep, and Helen lay with him for a while, thinking about what he had told her, until his quiet breathing eventually lulled her into a doze by his side. An hour later they woke to a gale blowing outside and the chairs pushed from one end of the balcony to the other. A storm had taken hold of Naxos.

Day opened a bottle of wine and pulled a frying pan from the cupboard. Pouring two glasses he went over to Helen, who was sitting on the sofa by the table, without book or laptop, just watching him. He handed her a glass and drank from the other himself, lodging on the table in front of her.

"It's all so hard to believe," she said, looking up at him, "If it turns out that the body in the cave is Christos, it raises so many more questions."

"Whatever happened to Christos, whether or not it's him in there, we have to leave it to the police. Ophelia couldn't have known there was a body inside that cave, she thought we'd find the Kállos inside, which means we're back to square one with no way to find her."

"It's not good, is it?"

"No, it hasn't been good in any way since the day she disappeared."

She looked at him and stood up. "What are you going to make for dinner? I'll come and watch you, and we can talk as you cook."

Day had no idea what he was going to make, especially as there was no meat in the house, but by chopping most of the vegetables he found in the kitchen and adding rice and spices and herbs and wine, there was eventually a good smell of hot food in the room. Cooking gave him space to let everything sink in. Helen too had apparently been doing some thinking.

"Can I say something a bit odd? I don't think this was ever really about the Kállos."

"Not about the Kállos? Why not?"

"Look, we've been assuming that Ophelia left a trail to the cave not knowing what it really contained. But what if she *did* know, or perhaps guess, that it was Christos in there? It would explain why she didn't want to be around when it was opened. I wonder if she could have been looking for Christos ever since she bought his book? Looking for the man, for Christos himself, and not the antiquities? What if she was never interested in them at all?"

"Sorry, darling, but I don't see how that can be right. We know she visited Naxos repeatedly in the last three or four years, James Sedge told us that, but Christos has been dead for a couple of decades. She can only have been looking for the Kállos. I can't make sense of any of it any more!" He stirred the contents of the pan more vigorously than was necessary. "It's all inexplicable."

He added more wine to both their glasses, and another splash to his cooking.

"For once, this red is at least as medicinal as it is enjoyable," he muttered, flexing his upper back and shoulders. "I'm not sure it's helping me to see any more clearly, but maybe tomorrow I'll have some ideas. Oh God! I'm not sure we'll ever get to the bottom of all this without Ophelia."

25

The bad weather set in. For the next two days and nights the Meltemi wind battered Naxos relentlessly and was as strong inland as on the coast. At Chora a small boat broke its mooring and damaged an expensive yacht. Outside the tavernas in Filoti the tables were stacked away out of the wind, and all outdoor life on Naxos seemed to be put on hold. Helen developed symptoms of a cold and spent her time reading.

Day, however, became more and more restless. He was normally quite happy spending hours working at his desk, but now he was unable to settle. He had heard nothing from Kyriakos about the result of the autopsy and felt it was too soon to call him. He tried to tackle the programmes on Greek excavation sites, which was a subject that genuinely interested him, and he achieved just enough to email Maurice with a skimpy progress report. He received a witty quip by return: Maurice had known him a long time.

On the second afternoon of the storm, desperate to get out of the house, Day dug out a coat and walked through the wet wind into Filoti to buy something to relieve Helen's worsening cold. He bought a newspaper, went to the pharmacy and visited the mini market for milk and bread. As he walked home the persistent sound of the phone in his pocket trumped the noise of the wind. It was a number he didn't recognise, one with a UK code.

"Hello?" he shouted, half closing his eyes against the weather.

"Martin? This is James. Can you hear me?"

"James?"

"Sedge. From Cambridge. It's a terrible wind, isn't it?"

For a moment Day was confused. Then he realised he could hear the same wind at James Sedge's end of the line.

"Where are you, James?"

"I'm on Naxos. I arrived last night on the only ferry willing to go to sea in this weather. Awful crossing. I'm in the Hotel Philippos in the main town. I need to see you."

"Why? Why on earth have you come?"

"I know why Ophelia came to Naxos. I know quite a lot, actually, and you need to hear it. I was wrong not to tell you before. Please, we need to meet. You see, I knew her husband Tim."

Day stepped back into a doorway out of the wind and wiped the rain from his face with his free hand. He hesitated. His instinct was not to trust this man, but unless he found more information from somewhere he had no chance of finding Ophelia. James's claim was intriguing and the opportunity could not be passed up.

"What do you know about Tim?"

"I met him in the States before I moved to Cambridge. Look Martin, I can't do this on the phone. Tim told me something very important just before he died…"

"All right, stay where you are. Stay in your room. I'll come as soon as I can. It'll take me about an hour. You'll be there, Hotel Philippos?"

"That's right. I'll be here."

"I'll have to involve the police. If it's about Ophelia, they need to know."

"Just hear me out, Martin, then call the police if you want. I'll tell them the whole story, I give you my word, but for Ophelia's sake please just listen to me first."

Nodding as if James could see him, Day ended the call. He thought about the conversation all the way back to the house through the force of the wind, and by the time he reached home his reluctance had been overtaken by a deep-seated excitement.

"Helen?"

"In here." She had gone back to bed with a cup of tea and was lying against the pillows surrounded by books. He put the bag from the pharmacy and the newspaper on the bed next to her and told her about the call from James.

"Be careful, Martin. I haven't even spoken to the man, but none of this sounds right. He's arrived out of the blue, he doesn't want the police involved, and suddenly he knows a lot about Ophelia … It sounds like it's James himself who has the problem with the law. You could be taking a risk, going alone."

"I'll be on my guard, don't worry. I don't think he's the violent type."

"You've not been the best judge of that in the past!"

He gave her a rueful look and asked if he could bring her anything before he left.

The wind buffeted the little Fiat as Day drove to the Hotel Philippos. The grey sky above was full of rushing, bright clouds with sullen undersides blowing inland from the sea. It was already darker than it should be, as if night was about to fall in the mid-afternoon. He was forced to change his route by a road closure near Halki, and found himself driving along the coast road in Chora. There were very few people about in the streets, and those that were braving the weather walked collar-up against the wind. Along the shore the masts of the moored boats swayed together and the exotic branches of the palm trees lost their dignity to the force of the Meltemi. At the port the stoical *Express Skopelitis*, undeterred by the state of the sea, had just released its thankful passengers. Day drove along the road towards the Portara, where the wind-driven waves splashed over the causeway, and continued up the coast towards Grotta and the Hotel Philippos.

The Philippos was a family-owned hotel in a large white building with a traditional stone balcony running the length of the first floor. Its best rooms were the three with glazed doors leading onto this balcony; at the rear the rooms overlooked the countryside and the turbulent sea. It was still early in the year, before the demands of the tourist season brought the young professionals of the family to run the hotel, and the elderly man at the computer did not see Day at first. Day said hello and asked him to let one of his guests know that he had a visitor.

While the call was being made, Day looked round the foyer. It smelled of polish and stale air, as its doors had been closed against the wind for two days, but it was welcoming and recently redecorated. There was a small but pleasant bar, the furniture was new, and some original paintings of Naxos brightened the walls. A crime had been committed at this hotel the previous year: a visitor from New York had been killed in one of the rooms, a man whom Day had known. It was a strange thought that perhaps James Sedge was waiting for him now in the very same room.

"Kyrie Day? Your friend is in Room 201. The lift is on your left."

Day thanked him but took the nearby stairs, two at a time, to the second floor. Room 201 was the last of seven doors on that landing and faced away from the road. The door was opened by a man about ten years younger than Day with a high forehead from which the curly chestnut hair was prematurely receding. His warm blue eyes were surrounded by smile lines. This was not how Day had imagined James from his voice.

"Martin? Come in." Shaking Day's hand and standing back to let him pass, James closed the door noisily behind him. "Take a seat. God, I've been dreading this, but now that you're here I'm really rather keen to get it over with. Sorry, you can have no idea what I'm on about."

"Take it easy, there's no rush. What's so serious that you needed to come to Greece when we could have set up a call?"

Day took the only chair in the room, a pink bedroom armchair, which left James to perch on the uncomfortable stool from the dressing table. He shot Day an appraising look.

"I don't quite know where to begin," he muttered.

"Shall I start then? Why did you take the position as Ophelia's research assistant?"

James's chin shot up and his lips tightened in a grim smile.

"You're very astute. I knew you would be. But that's not the place to begin. It was when I was in New York, about four years ago, finishing my doctorate in the department where Tim Mitchell taught. Coming from Cambridge, Tim was welcomed with open arms by the Faculty. He had a good reputation, some impressive publications, and a likeable nature. He was a born teacher, though I soon found out that teaching didn't mean that much to him. He was a man of great ambition. He wanted to do something important, something that would make his name. I admired him, everyone did.

"I realised after a while that he saw me as a friend rather than just another doctoral student, and I was flattered. Somebody like that is always worth having on your side, and I was ambitious myself. Anyway, as I got to know him better, I began to see that his confidence, his jollity, they were just a front. The more he pretended to be that kind of person, the more transparent it became that he was not. I noticed that he was drinking a lot too, and it soon became hard to hide that he was drinking excessively."

James broke off, looking for the strands of his narrative, sidetracked by his memories of a man Day had never met.

"When he was with me Tim was nothing like the man everyone thought he was. He mooched round with a cloud over his head. One day, when we were crossing Central Park talking about some lecture we'd just attended, he asked me back to his place for a drink. I tried to make an excuse, but then he wouldn't take no for an answer. I could tell something was wrong, but I had no idea how serious it was.

"We had quite a lot to drink in his apartment, and it got dark. Then he said that he wanted to get something off his chest. When I made a joke of it he actually begged me to listen, so I had no choice."

James fell silent and seemed to be searching among his memories.

"Were you shocked by what he told you?" prompted Day.

James shook his head. "Not at first. It was a love story about how he met and married Ophelia. He said that Ophelia was recovering from a broken relationship when they got together …"

James looked slyly across at Day.

"Was that relationship with you, Martin? Tim didn't give a name, but something Ophelia once said …"

Day shrugged with a small movement of his head that both deflected and acknowledged the question, but his lips remained shut and his eyes fixed on James.

"Well, they got married quite soon after they met. Tim wouldn't want to lose Ophelia, would he? Not only was she gorgeous, she was an excellent investment. Even at that age she was obviously brilliant. She had a good position at Cambridge and was going places academically. That mattered a lot to Tim. I'm sure he cared about her too, it was clear from what he told me later that night.

"Then one day Ophelia found a book online and ordered it. That book changed everything for them."

He paused and waited for Day to say something, but Day was ahead of him, mind racing, and he intended to keep his thoughts to himself. James was forced to go on.

"Tim said he'd always known that Ophelia would change his life, and that's exactly what happened when she showed him the book about the Kállos. Tim recognised the massive opportunity it gave him. He could get a huge amount of kudos if he found the location and discovered the antiquities. It would mean he could step up to the top flight of archaeology, his career established once and for all. He had no doubt that he was going to find the thing, no doubt at all. That was just how he was.

"Ophelia was only interested in the story behind the writing of the book and was curious about its author. It was Tim who studied the legend, looked at old maps, did everything he could to narrow down the search he was now determined to make. Then he told her he wanted her to go to Greece with him, find Nikolaidis and get the full story out of him so he could finish the task of finding the Kállos. Tim didn't want to go alone, I think he needed Ophelia's support, and he really put pressure on her. Eventually she gave in and agreed to go. It was a chance to meet Christos Nikolaidis."

"When was this?"

"I think it was the same year they were married, seventeen years ago. Soon after Ophelia bought the book."

"I see. Go on."

James shifted on the stool, trying to find a more comfortable position.

"Listening to the story that night in New York I could already tell that it wasn't going to have a happy ending, but I had no choice but to hear him out. Tim managed to speak to Nikolaidis on the phone and got the impression he was a timid, scholarly little man who wouldn't cause any trouble. It was agreed that Ophelia and Tim would meet him at his home, so they booked their flights for Naxos.

"When Nikolaidis heard that Tim wanted to find the Kállos, he replied that he doubted it was possible but offered to take them to a small island called Iraklia and show them an interesting cave. Once they had seen it, he said, he would tell them the whole story, which would explain everything. So they went in the Greek's boat, and there was a long way to walk before they reached the cave, at which point Tim expected to find either the Kállos or something that would tell him where to look for it.

"When they had walked for a while, Nikolaidis showed them a small opening in the hillside. Tim was sure this was the right place. The location fitted with what he expected. He set to work to widen the entrance and they all went inside, Tim full of anticipation. When he put on his torch and looked around, that was when he realised there was nothing there at all. Nikolaidis said that was what he had wanted them to know.

"Tim lost his temper. He turned on the man and accused him of all kinds of treachery. Nikolaidis protested that this cave was the right place, but that the Kállos had been taken by looters. He hoped that now that Tim had seen the cave for himself he would tell the world the true ending to the story, which had only become clear to Christos after the book had been printed.

"As Tim was talking to me, Martin, I literally felt the skin on my neck crawl. I could hear the tremor in his voice, as if he was still angry. I knew something bad must have happened. Nikolaidis, you see, didn't know that Tim had read a letter written by Nikolaidis himself saying that he had found the Kállos but planned to keep the location a secret.

"He grabbed the old man by the shoulders and threatened to hurt him if he didn't tell him the truth. Tim swore to me that he only shook him, he just wanted to frighten him. The cave floor must have been uneven, I don't know, but they lost their balance and fell together onto the ground. Tim landed on top of the old man."

James stared out of the window for a few seconds. Day let him take his time now, sadly certain of what he was about to hear.

"Tim was winded and didn't get up till he heard Ophelia crying. He realised that Nikolaidis hadn't moved. He had knocked his head on a protruding rock, there was a lot of blood, and he was unconscious. I don't know what happened next, what Tim and Ophelia could possibly have said to each other. They were miles away from the nearest help. It wasn't long before poor Nikolaidis died.

"Oh my god, this is awful! Tim then blocked up the mouth of the cave with the body inside. He moved all the rocks he could find, rolling some from quite a long way away, and filled up the opening completely. He packed smaller stones and soil into the crevices between the rocks to make it look natural and hoped that the weeds would eventually grow over the place. They went back to Naxos in Nikolaidis's boat and set it adrift to make it look like there had been an accident at sea.

"They went back to Cambridge and said nothing about what happened. Even now I find it hard to believe, Martin. At the time Tim never faced the fact that, accidentally or not, he'd actually killed someone. They adopted the little Nepali boy, and for a while everything seemed to be fine.

"Then something happened inside Tim that changed that. He didn't say what it was, but it was like his guilt was no longer possible to bear. He didn't want to stay with Ophelia, because with her he could never forget what they had done. He told her he was leaving her, resigned from his job and went to America, hoping to leave the memories behind. It was stupid, obviously, and it didn't work. It was never going to be possible, but Tim didn't see that at first. The night we talked in New York he had just accepted that there was nothing he could do any more to escape his guilt.

"I stayed another hour or so, drinking with him, letting him tell me whatever he wanted, but they were small details, disjointed bits and pieces that came into his head. I left him eventually, telling him to sleep it off and I'd see him over the weekend. I didn't get a lot of sleep that night myself..."

"And you didn't see Tim after that?"

"No. That night he hanged himself in his apartment."

26

"So, let me put my first question to you again," said Day. "Why did you take a job with Ophelia after Tim's death?"

James raked his fingers through his heavy, curly hair and heaved a sigh.

"Tim's suicide was an awful shock! Afterwards I thought a lot about what he'd told me and what I should do about it. Tim had been genuinely remorseful, I truly believe that, and what happened to Nikolaidis sounded like an accident. Tim exonerated Ophelia, although she probably watched him close up the cave and agreed to keep the secret. I decided I would keep their secret, and I told nobody. What would have been the point?

"The point would have been doing the right thing, I would have thought," said Day quietly. James nodded reluctantly.

"Then we started to hear about the excavations that were taking place on Naxos and Keros," he continued. "It was exciting stuff, important discoveries were being made. I began to think that Nikolaidis might really have been on to something, and I couldn't get it out of my head. I wrote to Ophelia asking her to consider me as a research assistant. I'd never been in contact with her before and I didn't tell her I'd known Tim, but maybe the fact that I'd been a student in his department went in my favour. I got the job, anyway. Ophelia didn't talk much about Tim, which suited me. I'm afraid by then I had ambitions of my own: I wanted to find the Kállos myself, and thought she would lead me to it."

Seeing the expression on Day's face, James flushed.

"I know, I'm no better than Tim. The same ambition that drove him to kill poor Nikolaidis was driving me mad. I practically haunted Ophelia. I may as well tell you everything. I followed her a couple of times, no idea why. I even got into her house and had a hunt round while she was out, to see if there were any papers or anything…"

"Twice," said Day.

"Yes, it was twice. How did you know that?"

"Never mind. Go on."

"I'd have been pleased with the slightest clue, but I didn't find a single thing. She didn't suspect me for a long time, but after a while she stopped talking to me unguardedly and I think she'd begun to have a bad feeling about me. I knew about her visits to Naxos but she wouldn't say what she did there. It was all very frustrating. I thought she must be looking for the Kállos, but each time she got back from her trip she looked downcast, so I assumed she hadn't been successful. She did tell me a bit about you, Martin, actually, but I didn't know that you lived there. Perhaps she was seeing you?"

"She wasn't. I only moved to Naxos last year."

"Then last month we heard she was missing and I knew something terrible must have happened. I'd thought it was odd, her going to Naxos in April when she usually went in August. I knew I should probably tell people about the Kállos because it might help to find her, but for some reason I said nothing. Then you called, and I didn't know what to do."

"I take it that was because you wanted to find the Kállos for yourself?"

The young man acknowledged with a grimace that Day had the right to say such a thing, but shook his head.

"No, Martin, actually it was because I'd just realised the truth. I'd guessed the real reason for Ophelia's annual pilgrimages to Naxos since losing Tim, and it was nothing to do with the Kállos, not really. While he was still alive she'd protected Tim because she loved him, but once he was gone, especially once he was dead, I think she went to visit that cave and acknowledge her guilt, pay her respects, whatever."

"Whatever," Day repeated coldly. Whether Ophelia had mourned Christos or Tim on her visits to Naxos hardly mattered now. He would think about her another time, when he could be alone. Here in the hotel room with James was not the place.

"Is there any news at all about Ophelia?"

"No, there's nothing new," Day lied. He stood up. He had no intention of telling James or anyone else about the discovery of Nikolaidis's body in the cave on Iraklia, and Ophelia's curious symbols that had led him to find it. He had only one more thing to say to James Sedge.

"Well, I see now why you wanted to keep the police out of this. They may still have to be told. I suppose you'll stay here, in case Ophelia is found?"

"That was the idea."

"Good, please do. It will look bad for you if you leave. I'll be in touch."

Day headed back to Filoti in the dark, the little Fiat finding its way with very little input from its driver. When he reached the house he found that Helen had gone to bed, so he made himself a small plate of food from what he could find in the kitchen and found an open bottle of wine. Not until after the first glass did he feel able to swallow anything solid.

He allowed the room to remain dark, lit only by the desk lamp which he used when working on fine print. He mechanically ate the cheese, the ham, the bread and the tomato until the plate was empty and he could turn to the wine. For a moment he could see himself as he might look to a stranger, drinking alone in a dark room like Tim four years earlier when he had confessed to James Sedge. The difference was that Day's mind was energised and inventive.

He wedged his feet on the rung of another dining chair and leaned back, rocking slightly, holding his glass in one hand. James had been astute when he had said that Ophelia's annual visit to Naxos was like a pilgrimage. Day thought she probably went to the cave on Iraklia each time, stood outside the blocked entrance and imagined what she knew to be inside, and the condition in which it must now be. What a terrible thing to have to think about and to feel responsible for. She was now the only person who knew that Nikolaidis lay inside alone. Did she want a proper burial for him, for his body to be found? Would that matter to Ophelia? Day thought so.

He refilled his glass and wondered what he would have done in Ophelia's place. He could not imagine himself in her situation at the time of the accident, when love and loyalty had led her to make a choice that he found unthinkable. Since Tim's death, though, she had been free to act differently. In her position he thought he would have confessed to the police, but there would have been consequences. She would very likely have been accused of killing Nikolaidis herself. That might have seemed to her like an acceptable punishment, but she would have thought of Raj. It was impossible to imagine her dilemma, but he was sure it had caused her great anguish.

Now he thought he understood why she had sought him out. Now he could see the importance of her meeting with his friend Alex in London a few weeks ago. Had she deliberately arranged the whole encounter in order to track him down? Or had it really been just a stroke of luck that she and Alex had been at the same event? Either way, Alex's amusing account of Day's involvement in a couple of mysteries must have resonated with her. Her conversation with him must have been an epiphany for her, a moment when a plan came to her that seemed to answer all her needs. And finally, she had obtained Day's phone number.

So Ophelia had decided to put it all in his hands. She had parcelled up the book and letter, and included the note asking him to remember her kindly. She had booked her flight and called him. Paid in full for her hotel, knowing she would leave it early. Chatted with Helen and himself on her balcony, knowing her life would soon change. Knowing it would end? Did she intend to do as Tim had done, once she had given Day the responsibility of recovering Christos's body? He had no answer.

He resolved to think practically before going to bed, hoping his sleep would be dreamless. There was much to decide before then. One decision he must make soon was when and how to tell Kyriakos what he now knew about the skeleton in the cave: who it was, how he had died, and how his death was connected to Ophelia. Day was grateful for the hours ahead in which he could think before having to act. For some time he weighed up the situation from the only point of view that might overturn his instinct to do the right thing at once: how it might affect Ophelia. He would find it very hard to act in a way that would jeopardise her.

A noise from the bedroom distracted him, Helen coughing slightly. It broke into his thoughts and his concern for her took precedence, but then the house fell quiet again and he guessed she had gone back to sleep. He eased his back, stretched his neck gently, and fell to thinking again.

He started to imagine Ophelia still somewhere on Naxos, listening to the peaceful sounds of the Greek night just as he was. No, it was a comforting thought but he did not believe it. He had a strong feeling that she was nowhere near, for surely she would not have remained on the island after handing over the whole thing to him. He could imagine her much further away, in Turkey, Italy, or even Syria perhaps. He recalled what Alex had said about the refugee charity in which she was interested, and wondered whether that had offered her a chance to make some amends. It was pointless to speculate, and he thought instead about her marriage to Tim.

He supposed he could understand how attractive Tim's outgoing personality and infectious ambition might have been to Ophelia after her turbulent relationship with himself. Beyond that he could not go. He could not bear to imagine Ophelia and Tim together in the happy times of their early marriage, and especially not later, after Iraklia, the thirteen years of guilt and pretence.

He got up intending to close the balcony shutters, but instead he opened the windows and stepped out, letting the dying wind refresh his face. The storm was passing at last, and tomorrow might even be a sunny day. He picked up a pot of pegs that had been blown over by the wind, closed the shutters and the windows, and returned to his chair.

He must focus. He still had to decide how much to tell the police. Had Ophelia's only wish been that he should discover Christos's body and see it properly laid to rest, in which case he had already done what he could. Or had she wished for the whole truth of how he died to be made known to the police, to Christos's friends, and crucially to Raj? There would be consequences to his decision that would affect many people. Moreover, he only had James's word for the truth of Tim's confession.

The second decision involved an even more difficult question. Had Ophelia also wanted him to find the Kállos and vindicate Nikolaidis? Day took a good swallow of his wine, aware of the strange irony of this problem. Three people had already become obsessed with the problematic Kállos, and he had no intention of becoming a fourth. The three he was thinking of were Christos, Tim and James. In Ophelia's case, he believed there was very little such ambition in her nature, any more than there was in his own. The thought made him chuckle: he had always lacked ambition, otherwise he would not be leading the life of an academic recluse on a Greek island. Yet he had to admit that, having come so far, he was now curious to know the truth about the Kállos. He might not be able to resist its appeal after all.

27

To Ναξιακό

The Naxian Newspaper

BODY FOUND AFTER SEVENTEEN YEARS IN CAVE

The body of a local man who disappeared without trace over seventeen years ago may have been found on the island of Iraklia.

YesterdayInspector K. Tsountas of Naxos Police confirmed that a body has been retrieved from a sealed cave on Iraklia. Although a definite identification has not been made and indeed may prove impossible, police have not denied that these may be the remains of Kyrios Christos Nikolaidis.

Christos Nikolaidis, a former teacher at the College of Naxos, was best known for his work on the Legend of the Kállos, a folk myth which tells of hidden Cycladic artefacts on or near our island. His book on this intriguing subject became well known when it was published two decades ago. He was also a popular member of Naxos Open Water Swimmers, and many of our young people owe to him their participation in this adventurous pursuit. He lived near Kalados and was unmarried.

Kyrios Nikolaidis was reported missing from his home in 2003. He was sixty-one at the time. His boat was found drifting off the southern headlands and it was popularly assumed that he had died doing what he loved best, swimming at sea far off the coast of Naxos. An assumption of death was legally made some years after his disappearance.

Professor Evangelos Stenos, Director of Naxos College, recalls Kyrios Nikolaidis as "a scholarly man with a natural gift for teaching who was dedicated to the welfare and success of his students. The history of the Cyclades, its discovery and preservation, were very important to him and he will be remembered with respect and gratitude."

A police investigation into the circumstances of death is under way. The area is believed to be in the neighbourhood of the famous Cave of St John, a popular visitor attraction. The police have refused to comment on speculation that foul play may have been involved in the sad end of this much-loved local figure.

28

Day showed the newspaper to Helen across the table of Café Ta Xromata, where they were enjoying their first coffee since she had shaken off her cold.

"Look at this," he said. "I thought Kyriakos wanted to keep the press out of it. I wish he had."

"What's wrong with a simple report in the paper?"

"I'm not sure whether Ophelia should hear about it like this, though I don't know how else she's going to find out."

Day had been quiet all morning and had still not told Helen what had happened with the lecturer from Cambridge in the Hotel Philippos. She finished her cappuccino and put aside the biscuit that had arrived on the saucer. As the morning was rather cool after the Meltemi that had blown for the past two days, they were sitting at an indoor table next to the window that looked out over the valley. She glanced at the familiar view, but today saw no movement except a single motorcyclist on a track heading towards the village.

"I'd feel much better if this had been kept from James Sedge too," said Day. "It turns out he has a far greater involvement in the Ophelia/Christos matter than we thought. I deliberately didn't tell him last night about the discovery of the body, but he'll find out today anyway."

"Are you going to tell me what happened with him, Martin?"

He smiled at her. "Sorry. He told me a very long story. It's not easy to hear."

Though Day had a talent for weaving a good narrative on most subjects, even those with little to recommend them, he was reluctant to embark on this one. He had no interest in painting a sympathetic account of the young academic from Cambridge whose actions, arising from his friendship with a man bent on suicide, had ultimately been reprehensible. He was also concerned about its effect on Helen. He began by summarising James Sedge in a single line of description that included the phrase 'unrealistic ambition and lack of personal integrity.'

"You seem less than impressed with this man, Martin."

"Let's just say that I've no desire to befriend him and I think he has ambitions to be involved in the search for the Kállos. I suppose it's to his credit that when he finally decided to do the right thing he came all the way here to tell me his story."

"And what did he actually say?"

Day told her, careful not to leave out any details.

"He made a good job of describing Tim Mitchell's character," he concluded, "and I can see how one thing led to another up to Christos's death, but afterwards their guilt must have haunted both Tim and Ophelia. Tim paid for it in New York, and I'm afraid Ophelia may be paying for it now."

Helen said nothing, filled with a deep sorrow that had nothing to do with blame or recrimination. Like the myth of Oedipus, who accidentally killed his father and unwittingly married his mother, the story of Tim and Ophelia was one of tragic waste and lifetimes of regret.

"We can now piece together the truth behind the events of seventeen years ago," said Day. "Christos received a phone call from a stranger, Tim, announcing his imminent arrival. That phone call must have filled Christos with dread. He was still resolved to protect his discovery, not only from the kind of looters who would dig it up and destroy everything around it. He also needed to protect it from the sort of man whose arrival he was now expecting: a self-serving, ambitious adventurer. Can you imagine, Helen? He wanted to prevent the Kállos from falling into the wrong hands, and the same wrong hands were on their way to talk to him. So Christos made a plan, one which depended on nobody knowing that the Kállos had already been found.

"Christos had once genuinely thought that the Kállos was on Iraklia, as he had asserted in his book, so he decided to take Tim to the cave and claim that the contents had been been stolen from it a long time ago. Tim would accept this explanation and it would be the end of Christos's nightmare.

"If he had lived, he may one day have shared his knowledge of the Kállos's true location, but he didn't live. He didn't survive Tim's visit. He took them across to Iraklia in his own boat, which Tim and Ophelia used for the return journey and then set adrift. The cave, of course, was empty. What a moment that must have been. Christos didn't know that Tim had seen the letter to the Director of the British School that he had tucked into a copy of his book and forgotten about, the letter that said that he had found the Kállos.

"We know the next part from James. Tim's optimism and ambition had put him in a state of high expectation, truly believing he would find the Kállos on Iraklia. Faced with an empty cave and no further clues he became violently angry and lost control. He grabbed Christos and shook him hard, probably shouting and threatening him. He thought he could frighten the truth from him, I expect. Christos was older and smaller, and Tim was empowered by rage."

Day took a long drink from the glass of water that had come with his coffee.

"I have a picture of Christos in my head, Helen: a scholarly character with a love of swimming by himself in the open sea, where he could find peace and some relief from his obsession with the Kállos. The broken glasses in the cave must have been his, broken during the struggle with Tim. They speak to me of a mild-mannered man who knew that people called him Odysseus behind his back because he was the very opposite of a legendary hero. When he was faced with a real threat, he thought he could talk his way out of it. And there he died, in an undignified struggle, and was left in the cave to which he himself had brought his killer."

"You were always meant to find his body, weren't you? Ophelia made sure of it."

"I think so. I think she came to Naxos every year to visit the cave and was desperate to make amends in some way. I'm afraid that if she finds out that Christos's body has been recovered she might … I don't know, do whatever she needs to do. She has been waiting to make sure Christos was found."

"Are you saying she might harm herself?"

"It's a possibility."

"What an appalling story it is from start to finish. An irredeemable waste of many lives."

Day stared out of the window, tight-lipped. He made up his mind and turned back to Helen.

"If Christos's Kállos could actually be found and conserved, and the credit given to him, do you think that's what he would have wanted? Is it the right thing to do?"

Helen stared at him. He looked as uncertain as she had ever seen him.

"I thought you'd already made up your mind to look for it. Are you having second thoughts?"

"Possibly. You see, I think it could be done. I think I know now where to look. A lot has happened since Christos's death, as I've told you, in particular some good surveys of the south coast of Naxos. They found some evidence of settlements between Kalados and Panormos. This is the area where Christos grew up and where he lived after his retirement. The people he interviewed about the Kállos lived round there too. Iraklia might have been his first theory, but he found out he was wrong and kept looking. The south coast of Naxos, which faces Keros and Koufonisi, is on the sea routes of the Cycladic traders, and that's where I think he looked next. My feeling is that Christos found the Kállos somewhere there."

"Let's assume you could eventually find this thing that has already caused two deaths. I'll play Devil's advocate for a moment. We know Christos wanted to keep its location secret, so why would that be any different now?"

"I've thought about this. I keep coming back to his unposted letter to the British School at Athens - that is, to its Director. We know from Nina that the Director at the time was Michael Stanford, and that Christos had a good relationship with him. I've been asking myself why the letter wasn't addressed to Stanford in person. I think the answer is that Michael Stanford was dying - Nina practically said as much - and Christos knew it. He wanted his letter to be read by *whoever was Director when the letter reached the School.* He was still thinking of sending it, and he feared Stanford might no longer be there when he did. Then he delayed posting the letter, so we can't know what he would have done if he had lived."

"Even if you're right, we can't prove it."

"Christos left the British School several clues in the letter, though, I think. Why would he do that unless he wanted his discovery to be brought to light one day by the right people? Look, I'll show you."

Day opened his phone to the photograph he had taken of the letter.

"In the last paragraph Christos says: *Like seafaring Odysseus I roamed for many years in search of beauty and fulfilment, only to find it at last close to home.*' By 'beauty' we assume he means the Kállos, and he says that he has found it 'close to home'. And he doesn't miss an opportunity to repeat his nickname, Odysseus, several times in the letter. Odysseus, of course, spent ten years at sea exploring the lands he comes across. The location of the Kállos is right on the edge of the sea, I think, and Christos found it using his boat and exploring along the coast near his home, Kalados. It's in a sea cave, Helen, somewhere along the south coast."

"That's quite a leap, darling. Even if Christos did want the Kállos to be found, it's still a needle in a haystack. How long is that stretch of coast? Miles and miles."

"True, but most of it doesn't fit the topography. I might consult our friend Panos the fisherman. My guess is that there aren't too many places along that coast that do, and he probably knows it like the back of his hand. Then we'll have to search from the sea like Christos: the tracks overland are terrible and I don't have the patience."

On the table between them Day's mobile made a single sound to indicate the arrival of a message.

"Interesting," he said, having read it. "It's a message from a courier company. They've left a parcel at Yiasemi Villas for me - couriers don't often deliver to private addresses in Greece, only to businesses. Shall we go and pick it up?"

The trip to Yiasemi Villas and back took the best part of an hour, but they saved opening the package till they were home in Filoti. They knew it was from Raj in London, who had used a courier to get it quickly from the UK to Greece. Yiasemi Villas must have been the only business address he could remember, and he had emailed ahead to warn them.

The padded envelope now lay open on the table next to the small pile of its contents. Day opened Raj's letter, read it quietly and handed it to Helen.

Fern Street
London E3

Dear Martin and Helen,

Not long after returning home from Naxos I received a registered package from my mother, contents of which are enclosed. I spoke to her friend Mary and we discovered that Mum had left it in the College post room

with instructions to send it on a certain date, ensuring delivery to me no sooner than this week. It's another proof, if I needed one, that Mum planned all this. She enclosed a personal letter to me. In it she asks me to keep the contents safe and not show them to anyone, or tell anyone about them, unless and until (those are her words) I know for certain the right person to have them. She said she trusted me completely to recognise this person. I'm sure it should be you, Martin.

I can hardly bear to repeat what else Mum wrote, so I'll just tell you that she was saying goodbye. It sounded final. I'm desperate, Martin. Please, please, find her.

Raj

The other contents of the package were held together with a large elastic band. There was a blank envelope, the flap unsealed, from which he extracted a handwritten sheet of paper.

For the last four years I have been revisiting Naxos each August when the university vacation gave me the opportunity to travel. My interest on these visits was Christos Nikolaidis, author of a book on the Kállos of Naxos which I obtained many years ago. I had no interest in the Kállos, only in Mr Nikolaidis. I would stay in a small taverna with a room to let near Kalados, his former home, and ask people what they remembered of him. I told them I was hoping to write something to commemorate his achievements in Greek archaeology, something I would truly have liked to do. People were helpful, and it was clear that Mr Nikolaidis was remembered with respect. The matter of his disappearance some years ago was often mentioned, which affected me deeply.

In addition to Naxos I visited Iraklia on each of my visits for personal reasons, although Iraklia was also of importance to Mr Nikolaidis himself. It was, however, on Naxos that I believe his most successful work to have been done.

You will find several items enclosed, including some photographs of Mr Nikolaidis which were generously given to me by his friends. I also give you the notebook in which I recorded my thoughts and discoveries, notes towards the tribute I hoped to write about him, and various other items which you may find interesting. You have to decide what to do with these things.

Thank you ...

Ophelia Blue

Helen read this over his shoulder, and Day sensed rather than saw her wipe away a tear as she pushed her hair back from her face. She picked up a photograph showing Christos with two other men by a small boat. He was wearing glasses, the same as those found in the cave. There were other photographs too, all dating from about the time of his death, pictures kept by friends who had missed him. Only one did not contain the smiling face of Christos Nikolaidis. Instead it showed strange markings on a rock.

"What's this?" said Helen.

"I can't make it out."

Day got up and fetched a small box from his bookcase. He took out a magnifying glass which he rarely used and applied himself to the image.

"It's an ancient inscription."

"Come on, Martin. What does it say?"

"I think it's a boundary marker to a sanctuary. It's not very clear though …."

On the reverse of the photograph, in Ophelia's handwriting, he read 'discovered on a walk on the coast path.'

Day shrugged and brought out the final object. It was a rough map drawn in pencil, but was minimal in the extreme. Across the top of the page was a wiggly horizontal line with a similar one drawn beneath it. There were only a few other marks and words. The writing seemed to match Ophelia's.

"Is this meant to be a map?" muttered Day in frustration. A map was clearly what it was, however. At the extreme left of the upper line was the word 'Kalados', and on the right-hand end of the lower line 'Panormos'.

"Imagine these two lines drawn on a larger piece of paper," said Helen. "They're meant to be one continuous line but she couldn't fit it all on the sheet. It's the coast from Kalados to Panormos. You were right, Martin. Spot on!"

Excitement was now gripping Day in the belly.

"That must be Rina in the middle, there," he said, pointing to a familiar-shaped bay recognisable in the roughly-drawn coastline. "Remember the sea cave there which attracts visitors in their yachts and the tourist boats from Chora? But the Rina Cave is far too popular for our purposes and Ophelia hasn't even marked it's name. She's only made three marks on the whole map, and they're all hard to understand. This isn't meant to be easy, is it? This one here must be a church, I think: this is a cross and the letter A next to it, but they're quite a way inland. Then she's written 'AQ', and this curiously twisted arrow. What on earth, Ophelia? …"

"Take it easy, Martin. She drew this for you, so she believed you could work it out. Why don't you compare it to a real map?"

He spent the next half hour doing as she suggested. Helen left him to it. She returned to find him poring over a topographical map of Naxos with a new air of contentment.

"You've worked it out, haven't you?" It wasn't really a question.

"Yes, and it's surprisingly simple. The symbol of the cross and the letter A show the location of a beautiful church which isn't marked on this map but I managed to find it on the satellite image online. Its name is the Church of the Archangel, which would fit with the letter A. After that the rest followed easily. 'AQ' stands for Ancient Quarry, where marble quarrying took place in the Early Cycladic. This map tells us where Ophelia was searching, and she was surely following in Christos's footsteps. There can only be one place that fits. This is the Bay of Spedos."

"What do you make of the curious little bent arrow? Why not draw a normal one?"

"What about the sea cave idea? You know, it could be an instruction to get into the water, turn round, and look inside the cliff. I'll read Ophelia's notebook carefully next."

"So the hunt is on? There's just one thing, Martin. This search for the Kállos has already been responsible for two deaths …"

"I know," said Day, gently, "and I'm not going to be a third. If it's there and we find it, there will be no grand announcement, no fame and publicity, just the appropriate conservation of the artefacts. I think I'll see if Nick will help me, rather than going it alone. Does that reassure you? Finding this bit of Cycladic heritage is not only important in itself, it's something I can do for Christos."

Helen sighed. "And Ophelia? Will finding it help her?"

"Who knows? I think the best thing I can do for Ophelia at the moment is keep her name out of it."

29

Day was about to call Nick the next morning when he received a call from Naxos Police Station. It was Kyriakos.

"*Ti kaneis*, Kyriako? Is there some news?"

"*Kalimera*, Martin. Yes, I have some news, but I'm afraid it's not the news you're hoping for. I have the autopsy report on the body from Iraklia. They have concluded death by misadventure. The man certainly sustained a severe injury to the head, but they can't say for certain that it was the cause of his death. It's also impossible to know whether or not the blow was inflicted deliberately."

"I see. And what about the man's identity?"

"Inconclusive. The medical and dental records for our suspected victim are no longer available and there are no surviving relatives. Nothing has appeared in the searches. As we feared, everything suggests the body is that of Christos Nikolaidis, especially the discovery of the spectacles in the cave, but legally that is insufficient."

In the circumstances, Day wondered whether he should be relieved.

"I saw *The Naxian* yesterday," he said. "I was surprised to see the article about the body."

"A member of the public called the newspaper having seen our activities on Iraklia. The locals could hardly miss the transportation of a dead body. The newspaper approached me for an official explanation..."

"I see," Day said again. "Well, is that as far as it goes?"

The inspector said he feared it was, but promised to be in touch if there were any developments. Day stood for a moment with the phone still in his hand after the end of the call. He had not told Kyriakos about James Sedge's story, about his certainty that the body was Christos, about Ophelia's part in concealing the death, the parcel from Raj, or even his own plan to visit Spedos Bay.

He brought up Nick's number and pressed the call button. Nick and Deppi's yacht, the *Zephyro*, was used to take visitors for sailing trips round the coast of Naxos in the summer, and for their own pleasure. It would be ideal for the expedition Day had in mind.

"I need you to take me on the yacht in search of buried treasure," he said mischievously when his friend answered. He heard the laughter at the other end with satisfaction. "I think we might be able to find a piece of Naxos history in a sea cave off the coast near Spedos. That area is appalling to reach by road unless you have a four-by-four, and anyway I specifically need to approach from the sea. I'll tell you all about it if you're interested."

"Sure I am. Why don't you come over here and see the new house at the same time? When would be good for you? Tonight?"

"Tonight would be great. Thanks, Nick."

"You're welcome, mate. I can't wait to hear what's going on. Come about seven o'clock, you and Helen. I'll do an Aussie barbie."

Though officially in Plaka, Nick and Deppi had bought a house some distance from the long, sandy beach beloved of tourists. It looked down on the sand and sun-loungers from an area of high land, a converted agricultural building facing away from Naxos's tourist developments.

"What kind of place was this before you started work on it?" Day asked, handing Nick the bottle he had brought. "It was in quite a poor state, wasn't it?"

"It certainly was, and that was what attracted me to it. Come in and take a look round. It was a rambling old family home that was crumbling away through neglect. The bedrooms and bathroom at the other end of the house are on the footprint of the original building, but where we're standing now is all new. The upper floor is all new-build, the old structure was too weak to keep but the foundations were strong."

"You've done a really great job, Nick," said Helen.

They were standing in the room which comprised the entire ground floor of the new part of the house. There were windows on three sides and a structural central pillar. Four distinct areas had been created, divided only by artful, curved beams on the ceiling. There was a kitchen to the left and a dining room to the right, and inside there were sitting areas for adults and for children. Everything was white except the wooden dining table, the soft furnishings and various children's playthings. The evening sun threw a warm glow into the room through the many windows and glazed doors.

"I wasn't expecting it to feel so modern. I suppose it's because I've only ever seen your conservation work on historic buildings."

"Glad you like it, Helen. It was quite difficult for me to have such a blank canvas. With a historic building you're working to a blueprint and have to stick to it, but with this place there were no guidelines, almost too much freedom. Come outside and see the view round the back."

He led the way through sliding glass doors and round to the side of the house. Under a rustic canopy artfully made from reclaimed timber was a terrace overlooking the sea. It had a long wooden table and wide armchairs; the table was decorated with candles and the chairs softened by cushions. The canopy threw a slatted pattern across everything from the table to the pale blue shutters along the side of the house. Tiny bougainvillea plants and young vines had been planted in pots or holes in the paving to eventually scramble up the walls. At the far end was a brick-built barbecue.

The view from here was towards the popular beach of Plaka and the white houses of Chora in the distance; the island of Paros across the water seemed large and close in the clear air. Just beyond the terrace wall, in an area of sandy soil and wild plants, a footpath meandered away before disappearing downhill out of sight.

"That path leads down to a quiet bit of beach behind the old cedar trees," said Nick. "We treat it as part of our garden. We usually have it to ourselves. Admittedly you come across the occasional nudist, but nobody worries. We're very happy with how this house has turned out for us. We might feel differently one day if Plaka gets a lot busier, but I reckon the house will be saleable and we'll just find somewhere else."

"How could you bear to leave this?" murmured Helen, transfixed by the glitter on the sea and the outline of Paros behind which the sun would shortly set.

"Take a seat, guys, and I'll fetch some drinks. Deppi will be back any minute with Nesto."

"Nesto? Is that what he likes to be called now?"

"Yeah, that's right. Teenagers!"

"Isn't he only eleven?"

Nick laughed. "Eleven going on fourteen! Beer? Wine? G&T?"

He went inside and soon Deppi arrived carrying a tray of glasses with Nestoras leading the way. Day got up to take the tray from her and everyone began to speak at once. Nestoras again displayed the social confidence they had noticed on the evening of the Curator and Rania's anniversary. 'Nesto' had replaced the extremely shy boy they used to know, and before long he invited Helen and Day to go and see 'his beach'.

"Hang on, Nesto," said his father, arriving with a bottle of wine. "Helen and Martin have only just arrived! We're going to watch the sunset and then we're going to have a barbie, Aussie-style. You up for giving me a hand with it later?"

"Sure," said the boy, and went off to his room.

"He's growing up nicely," said Helen. "How does he feel about the new baby?"

"Great, though he wanted a brother and he's getting a sister!" laughed Deppi.

Nick passed his wife a glass of juice and began to open the wine.

"I thought the right thing might be this white from Santorini, since it's a warm evening. It's a Nykteri. I just love it that this grape used to be harvested only at night, and in some vineyards they still keep up the old tradition. This particular bottle is produced by a cooperative who support the smaller growers on the island. Well, here's to your health!"

"*Stin yia mas*!" said Day, and raised his glass to Deppi, imagining a little girl that might look very much like her. "And to the baby!"

"So, Martin," said Nick, "tell us about this new adventure of yours. What's it all about? And why do you need the yacht?"

Helen smiled and settled comfortably in her seat. She rather enjoyed Day's narratives, even those she had heard before.

"It started with an old friend of mine called Ophelia," Day began.

"The woman who came to Naxos and has now gone missing, right?"

Day kept it as short as he could, but his personal frustration and concerns came through as the story went on. He told them about the skeleton on Iraklia and how it had come to be there. He outlined the culpable ambition of Tim Mitchell and James Sedge, and Ophelia's life following the tragic death of Nikolaidis. He left out nothing that was essential. Finally he explained his decision to search for the Kállos of Naxos, which he was sure was there to be found.

"Is that what we're going to look for? The legendary Kállos?" said Nick. His voice betrayed his excitement. Day nodded.

"I've just received a parcel from Ophelia's son which contains things that will help us. I think it's clear that she wants me to look for the

Kállos, and she probably has a good idea where it is. There's a map, some photos and a notebook. Everything points to Spedos Bay."

"I know that area," said Nick. "It's between the Rina Cave and Panormos Beach."

"Exactly. The bay is less interesting than the spits of land jutting out on each side of it. We already know there's an ancient marble quarry and other signs of Bronze Age activity on one side. I want look closely on the waterline for any sign of access into the rock. My theory is we're looking for a cave with an underwater entrance."

"Do you need to go on land at all?"

"Unfortunately I do. There's an ancient inscription I need to find, and Ophelia's notebook and map give a few more pointers that will be useful, including a view to an inland church and an ancient symbol scratched into rock that she suggests is connected to the Kállos. By aligning these things we might get an idea of the right place to look."

"Okay, Martin, I'm happy to leave all that to you. I'll get you there on the *Zephyro*, and we can go ashore in the tender. That way you'll get to see the rocks close up and do all the searching you want on land. What happens if you're right?"

"I suppose we swim," said Day with a grimace. "Christos was an open water sea swimmer, so that might be how he found the Kállos. How's your swimming, Nick?"

"Good enough. How's yours?"

"Good enough. But I suspect you're being modest and I'm being optimistic!"

Nick refilled their glasses just before sunset. On the high peak of dusky Paros, which had mass but no describable colour, the tired sun rested as if hesitating. A halo of pure yellow hung above it in a sky that had the delicacy of smoke, and magenta light spread briefly outwards like an invitation to an embrace. On the gently rippling surface of the sea, a path of bronze illuminated a small fishing boat in which a man sat motionless. The group on the terrace watched until the sun slipped behind Paros, leaving only remnants of its beauty on the water and in the thoughtful sky.

"Wonderful," said Deppi. "So, is it time to cook, Nick?"

"Yes, right, I'll get on with it."

Nick had built his barbecue to be like the Australian one he'd enjoyed in his youth, and he worked over it happily for a while. He came back to the table while it heated up, and it was clear he had been giving Day's plan some thought.

"I suggest we take Orestis, my business partner, with us, Martin. You met him last summer, remember? He can sail the *Zephyro* as well as I can, so he can handle the yacht while we're not aboard. I'd be happier than leaving it unattended."

"Fine by me. Helen will come too, so she and Orestis will stay on the boat while we're ashore. We'd better choose a day when the weather's good, better from every point of view. Then, we'll need some kit … binoculars, I have a pair I can bring…"

"You should try and get hold of a waterproof camera," said Helen.

"I can bring along another pair of binoculars, and I have a waterproof camera that I bought for the tourist trips," said Nick. "It's not fancy but it will do."

"That's brilliant. Let's hope we find something to photograph. We'll need a pair of torches, powerful ones if possible, waterproof of course, and we'd better bring snorkelling gear. I don't have any but I'll buy a couple of masks and snorkels…"

"Don't bother, we keep some on the yacht. I'll bring an underwater torch too, we've got all that kind of thing for the sailing trips."

"Then I think that's about it. There's just one more thing, and we need to tell Orestis too. Nobody must know what we're doing. We may not find anything, but if we do we have a responsibility to protect it. I'll involve Aristos if we're successful. He can tell the proper authorities."

"Agreed. Right, I'll speak to Orestis tomorrow and start getting the kit together. When do you want to go?"

"That depends on the weather. You're in charge, Nick."

Nick grinned. "Okay, until the real search begins. Then it's all yours, mate!"

30

Two days later it was a calm and pleasant day from the moment the sun broke the eastern horizon. The previous night's weather forecast had been good, and on the strength of it they had decided to make the trip. Day had worked late and woken early, determined to be fully prepared. He dressed in shorts and a shirt, and put an old pair of swimming shoes in the holdall to protect his feet from the rocks. He drank the last of his coffee standing up, looking over his preparations critically.

He was not a field archaeologist, and would have been more confident in his preparations if he had had a bit more experience. He hoped he had picked up enough from his reading not to make a complete mess of this. He lifted Ophelia's notebook from the table and leafed through it, despite having committed most of it to memory. Holding it made him feel closer to her, whereas otherwise he felt she was very far away.

Helen came into the room just as he was checking the time on his phone.

"Ready?"

"Yes, it's time we got going. Do you have the binoculars?"

"In my bag. I'll need them to keep an eye on you once you leave the yacht. You won't do anything stupid today, Martin, will you?"

"Me?"

"Yes, you. You do tend to get carried away. I hate the whole idea of caves…"

They locked up the house and loaded the car. On the usual route through Halki and the olive-rich region of Tragea, the gnarled old trees looked dark and heavy against the terracotta colour of the cleared earth beneath their canopies. Slumped in the passenger seat deep in thought, Day was oblivious to the natural beauty through which they were passing. Helen wondered when his excitement would take over, when his touch-paper would catch light. It happened as they approached Chora. The heavy traffic on the road to the port woke Day from his preoccupations, and he began to talk at full speed about his plans. She drove down Papavasileou Avenue, the shore road, until they reached the *Zephyro*'s mooring, drove past it and found a parking space, and walked back to the boat. Orestis was the first on board to notice them. He strode confidently across the gangplank and carried their things onboard with the practiced balance of a seaman. Day followed Helen onto the yacht with as much poise as he could muster.

"*Kalimera*, Oresti! Thanks for coming today, we couldn't do this without you. Morning, Nick!"

"Hey, you two! We've got a great day for it. You got everything? If so, I reckon we can get going."

Day placed his sunglasses on his face and settled down at the back of the boat to watch the receding view of Chora, while Helen stood looking from the rail. Orestis, whose competence on the yacht was obvious, had already stowed away the gangplank and retracted the fenders, checked the storage compartments, secured moveable objects and made the required last-minute checks. He untied the mooring line and joined Nick at the wheel. They drew away from the jetty and cruised towards the harbour exit, displacing only gentle waves round the prow. It was achieved effortlessly and with few words.

Nick watched for other moving boats while Orestis manoeuvred the yacht. There was little traffic in the harbour. One or two small vessels were returning from early fishing trips, but only the *Zephyro* was moving towards the open sea. The yacht's engine was quiet while it was moving slowly. When they rounded the harbour wall, Orestis opened it up and the boat began to cut more keenly though the water. Nick joined Helen and Day.

"We'll have to use the motor today, I'm afraid," he said, "there's not enough wind."

"That's fine, we haven't booked a romantic sail," grinned Day, feeling a knot of excitement tighten inside him. "I'm more than happy with a good engine anyway!"

"We'll try and make good speed till we get to Spedos, then drop anchor and use the tender. The conditions should be perfect for snorkelling."

The journey was considerably easier than the trip to Iraklia on the *Express Skopelitis*, because Orestis steered a course close to land where the sea state was calmer. For the best part of an hour the *Zephyro* motored steadily towards the south-west tip of Naxos. Once past the three capes of Moni, Gaitani and Katomeri that formed the western tip of the island, the yacht changed course and turned east into the morning sun, leaving Iraklia behind.

The first inhabited place along this stretch of coastline was Kalados, one of the most sheltered of Naxos's isolated harbours and former home of Christos Nikolaidis. They left Orestis in charge of the boat and went into the cabin, where Day spread out Ophelia's notebook, map and photographs. For the next half hour he showed Nick the parts of the notebook that he thought were important, and explained the photographs and map. Nick listened without interrupting until he had finished, then put his finger on the map where a headland to the east of Spedos jutted out into the sea.

"This would be my guess."

Day nodded. "Mine too."

Here it begins, thought Day, watching the coastline pass on the port side. The high ridges and peaks of the southern hills of Naxos, steep escarpments that rose to around five hundred metres, created a natural barrier to this isolated coast. From them the land swept down to the sea, creating narrow beaches, stony fields, tiny harbours and the occasional sea cave. He had swum into the cave at Rina years ago, but he had no idea what to expect of a cavity into which nobody had ventured before, unless it was Christos and the keepers of the Kállos.

Smaller islands were now looming on their right, part of a submerged mountain ridge that had been drowned by the sea thousands of years ago. Naxos itself was part of the same range, Iraklia and Schinousa too, both behind them now. Ahead lay the isles of Kato Koufonisi and Pano Koufonisi, together known as Koufonissia, a single rock divided in two by a stretch of clear water. Beyond Koufonissia lay uninhabited Keros, where the hoard of Cycladic figurines had been found.

The *Zephyro* was heading straight into the sun and the surface of the sea was dazzling. The turmoil in Day's stomach was no longer caused by the swell of the sea, but by adrenalin. When the yacht drew in line with the tip of Kato Koufonisi they changed course and headed in towards the coast of Naxos. The stony peaks of the giant grey hills, which may have been aids to navigation for Cycladic seafarers, grew more dominant. Orestis cut back the engine and steered towards the entrance to a small bay, the bay of Spedos. Day scanned the western headland through binoculars; it was just a low hill on which nothing but scrub was visible now, but in antiquity an accessible seam of marble had been found near the surface.

"Getting shallow here," remarked Nick. The draught on the *Zephyro* was small, and as they approached the shallower waters he was using the charts and depth finder to decide where to drop anchor. Just outside the bay he signalled to Orestis and the main anchor was dropped. Nick deployed the lighter kedge anchor to stabilise the boat and make it safer to utilise the tender.

"Right, mate," he said, turning to Day. "We'll blow up the inflatable and drop it over the side. Once we've attached the outboard, we're set to go! It won't take long, this thing is top notch."

He was not exaggerating. Nick had bought top of the range when he invested in his tender, and he was proud of it. The inflatable rib quickly took shape when attached to its powerful pump, and Nick adjusted the seating to accommodate them both comfortably and leave room for the bag of equipment. He lowered it into the water from the swim platform at the stern of the yacht, securing it to the rails. Orestis heaved an outboard motor from its storage and took it to the stern, where he began attaching it to the floating tender.

By the time they were done, Day had scanned every inch of the shore through the binoculars. There was no sign of the gaping entrance of a sea cave, but he had hardly expected to see one. At one point to the east of the bay an area of rock-face rose more steeply from the sea, its stone shining in the swirling water, and this held his attention. He lowered the binoculars and met Helen's enquiring eyes.

"Nothing much," he said, before she could ask. "Would you like to take a look?"

Helen took his binoculars and steadied herself against the side of the yacht. The calm water in the bay of Spedos looked shallow and inviting, and the small sandy beach at the far end was undisturbed. In other circumstances it would be idyllic, but she had a bad feeling. The flight of a buzzard distracted her attention, and she raised the angle of the binoculars to follow it.

"Martin, there's a church up there! Can you see it? You can just about make it out high on the hillside."

She passed the binoculars back to Day, who looked in the direction she was pointing. A small church stood alone about two thirds of the way up the first peak. Its weathered construction, the stone wall that encircled it and the surrounding cedar trees made it blend into the background as if it grew there. Only the perfect shape of its rounded dome and its small painted bell tower made it visible.

"It's in the right place to be the one on the map. Well spotted."

"You're not going all that way inland, are you?"

"No, I don't think I need to. My plan is to get to the higher ground beyond the beach, line up the church and the ancient quarry, and start to look for the other indicators."

"You're making it sound like a search for pirate treasure, Martin. X marks the spot and all that."

He laughed and stowed his binoculars in the holdall, leaving Nick's for Helen to use on the boat. Picking up the bag he made his way to the swim platform, where he hesitated briefly. Nick extended a suntanned arm, laughing.

"Not too comfortable, Martin? I'd be worse in front of a TV camera, I promise you. Jump in!"

Once settled in the centre of the rib, Day felt better. Round his feet were masks and snorkels, and the rest of the equipment was stowed neatly in the prow. He looked back at the yacht as Nick started the Honda outboard motor and they revolved in the water to face the beach. Helen was watching them go with a solemn face, the yacht's binoculars round her neck. He waved and turned away towards the bay. Ancient quarry on the left, beach and church ahead, rocky headland on the right. Spedos Bay became more and more shallow, blue turning to turquoise and then to sand. The inflatable beached itself gently and they both waded out.

Only when they pulled the boat from the water did Day notice the heat of the sun. They took what they needed from the tender's storage box - binoculars, camera and the map in a waterproof bag. The rest of Ophelia's documents were safely back on the *Zephyro,* and they didn't need the swimming gear yet. They stood on the sand looking for any signs of life, but they were alone. A flash of blue crossed the shallow water and disappeared into the rocks, a kingfisher of some sort, which Day decided to take as a good omen, as might the legendary Odysseus have done. As for the modern Odysseus, their friend Christos, had he too been here and stood on this spot with the same thoughts and hopes?

"Right, up to the top," said Day, leading the way. "We'll get clear of the beach and head right, past those cedars and onto the headland."

The sun was almost at the zenith now and shone with a fierceness unusual for April. Before they had climbed very far Day stopped to look round. The bay below was almost semi-circular and the beach a mere strip of sand between the sea and an area that showed signs of cultivation. The flat ground had been divided by many drystone walls, and a small stone hut lurked against one of them. Despite a dozen old olive trees that remained standing, he could see no sign of recent human activity.

In the other direction, looking out into the Aegean, the mountains of Koufonissia were clearer now, the sun was falling directly on their rocky flanks and scrub-covered lowlands. In the otherwise pure blue sky, a horizontal white cloud hovered over the summit of Keros. The *Zephyro* floated serenely at anchor at the lip of the bay, and Day thought he could see Helen at the rail. He waved, and the figure waved back.

"So, where do we go next, Martin? Up there?"

He indicated the steep eastern headland and correctly interpreted Day's grin. It looked like a huge pile of debris had tumbled into the sea, leaving impenetrable scrub and weather-beaten cedars on the top. "We'd better keep an eye out for snakes."

"Good point. Right, see you at the top. You know what to look out for!"

Day chose what he hoped was the easiest route up the first steep slope and made as much noise with his feet as he could to alert basking snakes. Behind him Nick did the same, though taking a slightly different path. Both went slowly, looking around them for anything that might resemble an inscription. Day didn't expect to see one: the rocks and stones were broken and small here, as if erosion and rockfalls had ravaged that hillside for hundreds if not thousands of years.

271

After a while he stopped to wait for Nick. They were not far from the highest point of the headland, where the scrub was thinner and the heat rose fiercely from the sandy-coloured rock.

"Anything?" asked Nick.

"No. I don't think this is the place."

"Why not?"

Day was prepared to accept that Ophelia could have come to Spedos Bay in a hired boat, but he couldn't see her clambering up this headland. If she had, he would have to reappraise her determination.

"I don't know, to be honest. Let's just keep going. We'll take stock when we get to the top."

When they met at the top they were dumbfounded by the spectacular view. The sea, the islands sitting squatly on its surface, the *Zephyro* turned sideways by the current, the turquoise water of the bay and even the deserted farmland, it was beautiful as far as the eye could see. Inland a vast tract of rugged plains and scree rose to the hills and further mountains, with areas of wild *maquis* and cedar forest. Through it all, tortuously winding and empty of life, was the mountain road. A rough trail led from the road down to the fields, perhaps the route once taken by the farmer.

'That's some road," said Nick, shading his eyes. "I wouldn't fancy that in your Fiat 500, mate. You'd be better on an mule."

"I don't think so, my friend! You will never see me on a donkey, not even if it meant missing a chance to find Atlantis."

"That's your line in the sand, is it, getting on a donkey?" Nick laughed. "Well, good job we came by sea."

Day extracted the map from its pouch and held it out between them. "So, we must be about here. The ancient quarry should be over there."

He brought up his binoculars and scanned the opposite headland. There were several places where exposed rock might indicate the location of the old quarry, though it was impossible to be certain. He handed the binoculars to Nick.

"We might not be able to see the place from here, but can you see those slanting, exposed rafts of rock near the water's edge? I guess that could be part of it. Anyway, the exact spot doesn't matter too much, we know it's there somewhere. So now, can you see the church, inland over there?"

The little church was visible from where they were standing. It huddled on the hillside by the road that came down from the north. A Naxos flag fluttered from its roof, meaning that it was still in use. Perhaps he should not be surprised: there were more inaccessible churches in the Cyclades than this one.

"Got it. Look, the church, the quarry, the bay. It fits Ophelia's map so far. Now we have to find the difficult things - your ancient inscription and a rock with a spiral mark. There's no shortage of rocks around here, Martin. A needle in a haystack comes to mind. Where do we start?"

"We'll make our way further round the headland. As long as we keep the church and quarry in view, we're in the right area. Keep looking. Remember - graffiti, spirals and snakes!"

An hour later they had discovered only that their shoes were not ideal for the terrain. A small breeze had started up, bringing with it the aromas of the hot inland: baking rock, desperate spring flowers and dust. The cooler sea air wafted in occasionally from the other direction, and the sweat began to dry on their faces before breaking out again.

"How much longer do you want to search, Martin? I'm up for it, just asking."

Day could not reply. He had simply reached the point when he could not give up.

"Change of plan," he said instead. "We're probably in the right place, so I don't think we need to keep the church and the quarry actually in sight. I'm going to take a look over the ridge there, where the headland drops down to the sea. I think I can see a track. You can stay here."

"Not on your life, mate. Lead on!"

Day started to move cautiously towards the brink of the headland. There was indeed a vestige of a path made by sheep or goats. It was an exposed, weather-beaten and dangerously mobile stretch of loose stones, and he stopped when he neared a place where the ground began to descend more steeply. He didn't fancy falling downhill from here. Nothing would stop him before he hit the sea.

It was then that he noticed an unusual grey boulder off the path ahead of him on the landward side of the headland. Its rounded shape, the way it had been blackened by the years, made him think of ancient marble. Alone among the surrounding stones it was untouched by the prickly, determined, drought-impervious vegetation that clung to whatever surface it could find. He went closer. On the uppermost face of the rock, the part that faced the sea, he saw the unmistakable trace of ancient lettering.

"Here! Nick!" he yelled, and his wave confirmed the urgency of his excitement. "The inscription, I think."

He knelt by the boulder and gently dusted off the surface with his hand. All the marks were faint. Some of the letters were almost worn away, which explained the difficulty with Ophelia's photograph. There were fourteen shapes carved in two lines, one beneath the other, and nothing to indicate individual words because spaces between words were not used in old inscriptions.

"What does it say? Is it what you're looking for?" asked Nick when he arrived.

"Yes, it's the right thing. Ophelia's photograph wasn't clear, but this matches what I could make out on it. It says 'Boundary of the Sanctuary of Zeus Melosios.' Melosios means Zeus in his form of the Guardian of Sheep!"

"Excellent! How fitting. I've seen sheep droppings all the way up! So this is the place? She meant you to find this stone?"

Day took a photograph of the inscription. "I'm pretty sure of it. We must be getting close. I hope so, it's like a furnace up here!"

He wiped the back of his hand over his face, which only succeeded in spreading the sweat. When he opened his eyes again he looked round for the one remaining marker he wanted to find, the petroglyph that Ophelia had written about in her notebook. Would it be the ancient spiral symbol which marked a burial or a settlement? There was nothing to be seen except a half-dead olive tree near the edge of the cliff, where erosion would eventually end its long life and drop it into the sea.

Leaving Nick examining the inscription, Day walked carefully over to the tree. He liked old olive trees, they were a symbol of Greece to him. Its huge bole, almost as wide as it was tall, was hollow, misshapen, bleached by the sun and mostly dead. A bird flew from the living branches in alarm at his approach, startling him, so only when he was very close did he notice something leaning against the far side. Facing out to sea towards Keros was a small rock, propped up like a headstone. Day edged round carefully to get a better look. There were words scratched roughly into its surface, this time in modern Greek. **Κάλλος του Νησιού**. He called Nick over to see it.

"Beauty of the island? What do you make of it?" asked Nick. "It looks like a gravestone. Are we supposed to dig here or something?"

"I don't think so - just as well really, the ground's unstable. No, my guess is that this is recent, either made by Christos or by someone who discovered the Kállos before he did."

"No spiral, though."

"Indeed."

They moved back to safer ground and Day took out Ophelia's map again.

"This strange little arrow is pointing to somewhere just about directly below us," he said. "I think I know what it must mean: we have to search in the rocks right beneath us. We'll have to make the attempt from the sea because there's no way down from here."

He refolded the map and smiled at the enjoyment on Nick's face that probably reflected his own.

"This could be it. Ophelia, and perhaps Christos too, thought that somewhere down there, under our very feet, lies the Kállos of Naxos."

31

Day took photographs of the headstone and they retraced their steps back to the beach.

"I guess we leave the boat here," said Nick, beginning to stow their things in the tender and pull out the snorkels. "From now on we'll have to swim."

They left the binoculars and map in the rib, threw their shirts and sunglasses into the boat too and loaded themselves up with the equipment they now needed. Nick attached the underwater torch to a glove on his right hand that held it pointing ahead, and Day clipped the diving camera to a belt round his waist. On the *Zephyro* Helen could be seen watching as they waded into the water, and Orestis sat in the shade of the cabin. Not for a moment did Day wish he was there with them. They waded from the beach through the cool turquoise water until, when the land shelved away, it was deep enough to swim. Despite not having used a snorkel for twenty years, Day enjoyed the sensation of freedom it gave him and his easy motion through the water. Nick soon passed him, swimming strongly. Half way along the headland Day caught up and they pulled down their masks to talk. There was a noticeable current below them.

"You swim well," panted Nick, unable to conceal some surprise.

"Drummed into me as a boy," Day muttered, wiping the water from his eyes. "I haven't swum that far since the last school swimming gala, as they called it. Do you reckon this is the right place?"

"Let's go another twenty metres. The old olive tree was further along, opposite that gash in the opposite headland."

"Right. From now on we look out for any kind of opening in the cliff."

After fifty yards they saw two small openings about five feet above water level which seemed worthy of a better look. They could stand up in the shallow water there. The first opening, which Day checked out, opened up into a space about three feet high at its tallest point. It was completely dry inside and out, and the rock shone white in the sun. Part of the cliff to one side had fallen away, revealing the rust-coloured sandstone of the headland's heart.

"This one only goes in for about four feet, and it's empty," shouted Day.

"This one's even smaller. Empty too."

They got back into the water and Day set off ahead of Nick. The current was more noticeable now, pulling gently towards the open sea, but he allowed it to assist him towards the tip of the headland. The boulders here were larger, the edge of the headland less uniform and less benign, but something caught his eye. He swam closer and heaved himself out of the water, pulling his mask off his face again and letting it dangle round his neck. Nick caught up a few minutes later and looked to see what he was squinting at.

"Holy Mother! Is that it? The spiral thing you were talking about?" He was treading water a few feet away where it was still deep. Above them, on a sheet of rock with a flat exposed surface, a spiral groove about seven inches in diameter was cut into the stone to a depth of half an inch. The rock was lodged at a strange angle as if it had fallen there. Thanks to the absence of tides and its position above the waterline, it had survived in reasonable condition but looked curiously out of place.

"Rockfall?" said Nick. "Maybe this part of the headland collapsed and the stone was dislodged? The same rockfall could have buried the Kállos somewhere inside all that."

Day nodded. It would explain how the Kállos, which local people had once been able to see and describe, had apparently disappeared and become folklore. It might mean the end of their hope of finding it.

Nick replaced his snorkel and swam out into the bay, stopped to look back at the land, and swam on again towards the open sea. Day knew he must be checking the location of the old olive tree on the headland above. When Nick buried his head in the water with conviction and headed back, Day lowered his mask and joined him further along the cliff face.

"We hadn't gone far enough," panted Nick. "This is more like it, the tree is right above here. Let's take a look underwater."

He dived and Day did the same. The water was cold and clear beneath the surface froth where it swirled round the rocks, and visibility was good. They dived repeatedly, but the land was solid, there was no sign of any cave. Each time they surfaced they were further from Spedos bay and considerably closer to the *Zephyro*. Day made a final dive, drained of energy and frustrated, barely a thought in his head worthy of the name.

The cave, its gaping entrance below the surface, had nearly eluded them. Day found it first. It was about three metres wide and nearly as tall. Large as it was, the last thing Day fancied was to swim inside its dark interior. He had a particularly strong survival instinct, as he was always happy to admit. Yet before he had time to think, Nick had passed him swimming strongly towards the cave, following the beam of light from the torch on his wrist. Day surfaced to expel the water from his snorkel and take a deep breath, submerged again, and saw no sign of Nick. He had no choice but to follow him and dived into the black hole.

He surfaced just before panic struck him. He could breathe air, and Nick was shining the torch in his face. As their eyes grew accustomed to the dark they saw the cave was large and irregularly shaped, its roof low in places but higher at the far end. The water was deep, but as Day explored further in he felt the bottom with his feet.

"I can stand here," he called. "And there's another opening…"

Nick joined him and shone the torch through the gap. He sniffed and peered inside.

"The cave must be connected to the open air somewhere. I can't see a thing in there. I'll try and find another way in - this gap is too small."

Day was left almost in darkness as Nick crawled, swam and paddled round the cave, looking for another opening.

"Nothing," he said when he returned. "What else can we do?"

Nick's tone suggested defeat, and Day's reply surprised him.

"I can get through. I'm going to go in. Take my stuff and pass me the torch."

He gave Nick his mask and snorkel in exchange for the torch, which he attached to his right hand. He twisted the belt round his waist so that the camera was behind his back and less likely to be damaged. That done he took a last look through the fissure into the second cave. He made out a sand-covered rocky floor rising clear of the water, and a solid roof hanging low above it. Day was tall but thin; he thought he should be able to force his body through the opening and crawl along, and nothing else mattered to him at that moment.

Scraping himself on the rough edges of the opening, he squeezed into the inner chamber. Nick was now alone in the complete darkness of the main cave. Day became aware of small noises, as if he was in a vacuum but for the distant sounds of the sea outside. He lay on his side under stalactite formations and wet-looking drips that seemed frozen in place, and shone the torch round the roof, which was too low for him to sit up. Then he saw one place where it became higher, brought up his knee and began to edge with difficulty towards it.

"Martin? You okay?" Nick shouted from outside.

"I'm okay. It's cramped in here, but it looks better further in. I'm taking a look."

When he could move on all fours it was an improvement, and finally he could sit up. He turned round and sat with his head hunched over his chest, shining the light all around. The roof of the chamber was just above his head and he was sitting on a bumpy floor in a dust of fine sand. The air smelled bad but was good enough to breathe. It was coming from behind him, and he noticed two chunks of stone in that direction which, with the eye of experience, he recognised had been shaped by human hand - quarried, split open, chiselled, or in some way purposefully cut. They could have been part of an original burial chamber or a flight of steps, or perhaps only a drain. They were too deep to be the foundations of a building.

He edged carefully on all fours towards the shaped stones. Using his free hand to support him and directing the torch with the other, he made slow progress. Then something beneath his free hand sent shock waves through him and he froze. He had been prepared for rock as sharp as glass or as abrasive as pumice, for sand, for shells, even - in a moment of nightmare - for a scorpion, but not this. The object under his hand was like smooth, round stone and felt nothing like any rock he had come across so far.

He pointed the torch onto his hand, managing not to snatch it away. Then with mounting excitement he dusted away the sand that covered his discovery until enough of it was visible for him to stop and think. He was slowly revealing a large piece of ancient marble. He felt it over again with no less passion than he would a real woman. The torch confirmed it: it was the face of a supine Cycladic figurine.

"Nick! We've found it! We've found it! Are you there?"

"Did you say you've found it?"

"Give me ten minutes, that's all. Okay?"

"Okay."

He crawled round the recumbent figure, carefully wiping it with his hands to reveal more of the statue. It was aged and ugly in its current condition, but beneath the dark exterior, Day knew, lay Naxian marble. Several thousand years had passed since this figure had been carved. He managed to extract the camera and take pictures using the torch and the camera's inbuilt light, then searched round for anything else the chamber might contain. There was nothing that he could see. The single Cycladic figure, about a metre in length, seemed to have spent the long years alone.

For the first time Day considered his situation and was struck by a debilitating wave of claustrophobia that gripped him for several minutes. When it faded a little he knew it was time to get out. He crawled carefully back towards the narrow opening where Nick was waiting in the darkness of the main cave, waist high in sea water.

"Let's get out of here," said Day, giving the torch back to Nick and once again grazing himself comprehensively on the rough rock wall climbing out. Nick passed him a mask and snorkel and began to rinse out his own.

At that moment the light disappeared. The torch had given out and they were left in pitch darkness. With appalling certainty Day realised he had no idea how to find the exit to the sea. He would be completely dependent on Nick.

"This way. See you on the other side," came Nick's voice, followed by a splash and then silence.

If he hesitated he would be going nowhere, so he pulled on his mask and dived in the direction of the noise. He felt the thrust of water from Nick's beating legs and followed it blindly. After what seemed a long time he felt the grip of strong hands and saw the brightness of the Cycladic sun..

"All right, mate?"

"Fine." You said it because you were English, Day thought, but nothing mattered now. "Let's get back to the boat."

They swam the length of Spedos bay towards the shore until the water became warm and shallow and they had to wade. The little tender, grounded on the beach, looked considerably more attractive to Day than it had before. They pushed it off the sand and clambered in clumsily. The outboard started with a pleasing willingness and Nick turned the boat towards the *Zephyro*.

"Better put this on," said Nick, throwing Day his shirt. "You don't want Helen to see the state you're in."

The shirt stuck to Day's grazed skin, but nothing seemed to hurt; he was far too elated for that. He turned to face the *Zephyro*, pushed his wet hair back from his forehead and enjoyed the wind against his body. Nick opened the throttle and the inflatable bounced back towards the yacht. They both looked across at the headland and the old olive tree as they passed. Day glanced at Nick and grinned, because Nick's expression matched his own.

"You can't beat one of Martin Day's adventures," laughed Nick, as they sat on the deck in the sun and Orestis took charge of the *Zephyro* on the return journey. "I really wish I could have got through into the inner cave and seen what you saw."

"There was no room for two in there anyway," said Day. "I had to crawl like a snake at one point, then all fours. I could only sit up at the far end."

"Do you remember somebody said that only a fit young man could reach the Kállos?" teased Helen.

"Ha!" said Day, "Not exactly young. Nor in fact particularly fit."

"And that word *bousoulo* that means 'to crawl' - that turned out to be right too."

"So it did. And the scratches on a rock. Some of the legend was more than just a good story."

"What are you going to do now?" asked Nick. "Now that you've found the Kállos?"

"Aristos can tell the Greek Archaeological Service. And I need to think about how this might affect Ophelia, and what if anything I can do about it."

Helen sighed and put her hand on his. "You and Nick have already achieved more than anyone could possibly expect, especially Ophelia. I'm not sure there's much more you can do, Martin."

"Perhaps."

"How do you think the figurine came to be down there, Martin?" asked Nick. "Was it buried during a collapse of the headland? In an earthquake, maybe?"

"There might have been a rockfall on the headland, certainly. That would account for the odd lie of the spiral-motif petroglyph and the closure of the land access to the cave. If I'm right, though, and the figurine is the only item down there, I don't think this is a burial chamber. Looters could have taken the smaller things, of course, but I'm sure they'd have smashed the figurine and and taken the pieces, or something equally barbaric. But if it wasn't a burial chamber, perhaps the figurine was hidden down there to keep it safe. Raiders from the sea have always been a scourge in the Aegean, so it could have happened a very long time ago. The two stones shaped like blocks could have been part of a flight of steps leading down into the cave, which might have been how the figurine was carried there. The entrance could have been closed up deliberately, or in a landfall, and the legend that Christos heard could have begun when the opening happened to be accessible for a while. Who knows? I'm happy to leave it to other people to work that out."

He leaned back, tired and increasingly sore, not sure that he was making much sense any more. There were too many possibilities and no way to choose between them. Nick got up and went to join Orestis at the wheel. Helen stroked Day's shirt, having noticed the bloodstains that were beginning to show through.

"Do you think Christos actually found the figurine?" she asked.

"I like to think so. If so, he must have got to it from the sea like we did. He had a boat, he was small and thin, and a strong swimmer."

"Do you remember the woman who saw the Kállos when she was a child?" she continued. "She said that she'd walked a long way to get there, and stood afterwards staring out to sea. I wonder if she was here too."

"I suppose she was, at the time when it was still possible to get into the cave from the top. She might have been one of the last people to see the figurine, apart from Christos. She was frightened by what she saw, said it was like a woman from the sea. It will turn out to be a female figure, I expect, most of them are, and the marble is dark and aged."

Day leaned back against the side of the cabin, suddenly very tired. The sun shone through his closed eyelids reassuringly. He felt Helen take his hand and the comfort of her shoulder next to his. He would have to call Raj tomorrow, tell him what had happened, but admit that he could do no more. It was up to Ophelia now. The last thing he thought of before he dozed off was a spiral.

32

Day eased himself out of bed the next morning and paused to consider his aches and pains. It was no longer so easy to overlook the passing of his fortieth birthday. Helen eyed him from her pillow as he stood up and stretched, opened the shutters and went for a shower. He was quite glad that the flow of water was neither powerful nor hot, and waited for the warmth to soothe his entire body before taking a closer look at himself.

The damaged skin was less angry than it had looked the night before, and the bruises had not yet darkened. There was nothing too serious and he had earned his wounds in a search that would surely remain one of the most unlikely successes of his life. By the time he turned off the shower he even felt quite proud of himself. He chose a long-sleeved cotton shirt and his most comfortable trousers and dressed carefully. He could hear Helen making coffee in the kitchen. He found her carrying it out to the balcony.

"Coffee! Wonderful!"

"You look like you need it. Sore this morning?"

"It's not too bad. Nothing shows now I'm dressed, at any rate." He sat down happily in the chair. "What's the matter?"

"You!" she said, crisply. "The cuts and bruises will heal, I know that, but what if something really bad had happened? Nick wouldn't have been able to get in to help you, he might not even have made it out himself. I'd have waited and waited for you to reappear, and then I suppose I'd have called your new policeman friend."

She bit back the rest, poured the coffee and took a long comforting swallow. A pair of white pigeons landed with a clatter on the cane canopy above them and proceeded to try to impress each other with the amount of noise they could make, before one flew away across the neighbour's garden and the other, belatedly, followed.

"I'm really sorry. I hadn't thought of it like that."

"No. Anyway, all turned out well, and you're both still here. But you do take risks, Martin. I worry about you."

"I know," he smiled, "I know you do. Thank you. I'll try to be more …"

She had to laugh when he didn't finish the sentence. "More what? Considering how clever you are, and the sense of self-preservation you're always talking about, you're impossibly impulsive."

"'Clever'?" he teased, leaning towards her and kissing her gently on the cheek.

"Mmm, and brave, actually. But don't let it become a habit! And you'd better not roll your shirt sleeves up for a few days. It's not a pretty sight, and people think you're an academic."

"I am an academic! And I'm going to prove it. I'll get on with work just as soon as I've spoken to Aristos. I'm going to see him today.

We can't keep the discovery of the Kállos to ourselves, it wouldn't be right, but I'm worried it might push Ophelia to do something desperate. Now that both Christos and the figurine are found, there's nothing left for her to take care of."

"There is a different way of looking at it, surely? When she hears that the Kállos is in good hands, which she inevitably will, and knows that you've done it for her, she might actually contact you. I'd have thought she owes you that. She might tell you where she is and what she's going to do next."

He gave that some thought; it was the best outcome he could hope for.

"I like that, at least it's positive. I'll speak to Aristos after coffee, tie up one or two other things and then get down to some real work. At least that will please Maurice."

"Which project are you going to start with?"

"The TV series on Greek excavation sites. I think I can tie that one up in a couple of months."

"I'll work too. The novel won't write itself."

"Back to normality then. Right, I'll give Aristos a ring."

He collected his phone from the bedside table and sat at the little desk in the bedroom where he did some of his best thinking. This call, at least, required no thought at all.

"Aristo? *Ti kaneis? Poli kala.* Can I come and see you? I need to tell you something - I think you'll like it."

"You don't want to 'pick my brain', then, as you always say?" the Curator chuckled. "I have nothing planned for this afternoon, Martin. Would that suit you?"

"Perfect. What time?"

"Let's say half past two." The Curator put a great deal of store on lunch, for which sufficient time had to be allowed.

"I'll see you then. Thanks, Aristo."

"What's it about?"

"I'll tell you later."

Day smiled and ended the call. Aristos would even now be making connections - Ophelia, Christos and the mysterious Kállos, not to mention Day's evident good spirits. By half past two his friend the Curator would probably have worked out that the news was good.

With a sigh, Day pondered the three other things he must do. The most important was to speak to Raj, but it was too early in the UK to make the call. He had to start with the person he least wanted to speak to. He brought up James Sedge's number and pressed the button.

"Hello, Martin."

"James."

"Is there news of Ophelia?"

"Sadly not, but there is news of the Kállos. I'll be brief, James, the Kállos has been found. All I can tell you is that the Greek authorities are involved, and it's completely out of both our hands. In fact, this call is confidential. If I were you, I'd go back to England."

"Where? Where was it found, Martin?"

"You'll get the details when they're made public, like everyone else."

"But it's a huge and important discovery!"

"One in which I'm afraid you've given away any right to be involved. Let me be clear. If you try to involve yourself in this excavation, I shall have no qualms about reporting your behaviour towards Ophelia."

"You're threatening a colleague?"

It was the word colleague that really annoyed him, and he could not reply. He had said everything that he wanted to say, and he ended the call.

His own rudeness upset Day until he reflected on James's behaviour towards Ophelia. At least he had spared the younger man the involvement of the police. Day hoped this was the last he heard of James Sedge. It was time to call Kyriakos Tsountas.

He left a message and the inspector called Day back within ten minutes; that was when he learned that the Kállos of Naxos had been found in a sea cave off the south coast.

"The Greek Archaeological Service will arrange for its protection and excavation," Day told him. "Until then, the location will remain a secret. My name will be kept out of it."

"Remarkable," said Kyriakos. "Congratulations, Martin. What help do you need from the police?"

"Nothing, as long as word doesn't get out. If it does, there might be a need for some protection at the location. It was simply that I wanted you to know about it."

"I appreciate that. You can call on me for help at any time. The matter will remain between ourselves."

Day was about to say goodbye when he heard the policeman clear his throat.

"I too have some news, Martin, personal news. Angeliki has accepted a job in a private medical laboratory close to the hospital. She will be here on Naxos next month."

"I'm truly pleased for you, Kyriako. That's very good news."

Day said goodbye and put his mobile on the table with a smile. He now had only one more call to make before going into Chora to talk to Aristos, and the thought took the smile from his face.

"Raj. Hi, this is Martin."

"Have you found Mum?"

"I'm afraid not, but there's some good news. I've found the Kállos, the thing she wanted me to find. Your parcel arrived a few days ago, I collected it from Yiasemi Villas. The things your mother sent led me to the right place. She'd worked it all out."

"Did you say you've *found* it? What is it?"

Day told him as much as he could of the search and the discovery, answering all the questions fired at him from the other end.

"Your mother wouldn't have been able to get to it on her own, the access was all but impossible. She needed help and that's what this has been about."

"I see. But why didn't she just ask you directly?"

"I think she has things on her mind that she wants to resolve alone."

"Perhaps she'll come back now, when she hears what you've done."

"Let's hope so. It might take a little time, because the discovery won't be made public for a while."

"I'm not going to wait for that. I'll look for her until I find her."

"So will I," Day said, but even as he spoke he wondered what more he could do, and how much he still believed he could achieve. "Come and visit us on Naxos, Raj. Any time. Just give me a call."

"Thanks, Martin, and thanks for all you've done. I can't think who else could have worked it all out like you have. I guess that's why she chose you. I'll give you a call in a few weeks."

Grateful for Raj's optimism, Day went to find Helen. She was working at her computer, several notebooks open around her and a half empty cup of tea abandoned on the table. She looked rather studious, which made something inside him quiver.

"If the book turns out as good as you look, it will be a huge success," he said, folding himself into an armchair near her.

"Thank you. All well? When are you meeting Aristos?"

"Half past two at the museum. I think I'll go early and look round a bit till he's back from lunch. Are you still planning to stay here and work?"

"Yes, might as well. Would you mind picking up some milk while you're out?"

"Will do. You know what? That makes us sound like an old married couple!"

As he drove into town he wondered why he was setting out so early for a meeting that was still more than two hours away. He felt restless and unable to settle to anything; although his body hurt in many places, it was not physical discomfort that he felt. Perhaps he was suffering from anticlimax after finding the Kállos? It was certainly true that nothing could match the elation of yesterday, but again, he was not someone who sought constant excitement. He gave up worrying and concentrated on the road and on his meeting with Aristos.

He parked in one of the outlying car parks to give himself some exercise. A footpath led to the hill of the Bourgo, the labyrinth of old buildings built in the thirteenth-century around the Kastro by the Venetian bourgeois. Soon he was following the quiet lanes between the houses. The buildings often extended over the narrow street at first floor level, creating sheltered walkways paved with stone. Day enjoyed coming here. He liked the twisting paths and the stone staircases that led to doors high up in a wall. Today the Bourgo matched his mood. It was convoluted and lacked direction, and was rooted in the past. Walking without purpose among buildings that seemed to grow out of one another organically, he felt strangely comforted. He wandered uphill along arched alleyways and round blind corners until he entered the ancient acropolis of the Kastro. Here the narrow streets between the old mansions were no less contorted than in the Bourgo, but they spoke of gracious and privileged living, wealth and security.

At the Della Rocca Barozzi Tower he waited while a group of tourists emerged into the lane from its small museum. He passed the Castle, the Catholic Cathedral and the old Orthodox Church, all basking in the sun. The peaceful coexistence of the two religions was common in the Cyclades, and although Day was not religious he liked the architecture of both churches and respected their peaceful coexistence. At the Capuchin Monastery he faced the prospect of the short uphill climb to his destination, the Naxos Archaeological Museum. He pulled out his phone to check the time. It was too early: Aristos would still be at lunch in one of his much-loved tavernas. It gave him an idea.

He turned and retraced his steps, taking a sharp left down a narrow lane past the old stone walls of the castle. There was a bar somewhere in these streets, a rooftop place with a stunning view over the Bourgo where he had been one night as a student on a trip to Naxos with friends. They had sat drinking long into the small hours of the morning. The bar should be quieter now, and he fancied a good coffee and space to think.

He recognised the entrance at once, no more than a door on the street. The sign was small and discreet, Bar Paravoli, and the door was open. He walked up the stairs and out onto the rooftop, where for the first time he saw the beauty of the view in the daylight. Four or five couples were already sitting at round tables with white cloths. Day chose a small one for himself and sat facing away from the other people. When the waiter arrived he ordered a Greek coffee, something he rarely did, but today it was the only thing he wanted. His *kafes* arrived in a traditional cup with a miniature *koulouraki* biscuit on the saucer. The biscuit was wasted on him, but the smell of the coffee carried all the comfort of Greece.

He knew what was wrong; it was not so very difficult to see. He had done what Ophelia wanted, but even so he had failed to help her. It was finished: he had no possibility of finding her or rescuing her now, and he feared for her. This was a failure he would have to accept. There was something else, too, if he was honest, and he wanted to be honest. He was troubled by what he now knew about her, how she had concealed what had happened to Christos. He would have to accept this too.

He opened his memory and forced himself to recall for the last time the details of his relationship with the twenty-seven-year old

Ophelia. He remembered one incident after another, they came thick and fast to his mind, all in the wrong order as memories do. There were exciting one-to-one tutorials and magical times when they had laughed till it hurt. They had had the most appalling rows and he had made her cry. Predominantly, there was wonderful sex. Day allowed the film to play in his head unexpurgated, but he looked on from the distance of years with a certain fond cynicism. He drank the last of his Greek coffee carefully, mindful of the thick grinds at the bottom, while all the time the unstoppable memories filled his mind. When he felt the tears prick behind his eyes he knew it was nearly done. He reached out for the glass of water that they had brought with his coffee, and drank it all. He didn't know if he would ever see Ophelia again, or even if she would ever again be seen by anyone. He knew he had done as much for her as he could, and had not let her down, and that would have to be enough for him. He had been given the chance to revisit the part of his youth that he had spent with Ophelia, and accept both its disasters and its triumphs. This final disaster was now part of her story. She too had a chance, thanks to him, to face her past actions and decide how to move on. It was a decision that nobody could make for her.

It all came back to a Cycladic figure known as the Kállos. How ironic, he thought, that the disasters for Christos, for Tim and for Ophelia should have arisen from an object known as the Beauty. In its current condition the Kállos was not beautiful at all, nor were the emotions it had generated in people, yet the search for beauty is a powerful drive and has been since the dark days of prehistory. For many people it is not an easy quest.

Day raised his eyes. He looked across the tiled roofs of the Bourgo to the distant Portara and the Aegean. The islands of the Paros, Iraklia and Keros sat at peace in their setting. For the past few minutes he had stared at them but not seen them, and they swam into focus now as his mind cleared of its memories. He must leave it to Ophelia to conclude her quest in whatever way she chose. He would like to know the final outcome, but that particular wish was unlikely to be granted. She had asked him to think well of her and try to understand, and those were things he could do.

He must also acknowledge his own quest, his personal search for beauty, and not feel guilty about accepting that for him there was a happy outcome. He had found his own Kállos, and he did not mean the recumbent marble statue that had been the cause of heartache and death.

He sat for another fifteen minutes before summoning the waiter and paying for his coffee. He had something important to do before meeting Aristos and telling him about the sea cave of Spedos bay.

33

With his new purchase safely in his trouser pocket, Day took the wide stone steps from the museum's lobby to the Curator's office. Half way up he diverted on impulse into the Cycladic Gallery, which housed most of the museum's figurines. He had a favourite and wanted to see it again. He stood in front of it enjoying its perfect symmetry, the roundness of its curves, the precision of the incised lines that indicated its neckline and belly, the simplicity of its face. It had been found on Keros and, like most of the figurines that had yet been discovered, was a fraction of the size of the Kállos. Little wonder that the Kállos had become the stuff of legend.

He knocked on Aristos's door and found it was ajar. The office was in its customary state of comfortable disarray, and Day threw himself into the only spare chair in front of the Curator's desk. They played a short game of not being the first to speak.

"So," said Aristos, losing the game, "I think you have something new to put in my safe. You have that look about you, Martin."

Day grinned. "Your safe, excellent though it is, wouldn't be big enough, my friend!"

"You've found the Kállos."

"I know where it is. Would you like the story, or should I just tell you straight away what it is?"

"I can wait. I think I'd rather hear the whole thing. Just tell me where it was in the end? Naxos or Iraklia?"

"Naxos. The south coast, where you suggested in the first place. A few days ago, Raj sent me a parcel containing a map, a notebook and some photographs from Ophelia. I also found out that she has visited Naxos every August for the last few years following the trail left by Christos, but had reached a point where she couldn't get any further on her own. She thought she knew the right location but it was inaccessible. That was why she left it to me to recover the Kállos.

"Based on what she sent me I thought I'd take a look at the Spedos bay area, and asked Nick to take me there on the yacht. Ophelia had sketched a rough map with an arrow in the water, so we looked for a cave with access from the sea. To cut a long story short, we found it. It was a sea cave that went a long way under the headland, with a rather difficult underwater entrance."

"I didn't even know you could swim, Martin," remarked Aristos drily.

"Ah well, it seems I can when I have the right motivation. The cave is beneath the eastern headland of Spedos bay. Luckily there was fresh air inside, which means there must have been access from the ground above, probably all but closed off now. There's an old olive tree directly above the cave, and a kind of headstone leaning against it on which someone has scratched the words 'The Kállos of the Island'. Modern Greek, recently done. Before you get to the tree, there's an ancient boundary marker like the one on Mount Zas, dedicated to Zeus the Guardian of Sheep."

Aristos nodded. Nothing would surprise him about one of Day's stories, he was sure.

"Inside an inner chamber there are two squared-off stones that could be from a drain or possibly a tomb, but I don't think so. I think they may be part of an old series of steps… There's just one object down there, as far as I could see…"

"One?" Disappointment vied with surprise in the Curator's voice.

"Yes. A single Cycladic figurine, and I'm willing to guess it's in one piece. I'll send you the photos I took."

"That doesn't sound like either a grave or a ritual site."

"I agree, unless the looters have got there before us. My theory is that the figurine was so precious that it was hidden down there, either by the original inhabitants or more recently, to keep it safe."

"That makes some sense, I suppose." Aristos was still trying to conceal his disappointment. The Kállos legend had promised more than a single figurine.

"So, will you take over from here, Aristo? I want to keep my name and Ophelia's out of it, and you know the people in the Greek Archaeological Service. It won't be easy to get the statue out."

"Of course, with pleasure. Congratulations, Martin, it's extraordinary what you've done. I'll get the wheels in motion tomorrow morning. Tell me, when you went into that cave, was this what you expected to find? Just one figurine? I was expecting something a lot more significant, something amazing that had inspired the folk-stories, the imposing name of Kállos, and particularly Christos Nikolaidis's obsession."

Day smiled.

"You were quite right to expect something astonishing, Aristo. You won't be disappointed. I reckon it's one of the largest complete Cycladic figurines that's ever been found."

Calling out to Helen, Day opened the front door of the house in Filoti, and for the hundredth time was thankful for his decision to put his entire inheritance from his father into buying it. Helen was sitting out on the balcony with a glass of fruit juice, basking in the warm afternoon sun. Already her pale winter complexion had turned golden. He sensed their long, Greek summer was now under way.

"I'll be out in a minute," he called, and went to the bedroom, where he placed his purchase in the pocket of his jacket behind the door before going to the bathroom to splash water on his face. In the kitchen he poured himself a glass of juice and joined her on the balcony.

"How did it go with Aristos?"

"He was suitably delighted. It's all in his hands now. I expect he'll speak to his friend Aliki first and between them they'll take care of everything."

"Aliki from the Archaeological Service? Good. Will you be involved in the next stage?"

"No, I asked Aristos to keep my name and Ophelia's out of it."

"How's that possible? Your name, I mean? The Kállos didn't find itself. Christos has been dead for seventeen years."

"I know. Aristos will arrange it somehow, that's why he's the right person for this. They respect him too much to argue." He sighed heavily and happily. "The figure will be excavated in the fullness of time, and until then they'll do whatever is necessary to protect it. Christos will be vindicated in the end, Helen, and get the credit for all his work and perseverance. It may take a few years, but it's already been a long time."

"You did that for him, Martin. I hope you're a bit proud of yourself?"

"I'm very happy about it, but it took many people to find this figurine - Christos, Ophelia, even Tim to begin with, then Nick, you and me. Aristos himself. There's one more thing I want to do, which is to write about Christos and leave a record of his achievement. Ophelia planned to do it but that won't happen now, and it should be done."

"What about Ophelia?" said Helen. "Do you think we'll hear from her?"

"We might, but I don't think so. I've been thinking about her today. She made a bad decision when Christos died. She made it because she loved Tim, but all the same it was the wrong decision. That must be hard to live with. I think she will cut all ties with her past, one way or the other."

Helen turned back to the valley. She watched a pair of birds fly over the green landscape and the stone walls of abandoned terracing until they were out of sight. For a few minutes she was absorbed in her own thoughts.

"You forgot to get the milk, then," she said at last.

"Ah. Yes. Completely slipped my mind. I'll walk into the village and get some. I don't feel like starting work yet anyway."

"Forget it," she smiled. "We can do without milk."

She got up and stood in front of him. Her skin was warm from the sun and her eyes shone. He needed no further encouragement.

34

Time passed and there was no word of Ophelia. Kyriakos ordered another search of the hospitals, hotels and all the accommodation on the island, but the result was as disappointing as before. Raj involved the British police and informed the British Embassy in Athens, but finally he too ran out of things to try. Day and Helen filled their time with work, gradually having to accept that Ophelia had disappeared from their lives as abruptly as she had arrived. Day began to believe that she had begun a new life somewhere far away. He liked to think of her making a fresh start, finding a way to make amends. If he lost sight of that belief, which happened from time to time, the Pre-Raphaelite picture of Shakespeare's Ophelia came to his mind, the lady in the stream surrounded by flowers at the moment of her death.

On Naxos they enjoyed the arrival of summer. The landscape was still green, but the wild flowers were now less plentiful. The air was full of the glorious scent of warm herbs, grass and sea salt, and the sun heated even the darkest recesses of the houses on the coast and in the hills. Day worked on the balcony table, spreading his books round him and trailing a cable out to his laptop. Helen turned the room that had once been her bedroom into a writing room, throwing open the windows to allow inside the soothing sound of the chattering sparrows and the fresh air of the valley. After meeting at six for a drink they would usually walk to Taverna O Thanasis for dinner, which gave them a change of scene and a few hours to relax. The rhythm of the Naxian summer was reasserting itself.

Day was working on the balcony as usual when Aristos rang with news, three weeks after taking responsibility for the discovery. The new find on Naxos had been given priority by the Archaeological Service, who would undertake an initial survey of the cave in a fortnight's time.

"That's very quick, you know, considering funding constraints," said Aristos. "Do you want to be involved when the team arrive?"

"Not really. I'll give you an accurate description of the location, so they shouldn't need me at all. I presume they'll search for a way to access the cave from up on the headland before they try the underwater entrance?"

"That's the idea, but of course they have divers if they're needed."

"Divers?" laughed Day. "Well, I wish them luck! Thanks, Aristo, I'm grateful to you for taking over, I really am."

"My pleasure. I hope you realise how important this is, Martin, and what a valuable discovery you've made? Once it's made public, there's going to be quite a fuss."

"I understand, truly, and I know it will be hard to avoid some explanation of how we came to find it, but perhaps it can be kept between us and the Archaeological Service?"

"For a while, maybe. I think you'd better give it some thought, Martin. I can't actually lie about it, you know."

Day smiled into the phone. "I know. I'm not asking you to."

"I know you have your reasons, Martin, and I don't need to know what they are. Now, on a personal note, can I persuade you and Helen to come and see us soon? This weekend?"

"You don't know how good that sounds. It would be wonderful."

"Let's say Saturday, then, about seven. I'll see if Panayiotis has any more of that good Nemean red."

Day put his phone back on the table with a small sigh of relief. He had a sense that a corner had been turned. He and Helen would be able to move on soon, return to something like the life they were living before Ophelia had called from England. He stared out at the valley that unfolded beyond the balcony, the vivid greens of early summer, the bright orange lichen across the rocks, the shadows of midday pooling beneath the solitary trees. The olive trees were in blossom in the neighbour's garden, their small white flowers in clusters amongst the older, grey-green leaves, while at the tips of the branches the new growth gave an unmistakable sense of emerging life. In contrast, on the dark-leaved pomegranate tree, the luscious orange-red flowers had begun to appear, and in the vegetable garden the soil was freshly dug over to accommodate new planting.

He stood up and went inside to look for Helen. He found her at her computer next to the open window in her room.

"Let's go out tonight, to the Kastro!" he said without preamble. "It would be nice to have a real night out, don't you think? We could have a cocktail somewhere and then a nice meal."

"A cocktail?" she said. "You never want a cocktail, Martin!"

"I know. All the more reason to have one."

"Well, yes, all right. That sounds nice."

"And we'll dress up. Also we've been invited to Aristos and Rania's on Saturday night."

"Lovely. Whatever will Thanasis do without us."

Day returned to his work but his mind was now on other things. He knew exactly where he wanted to take Helen for the cocktails, but he must book somewhere new for dinner, somewhere she had never been before. He intended to give her a very special evening. This recent madness had been none of her doing, yet she had thrown herself into it without complaint and worked alongside him for the sake of Ophelia.

He made three phone calls, did a little more work, and then the excellent Greek tradition of the afternoon rest beckoned. As he drifted off into a light doze, the warm air hardly moving the light curtain on his window, he smiled to himself in anticipation of the evening ahead.

Bar Paravoli remained open until three in the morning, but this was something that Day had no intention of experiencing. It would be much busier as the evening drew on, but when they arrived and were shown onto the roof terrace it was perfect. This was how Day liked a bar, humming but not overflowing. Their table was right against the terrace wall and gave them an uninterrupted view across the rooftops to the sea. The candle in the glass was already lit, but counted for nothing in the glow of the approaching sunset. The island of Paros had already become a spectral shadow.

"This is a stunning place," said Helen. "How did you know about it?"

"I came here once years ago. I was on holiday with some college friends. We drank quite a lot that night so I don't remember much about it, but I suddenly thought of it when I was early for Aristos last week. I came here for a quiet coffee. I didn't tell you because I wanted to surprise you tonight."

"Well, it's beautiful. And look at this enormous cocktail menu. I guess you're going to have a gin and tonic?"

"I think tonight I'll be more adventurous."

"I think I'll try their Kitron Margarita," she said, having looked down the list. "It says it's a Naxos speciality. Basically it's a Margarita made with the local Kitron liqueur."

"Good choice," he said, and at that point the waiter arrived at their side. "A Kitron Margarita, please, and for me a Kitron Martini."

The waiter thanks them and left, and Day turned back to find Helen smiling.

"Basically gin?" she teased.

"Not basic in the least, hopefully," he said.

As they sipped their cocktails the sun sank further into the horizon and their candle, augmented by the soft lights of the Paravoli bar, came into its own. Day had lost count of the number of times he had watched with Helen as the sun set over the sea, but this time he wished he could prolong the pleasure and delay its inevitable disappearance.

On the islet of Palatia a crowd of dark shapes were clustered near the looming portal of the Portara. A shimmer of bronze radiated over the tranquil water and cast a gleam over the marble of the ancient doorway, before the edge of the sea gently consumed the lower half of the sun, and the rest of it sank quietly after.

Estiatorio Thalia claimed to be the oldest restaurant in the Kastro. It had caught his eye during his pensive walk to meet Aristos and was only a short way from the Museum; he was surprised that he had not taken much notice of it before. Like the Paravoli, the restaurant was already busy. May had arrived bringing a noticeable increase in visitor numbers, and it was these people who filled the tables so early in the evening. The dining area on the first floor, open to the balmy night, was already full. White-shirted waiters passed efficiently between the tables with dishes held high. Day gave his name at the door and was surprised when the proprietor led them away from the busy restaurant.

On the quiet side of the pedestrian street, flanked by a pair of olive trees in pots, was a private courtyard belonging to the Thalia in which only a few of the tables were occupied and Greek was the only language to be heard. The high walls were bright with purple bougainvillea, and red geraniums in pots added splashes of colour. They were shown to a corner table from which they could both see the courtyard. Under a wooden staircase opposite was a life-sized statue of a woman with a carved ivy wreath round her shoulders and a stone trumpet at her waist. The walls were decorated with brightly-coloured plaster masks, symbols of comic theatre, and in an alcove behind Helen was the marble head of a woman, her hair dressed in a circlet of leaves.

"What a beautiful place," said Day. "I can't believe we've never been here before. At least, I haven't. Have you?"

"No, I don't think I have either. I didn't eat out much when I came to Naxos on my own."

"All the more reason to make up for it now," he said. "So, let me tell you about this place. They claim there's been a taverna on this site for centuries. It's named Thalia after one of the Muses. That must be her statue over there, and the bust behind you is probably her too. She was the daughter of Zeus from his liaison with Mnemosyne, the goddess of memory." He paused and grinned. "I had a Classics teacher at school who was obsessed with the Greek myths. It was excellent, we could get him to spend the whole lesson on stuff like this."

"Clearly! Thalia was the muse of comedy, wasn't she? That would account for the comic masks on the walls."

"Yes, but Greek myths are very flexible, Helen, so I shall choose to see her as the muse of all literary creativity, making this an excellent place to bring you."

She laughed. "Fair enough! She might even find it amusing to inspire your TV series."

"I'm sure she's a very generous lady, no problem at all. It could do with her help at this point."

A young man came to the table with their menus, a bottle of water and a basket of bread.

"*Kalispera sas*, Kyrie, Kyria. Would you like me to bring the wine that you ordered now, Kyrie Day?"

Day accepted and the man went away.

"You've already ordered the wine? Why?"

"I thought we could try something different tonight. This restaurant stocks a white wine made from a grape that was saved from extinction in the 1970s. A Greek botanist on his travels round the country collected samples of all the rare grape varieties he could find, including this one. He took them home and persuaded a winemaker to grow them for him. The winemaker realised what an exceptional grape this one was and grew it commercially. It's become very famous, it's called Malagousia. It inspired Greek growers to look for more old vine stock, but so far the Malagousia is still the best."

The young man returned with the wine and adeptly removed the cork. Day took the bottle from him to read the label before pouring a little into Helen's glass and then his own.

"Well, here's to the inspiration of the creative muse!" he said, twirling the wine gently in his glass and sniffing it.

"And to Malagousia wine." She tasted her drink and then took a slightly larger sip. "Mmm, I like it. We should try to get a bottle for Aristos. The clever grower who spotted the potential in this grape did very well."

"His name was Evangelos Gerovassiliou," said Day, slightly embarrassed for once at the extent of his knowledge, but there was a point to it this time. "Evangelos means 'a messenger with good news'. I think that's rather apt."

After consulting the menu they ordered a gilt-head bream, called *tsipoura* in Greek, for the highlight of the meal. It would be baked in parchment with olive oil, lemon and oregano. While the *tsipoura* was being cooked they started with a small plate of tender baby squid, the rings and frond-like pieces of tentacle dusted in flour and fried to perfection. With this came the yellow split-pea dip called *fava*, served slightly warm with a sprinkling of chopped onion and a drizzle of olive oil, to be scooped up with bread. The last little side-dish was a Greek potato salad made with the fine produce of Naxos dressed with chopped spring onions, olive oil and fresh herbs.

Over at the courtyard entrance the young waiter stood waiting, and on hearing his name he crossed the lane to the restaurant's kitchen and returned with a large platter. He brought it to their table and opened the parchment to reveal the *tsipoura*, fragrant with lemon, herbs and a warm smell of the sea.

"*Kali orexi!*" he announced, and left them to enjoy their meal. Helen drew a knife gently down the central bone of the fish and drew away the skin. The white flesh of the bream came away from the bones easily, releasing fragrant steam.

"Now this really is Greek cuisine at its best - simple and fresh," said Helen. "No chips, though, Martin?"

He grinned and took a little more potato salad to show how happy he was. He was conscious of the slender package in his jacket pocket and the thought of it had even eclipsed his usual desire for chips. Once they had finished the meal and the plates had been removed he would give it to her.

Accordingly, when the young man had cleared the table and brought them both a complimentary glass of Mastika liqueur, Day laid his hand over Helen's. Before he could say anything, though, Helen forestalled him.

"Since we're in the garden of the daughter of memory, I have a question for you."

"Mmm?"

"How do you feel about Ophelia now?"

They had already exhausted the subject of Ophelia's predicament, so he knew she was asking him about the state of his heart. Over the years Day had perfected the skill set of avoiding this kind of subject, but tonight he felt differently. He knew exactly how he wanted to answer her. He had, after all, given it considerable thought over his Greek coffee on the rooftop of Bar Paravoli.

"Knowing me as well as you do, you might be surprised that I can answer that very easily. And thank you for not asking me until now, for trusting me. Thank you for supporting me when she asked for help. Ophelia meant a lot to me in Cambridge at the time, but my involvement with her ended many years ago, and it was right that it did. The truth is, she's in my past, but she's not in my present, and certainly not in my future."

He took his hand from hers and reached into his jacket pocket.

"I bought this for you after something you said on Iraklia."

He watched as she undid the paper envelope and drew out a small package of white tissue paper. Laying it on the table, she peeled it open slowly to reveal a delicate chain from which hung a finely-wrought pendant in the shape of a tapered spiral.

It had exactly the effect he had hoped.

Lightning Source UK Ltd.
Milton Keynes UK
UKHW021542250922
409421UK00007B/198

9 781838 453367